MCLEOD SECURITY

EVERNIGHT PUBLISHING ®

www.evernightpublishing.com

MCLEOD SECURITY

DEDICATION

For Sandy, enjoy 'your' men and Happy Birthday—again.

MCLEOD SECURITY

HER HUSBAND'S ARMY BUDDY

McLeod Security, 1

Doris O'Connor

Copyright © 2018

Chapter One

Male laughter washed over her, and Sandy grabbed the tray of after dinner treats tighter. Even so, the delicate china cups—a wedding present from the very man now occupying their dining room with his larger than life presence—rattled on their saucers, giving the tiny birds decorating the rims the impression of flight.

The metaphor wasn't lost on her as her husband's laughter rang in her ears. This dinner had been her idea, after all. Ever since she'd spotted both men together, leaving Zane's office, she'd known the truth. At the time, the bottom had dropped out of her world. As relieved as she had been that Zane's preoccupation and distance hadn't been due to an affair as her girlfriends had been so quick to assume, this … well, *this* was far more dangerous to their marriage.

Zane didn't miss his army career. Having been medically discharged due to the complete loss of hearing in one ear, he'd built up a successful security business, but he did miss his buddies. Sean, in particular.

Sandy knew their history, had believed her husband when he'd said that part of his life was over. The day of their wedding had been the happiest one of her life. She'd ignored the warnings of her parents, her girlfriends. They loved each other. They could make this work, and they had done so successfully for the last ten years until ... *he* left the service.

Now, well, now she didn't know what would become of them.

Sandy paused in the doorway and took in *that* smile. It had been so long since she'd seen Zane like this. Happy, playful, flirting. As much as it had hurt to admit this to herself, he'd needed this. She wasn't enough, not anymore. Had she ever been?

Fixing a smile on her face, Sandy stepped into the dining room, and both men looked up. Her heart missed a few beats, being under the scrutiny of two sets of male eyes. Sean Manson was altogether too handsome, too virile, far too much of *anything*. Six feet five of tightly packed muscles, he towered over everyone, and had a good couple of inches even on Zane. With his military buzzcut, and the stubble on his jaw, he oozed dominance, power, leashed aggression, and above all, danger. Never more so than when he was smiling like he was now. It softened his harsh features, brought out the dimples in his cheeks, and made his steely eyes lighten to the bright color of a summer's morning. That smile alone had the power to pull anyone into his charms, and Sandy was all too painfully aware that she wasn't immune to him. She ought to hate the man for what he represented, but the opposite was true. Sean Manson intrigued her almost as much as Zane had done from the moment she'd met him.

She'd instantly known Zane was her soulmate, but this man ... he was a threat to her marriage, to everything she and Zane had built together, and she shouldn't, couldn't be attracted to him.

"Let me help you with that, Sandy." Sean pushed away from the table, crossed the short distance to her with a few long-legged strides, and tugged the tray out of her hands. "This looks delicious. I'll have to hang around if you keep feeding me this well."

He winked at her, and when their fingers touched a current of electricity shot up her digits. She barely bit back her gasp, and Sean's grin turned sinful.

"You chose well, buddy." He glanced at Zane, and the smoldering look that passed between the two men raised the temperature in the room by several degrees.

"I know I did, Sean. My girl is one in a million."

Sandy's heart cramped painfully, hearing him call her that, and she blinked away tears when he held out his hand for her. She was far too aware of Sean's eyes on her ass as she walked toward her husband.

"Am I, still?" she asked. She hated the wobble in her voice, hated the concern she read in Zane's amber gaze even more as he pulled her down for a kiss. Not a peck on the cheek either. This was a full-blown assault on her senses, which made her forget where they were, as Zane's familiar scent and taste pulled her under his spell. Nothing else mattered but the feel of her husband's lips on hers, his grunt of approval when she opened up to him, and he deepened the kiss. She kissed him back with all the pent-up passion she felt, and whimpered in need when he pulled her down on his lap. His cock hardened under her ass cheeks, and she clung to him, pressing her breasts into the hard planes of his chest, as his hands fisted in her hair and tilted her head to his satisfaction.

Loud throat clearing eventually pulled them apart, but not before Zane kissed a path along her jaw and growled his confirmation into her ear.

"Always, baby, don't ever doubt that."

His voice, rough with need, pitched her own arousal higher, not helped one iota by Sean's deep grumble.

"Damn it, you two, take pity on the lonely bachelor here. Get a room, will you?"

Zane laughed, kissed her nose, and let her go.

"I would, but it would seem rude to leave you sitting here all by yourself, and besides, don't give me that lonely bachelor crap. I bet there's any number of sweet pussy you could dial up at a moment's notice."

Zane's unexpected crassness was as hot as it was dirty. Sandy gasped and attempted to scramble off her husband's lap, but Zane's hold on her tightened. "You stay right here, little girl, or else."

"Yes, Sir."

Sandy mumbled her reply, utterly unable to resist *that* tone of voice. It had been way too long since she'd heard that. Way too long since they'd last indulged in some kinky play.

"Good girl."

His murmured approval lit up the dark spaces of her heart.

"Well, I'll be damned. Guess that's my clue to make myself scarce." Sean put the tray down on the table with a loud thump that further rattled the saucers, and Sandy jumped.

"Don't be an idiot, Sean." Zane said. "We both want you here, don't we, sweetheart?"

Her heart missed a few more beats at the intonation behind those words. He couldn't mean what she thought he meant, could he?

A sharp tug to her hair focused her attention on her husband, and the steely determination in his eyes made breathing difficult.

"Sir?" Try as she might she was utterly incapable of projecting her voice above a whisper.

Zane smiled.

Sean swore.

"Fuck it, I didn't come here for this, Zane. She's your wife, for fuck's sake. I should go."

Zane smiled, and twisted her head so that she had no choice but to look at his old buddy. The heat in Sean's eyes took her breath away. Her already hard nipples tightened further, and she squirmed on Zane's lap, as her panties grew damp.

"She doesn't want you to go, and neither do I. Tell him, baby girl."

The air thickened in sexual tension, as Sean drew himself up to his full height, crossed his massive arms over his chest, and waited for her answer. He'd taken his jacket off earlier and rolled up his shirt sleeves, and she couldn't take her eyes off the way his biceps strained the fine cloth of his shirt. The edge of a tattoo, similar to the ones Zane had on his shoulders, could just about be seen as Sean's shirt sleeve rode higher, and she swallowed hard.

"I … that is…"

She dropped her gaze, unable to stand the intensity of Sean's stare and promptly wished she hadn't done so because it brought his groin into her eye line, and heaven help her, the man was huge. He was also as turned on as Zane was, his cock a hard, ridged outline along his tailored trousers. She licked her dry lips, and Sean groaned.

"Fucking hell, don't do that, or I'll be tempted to

take that as an invitation."

Heat flooded her cheeks at the implication, while Zane chuckled. A sharp tug to her hair focused her attention back on her husband.

"She does have the best mouth, and trust me, Sean, she knows how to use it."

Zane's voice had dropped further, taking on that delicious edge of command which made her want to sink to her knees and submit to him in all ways. His gaze rested on her lips, and every feminine cell in her body sighed in submission. Had they been on their own, she'd already be in position, and putting the mouth both men seemed so utterly focused on, to good use. Sandy had always loved going down on a man. There was such power in that act, the ultimate gift, especially with Zane, who always put her pleasure first.

"I'm sure she does, mate."

Sean's voice, too, had dropped to a guttural growl, which only served to pitch her further into a maelstrom of arousal. This was wrong, wasn't it? She shouldn't be this needy, wet, aching to be fucked right now.

Sean stepped closer, and a shiver of apprehension went down her spine when his boots appeared in her vision. Scuffed and well worn, they suited him. Besides, the man had arrived on a motorbike, so the boots made sense.

Heaven help her, he was every dratted bad boy fantasy come to life. She stopped thinking altogether, when his calloused digits grasped her chin and nudged her head up to make her look at him. The heat in his amazing cornflower gaze threatened to engulf her with silent promise. He ran his thumb over her lips, and she opened to him without any conscious effort on her part. When she licked that digit, Sean inhaled sharply, and

Zane swore.

"Fuck, seeing you two together is so damn hot. Kiss her, Sean."

A grim smile kicked up Sean's full lips, and he shook his head, as he briefly tore his gaze away from her and focused on her husband.

"I told you, I didn't come here for this, and if we do this," he glanced at Sandy again, and she didn't dare breathe under his questioning regard. "I won't come between you and your wife, Zane."

"You won't. Tell him, baby girl. Tell him whose idea this dinner was."

Zane's grip on her hair loosened. He slid his hand to her nape and massaged the tight knots forming there, as he nuzzled into her neck at the same time. His harsh breaths skittered across the sensitive skin under her ear, and she automatically tilted her head to give him better access. She felt his smile in the butterfly kisses he delivered before he bit down hard on her earlobe. That zing of pain shot straight to her clit, and she moaned her answer.

"Mine, it was my idea, Sir."

"Good girl, now tell him why."

Zane withdrew, and without his reassuring warmth all her previous insecurities rushed back with the full force of a speeding train. Sandy shook her head and tried in vain to blink away her tears. Zane swore when he noticed, and Sean swiped away the lone tear trailing down her cheek.

"Shit, I told you this wouldn't work. I should go, Zane." Instead of withdrawing, however, Sean's digits lingered, stroked along her jaw, and tilted her head back up again. It was the concern in his gaze that made her blurt her answer.

"Don't go."

Sean gave a sharp nod and smiled.

"I should though. I can guess what you must have been thinking, but I mean it. I would never come between you and Zane. I love him too much to fuck up his marriage."

Zane's thigh muscles tensed under her ass, and this time, when she scrambled off his lap, he let her. Sandy hastily put some distance between herself and the two men, and it was only when she put the table between them that she looked at them.

What she saw broke her heart all over again. Sean's hand curled into her husband's shoulder, the white-knuckled grip testament to how riled he was, whereas Zane looked up at his former lover with a look of love previously only reserved for her. Sean stared straight at her, brows drawn together in concern at her reaction.

Finding her voice from somewhere, Sandy nudged her chin up.

"Maybe you already have."

Chapter Two

The barely suppressed pain in his wife's voice served as an ice-cold shower to Zane's arousal. He shook off Sean's hand and glared across the table at the other love of his life.

"How can you say that, Sandy?" The deliberate use of her name stung as he knew it would, because Sandy blinked away more tears. Sean swore and thumped his back.

"Jesus, man, stop being an ass. She's your wife. Your first concern is and should be to her."

Zane shot out of his chair and poured himself a generous helping of Scotch whisky and then downed it in one swallow. The burn down his gullet was a welcome distraction from the ache in his chest. When he turned back round to face the room it was to see both of the people he cared most about in this whole fucked up world looking to him for answers.

Answers he wasn't sure he could give.

"Sir?"

Sandy's hesitant voice made his mind up for him. He knew he'd been a miserable bastard of late, and she deserved so much better. But the sudden reappearance of his old army buddy in his life had thrown him for six. Long suppressed feelings had reemerged. A part of his life that he thought long buried had come back to bite him on the ass.

While Sean and he had parted company amicably when he'd met Sandy, and realized she was the woman he wanted to spend the rest of his life with—rather than her being someone both men would share for a while— he hadn't counted on what would happen years down the line. He'd thought himself happy with Sandy, and they had been … until Sean had walked into his office two months ago, looking for a job.

To not take him on had been out of the question. Providing jobs for ex-special forces personnel was his company's specialty, after all, and one of the reasons why his security firm was considered the best in the country.

He employed the best, and thus his services were the best.

What he hadn't counted on was the fact that he wanted Sean in his life, in his bed with Sandy. Unable to determine how best to approach that hornets' nest he'd withdrawn into his work and had kept both Sean and Sandy at arm's length.

He would never, ever cheat on his wife, and besides, Sean was too honorable a guy to let him do that—one of the many reasons why he loved the man— but something had to give.

Sandy's suggestion of inviting Sean to dinner had been the perfect opportunity to bring all of this out in the open. Especially when he noticed the way Sandy and Sean responded to each other.

He knew his wife's body inside out, and her instinctive responses to Sean's dominant nature had been such a fucking turn-on. Without meaning to he and Sean had fallen back into the familiar pattern of wining and dining a woman they both wanted.

It wasn't wrong to want it all, was it? He was so sure he hadn't read the signals wrong, that Sandy wanted this. He knew one of her secret fantasies was to experience a ménage, and who better to give her that fantasy than the one man he trusted with his life?

Sean cleared his throat and grasped his jacket off the back of the chair he'd placed it on earlier.

"Right, well, I'm going. Thank you for a lovely dinner, Sandy. I'm—"

"Don't be ridiculous, stay." Zane interrupted the other man and got in his way. "It's late. You've been drinking, and your riding is bad enough when you're sober." He scrubbed a hand over his face and shook his head. "I'd never forgive myself if something happened to you. We have a spare room. You can crash in there for as long as you need to. I told you that before."

Zane had been outraged when he learned that his old buddy had holed up in a hostel. Sean had so far refused to take him up on his offer to stay at his place, however, and he still looked as though he would leave, until Sandy stepped forward.

"Zane is right, you can't go like this. I'll just go and put some sheets on the bed." With that she scrambled from the room as though the hounds of hell were after her, and maybe they were. The urge to go after her was strong, but Sean stopped him from doing so by his growled question.

"What the fuck, man? This was just dinner, and you turned it into … *fuck*."

Instead of answering him, Zane poured two more generous measures of the amber liquid for both himself and Sean, and both men drained their glasses before they slammed them down on the sideboard.

"Guess I didn't handle that all that well."

"You fucking think so? Hell, man, she looks ready to bolt."

Sean stared off into the distance, hands fisted into tight balls next to his thighs, and he blew out a harsh breath.

"I know how much you love her. You can't blow this, man. I won't let you."

Zane shook his head and sighed.

"I have no intention of blowing it. And get off your high horse. She wants to fuck you as much as you want to fuck her."

The fist to his jaw sent him reeling backward. He blocked the next move and shoved Sean away from him. He crashed into the table, sending the cutlery flying. Had it not been for Sean's fast reflexes, the man's wedding present to them would have ended up a shattered mess on the floor. As it was it narrowly escaped that fate when Sean caught the cups teetering on the edge and placed them back on the table.

"Don't talk about her like that. I want to do no such thing."

"Liar."

The words hung between them heavy and solid, as the tension grew until Zane couldn't stand it anymore. Fisting his hands in the other man's shirt, he yanked him closer and slanted his lips over his in a manner he'd wanted to ever since Sean had walked back in his life.

Sean pushed him away with a muttered no, but that one word was enough to grant Zane access. Grasping the other man's head, he pulled it down and shoved him backward at the same time. Sean's ass rested on the edge of the table, and Zane thrust his tongue into his friend's mouth.

Sean responded like he hoped he would, by wrapping his arms around Zane and kissing him back with all the underlying simmering passion that always flared to life between them. Sean had been the first and the last man Zane had ever been with, and this—the raw need and connection between them—was why.

Teeth clashed as they devoured each other's mouths. Tongues dueled for dominance in a dance that Zane never wanted to end. It was Sean who broke away first. Panting for breath he rested his forehead on Zane's and grumbled his denial.

"This is wrong. We can't do this, not without

Sandy."

The soft feminine gasp swiveled both their attention to the doorway. Judging by Sandy's flushed expression, and the way her breasts heaved against the fabric of her dress, she was as turned on as they were. Her nipples poked through their restraints like "come suck me" beacons, and her pupils were so dilated, her hazel eyes looked almost black. He could see the telltale clenching of her thighs. The little minx was getting off watching them, and that would never do.

"Stop that right now, baby girl. Who do your orgasms belong to?"

Her eyes widened further at his growled question, and Sean let him go with a low whistle of appreciation.

"You, Sir. I'm sorry, Sir. It's just. Please don't stop on my account. That was *so* hot. You two together is hot."

The whispered words were music to his ears, and Sean swore and approached her.

"I swear I didn't mean to … fuck. I want you in on this." He held out his hand, and Zane held his breath, wondering what his wife would do. She looked between that hand and him, and at his nod of encouragement slid hers into Sean's. The minute she did his buddy growled and, pushing her up against the wall, kissed her. Her whimper of need shot straight to Zane's cock. Already rock hard from the kisses he'd shared with Sean, seeing the other man devour his wife made him even harder. Sean brought his hands down to Sandy's ass and lifted her up. Her legs came around his hips, and it didn't take a genius to figure out what was going to happen next. The way those two were dry humping each other was such a fucking turn-on. She was close. Zane could tell by the little whimpers his wife was making, as was Sean. His hips rocked into Sandy's pussy with ever increasing speed, until the two of them came together in a spectacle so hot to witness, that Zane yanked down his trousers, pulled out his cock and pumped. He was so revved up it only took a few strokes before he exploded all over his hand. Thick ropes of cum shot out all over the polished floor, and he collapsed into the chair he'd been leaning against with a muttered curse as his legs gave way.

****

Over the blood rushing in his ears, Sean heard it. The unmistakable growl that signaled Zane reaching his climax. *Fucking A.* His own release soaked his boxers, and he smiled in grim amusement. It had been a hell of a long time since he'd come in in his trousers like a fucking teenage boy. Then again, with sweet little Sandy's mewls of surrender still ringing in his ears, her hot puffs of air racing across his neck, where she'd burrowed in in seeming embarrassment, he reckoned he wouldn't have been human, had he managed to hold back. The damp heat of her pussy against his clothed cock made his dick semi harden anew. Now *this*, he could work with. The recovery speed of his teenage years with the experience of a grown ass man. A genuine smile formed on his lips, as he glanced across at Zane. His buddy froze, mid tucking himself away again, seeing his raised eyebrow, and just like that they were back to their old dynamic.

Damn it, that felt good and had so not been what he'd been expecting when he sought out Zane. Unsuited to Civvie street, as he was with his particular skill set, he'd been down on his luck. Pissed off living in shabby hostels, he'd taken his pride in his hands and knocked on Zane's office door. He'd hoped for a job, not the instant connection that had sprung up between them again, made ten times more potent by the passage of time. The boy he'd known had grown into a mature man. A very successful business entrepreneur and above all happily married. To the very woman who stirred in his arms and tried to push him away.

Sean tightened his hold on her delectable ass cheeks in response, and a truly cock-hardening moan came from the woman in his arms.

"Please, let me go. This isn't me. I don't … mph."

Sean shut up her protests by the extremely expedient method of kissing her. She struggled for a few seconds before she went pliant in his arms. Her hands snaked over his shoulders and locked behind his neck as he lifted her higher, to enable him to deepen the kiss.

Sandy tasted of chocolate and coffee, mixed in with the dark spice that Zane used. In short, she tasted of home, salvation, hope, and dammit, he wanted her. Wanted both of them, writhing under his hand, as he took ownership of them both. Sean put all of his emotions into the kiss, all too aware of the heat at his back that alerted him to Zane's presence. Sure enough, when he broke the kiss and gently set his precious bundle of curves back on the floor, her husband was right there.

Sean handed Zane his wife and smiled at them both.

"Convince her this is indeed her, will you, buddy?"

"Yes, Sir."

Sandy gasped. Her eyes fluttered open, and the hazel orbs grew lighter as confusion warred with arousal. Sean ached to pull her back in his arms, to take her out of her head for a while until there was no room for doubt, but that wasn't his place. Not yet, might never be, because she needed to give her consent. They had both railroaded her enough.

Zane dropped a kiss on her button nose, and some

of her agitation fled.

"Tell me you didn't enjoy that, baby girl."

Sandy looked between her husband and Sean, and he could almost see the cogs whirring in her brain, as she connected the dots.

"What did you just call him?" she asked, her voice barely above a breathy whisper. Zane shot him a glance and Sean smiled in encouragement. From the little he'd observed of his buddy's dynamics with his wife, Zane had this.

Sure enough, Zane raised an eyebrow and lowered his voice.

"There's nothing wrong with *your* hearing, so I know you heard me." The intonation he put on that one word wasn't lost on Sean. Zane had borne the worst of the shell blast they'd both been subjected to all those years ago. An ice-cold vise squeezed his chest, making breathing difficult, as all the near misses of his career threatened to suck him under. Now was not the time, nor the place, dammit.

Besides, Sean was one of the lucky ones. He'd chosen to leave the service rather than being forced to retire by the medics, like his buddy had. Not that you'd ever guess Zane's disability. He'd hidden it well, and the tiny hearing aid needed to enhance the hearing in his one good ear was almost invisible to the untrained eye.

And the man had the delightful Sandy, who blushed the prettiest shade of pink, and lowered her gaze to the floor in sweet submission.

"I'm sorry, Sir, it's just … I mean … I wasn't…" She bit her lip, making both men groan, and gave up trying to justify herself.

"I take it you never told her about that side of our relationship, Zane?"

His buddy shook his head and Sandy tensed.

"Why not?" he asked.

"It didn't seem relevant at the time, but..." Zane paused, wrapped his hand back in Sandy's long auburn curls and tugged her head up to ensure she looked at them both. When she did the utter trust that shone from her hazel orbs took Sean's breath away. It also made that never far away ball of disappointment, of longing, bounce around his gut. He would have to earn that level of commitment from her, if she agreed to be his. Zane's next words brought that ball to jarring halt.

"Sean taught me everything I know. He wasn't just my commanding officer, he was and is my friend, my Dom, the one person who *got* me before you came into my life, baby girl. I trust him with my life, and I want you to trust him, too. He won't steer us wrong, not in a scene anyway." Zane smirked at Sean, and Sean's hand itched to turn his buddy's ass raw for that. It had the desired effect on Sandy, however, because her lips quirked in amusement, and she glanced across at Sean briefly from under her eyelashes.

"Well, if that's the case, Sir, might I remind you to watch your tone. If I talked about you like that, I dare say my butt would be red already."

Sean threw his head back and laughed, and Zane frowned.

"Let me worry over that, baby girl. If I was you I'd worry over your own behind. You came without permission, did you not? What shall we do about our naughty little girl, Sean?"

Sandy opened her mouth as though to protest, but one glance at both of them seemed to make her think better of it.

"I'll let you know that once I know for sure that Sandy is *our* girl." Sean dropped his voice on purpose, let it take on that edge he knew would get through to any submissive, and sure enough a shiver went through Sandy. He reached across to enable him to place his hand on her throat and squeezed. Not enough to cut off her air supply, just enough to make his intentions clear, and her pretty little bow mouth opened in a silent plea.

"I need to hear her say she wants this, and if she does I need to know her safewords, not that I have any intention of taking things too far, not tonight, at least." Another one of those telling gasps came from Zane's wife, and her heart rate went crazy under his fingertips.

The sweet musk of aroused woman hit his nostrils, made him rock hard again, and judging by Zane's grunt and the way he shifted from foot to foot, his buddy was in the same predicament.

"Well, little one, what will it be?"

Chapter Three

Sean's growled question left her breathless and so damn aroused she could feel the trickle down the inside of her thigh. The lacy thong—a matching counterpart to her bra—had long since stopped offering any protection from her own desire. Her pussy felt swollen and so sensitive after that delicious orgasm she'd ridden out against the massive bulge in Sean's trousers, it wouldn't take much to send her over the edge again.

Wasn't this her deepest, darkest fantasy come to life? They'd talked about in on occasion in the past, and Zane had always been too possessive to go through with it. Only at her last birthday, he'd apologized to her for not being able to fulfil that particular fantasy. In any case, Zane did such an awesome job with his cock and the help of dildos that she'd never felt like she'd missed out on the whole double penetration thing. It was one of their favorite scenes, in fact, but this… Being the meat in between this particular male sandwich … good grief, if she got this turned on just imagining it, what would the real thing be like? She'd never survive it, and more importantly what would that do to her relationship with Zane?

How could she love him like she did, yet be this drawn to his buddy? This was all kinds of wrong, wasn't it? Even as she thought that, she told the rational side of her brain to take a fucking hike. Zane wasn't only her husband, he was also her Dom, and she trusted him implicitly. As crazy as it sounded, the last few minutes since she'd walked in on the two of them kissing, she'd never felt closer to him. And if this was what Zane wanted, needed, as she was fast beginning to realize, then they could make this work. After all, he'd fulfilled every one of her fantasies over the last ten years, and plenty she hadn't even known she'd had, so if he needed this...

Stop thinking about it and just go with it. Especially as you want this, too.

Taking a deep breath in, she nudged her chin up, and searched her husband's expression. He looked pensive, tense almost, as he waited for her answer, and as for Sean? She could feel the heat in his gaze scorch her skin as though it was his hands not his eyes that devoured her. His steady hold on her throat, while Zane kept his hand wrapped in her hair in clear signal of his ownership of her, further grounded her.

"Is this what you want, Sir?" she asked Zane, and the flash of hope, of excitement in his amber eyes was all the confirmation she needed. "This won't change things between us?" She hated how needy that sounded, hated how she couldn't just shut off her brain and simply grab the pleasure on offer.

Zane shook his head and released her. Sean, too, let go of her, and, bereft of their combined possession, Sandy shivered in the warm room. She wrapped her arms around herself to chase away the goosebumps that seemed to invade every inch of her skin.

"It will change things, but I hope for the better." Sean's answer made her draw in a sharp breath. "I promise I'll take good care of both of you, and if this isn't working for you, I'll leave. The last thing I want to do is come between husband and wife, Dom and sub. This won't work without your consent, Sandy. But know this." He paused, rubbed his large hands up and down her exposed arms and swore softly under his breath. "Jesus, you're frozen. Perhaps we ought to shelve this for now. We all got rather in a mess earlier, and I think we need a shower, don't you, pet?"

Something warm and cozy uncurled inside her chest hearing her call him that. As generic as that title was her submissive side lapped up the concern, the care behind his words, and it made her blurt out her own question.

"Together, as in all of us?"

Sean's brows drew together, and Zane smiled.

"If we get into a shower together, you know what will happen, baby, and—"

"Maybe that's what I want, just for tonight?" Her cheeks heated at her having interrupted her husband, but in for a penny in for a pound and all that. "I mean you ask me if this is what I want, but how can I know that? How can I know if this will work without trying it on for size so to speak?"

Both men smirked, and she knew immediately that had been the wrong choice of words, as confirmed by Sean's amused laughter.

"Is your sub not only insulting the size of our cocks, but also our ability to satisfy her needs, buddy? Are you going to stand for that, Zane?"

Her husband crossed his arms over his chest and spread his legs in a move designed to let her know she'd just displeased him, and her heart turned into a jackhammer.

"I most certainly will not, Sean. Tell your Sirs your safewords, girl, before we turn that delicious butt of yours red."

Lordy, *your Sirs*, that sounded way too promising. From somewhere she found her voice. Admittedly a breathy porn star impression of her usual cadence, as she recounted the traffic lights system.

"Red for stop, yellow for I need a minute, and green for all systems go. I—yikes."

The world tilted as Sean lifted her effortlessly and flung her over his massive shoulder. The breath whooshed out of her lungs, and her scrambling hands were caught in Zane's as he grasped her wrists and grumbled his command.

"Hold still. What color are you now, girl?"

"Green Sir, I … ow."

The swat to her ass really stung. Sean hit much harder than Zane ever did, and he didn't stop as he rained blows on her ass that brought tears to her eyes, before he stopped and rubbed that area with one hand while the other dove between her thighs. She couldn't help her groan of need, as his questing fingers made contact with her slit.

"Hmm, our girl likes a spanking, I see. She's sopping wet for us, Zane. Here, taste."

Zane transferred both of her wrists in one of his hands, and then presumably licked her cum off his buddy's fingers. Sandy tried in vain to blow her hair out her face to see, but her hearing worked just fine.

Those slurping noises could only mean one thing, and she grew wetter still.

"Hmm, delicious, lead the way to the shower, so that we can properly enjoy her."

With that, Zane released his hold on her, and she was treated to the awesome view of Sean's ass cheeks clenching in his trousers as they started the trek up the stairs to their wet room. Her excitement grew with each step, not least because Sean swatted her ass with every step. Alternating hard swats with far too arousing rubs of his hands while he murmured his approval of her behind.

"Hmm, you really have the most delicious ass. I can't wait to bury myself balls deep in it while Zane fucks your sweet pussy. Would you like that, pet?"

"God, yes, green, Sir."

Sean's big shoulders shook in silent amusement, and Zane, too, laughed.

A door opened and banged shut, and then Sean

slid her slowly down his front.

"Here we are. I've had some additions made to this room over the years, as you can see," Zane said. The deep, rough timbre of his voice caused a renewed ache in her pussy, as Sean stood her gently on her feet and looked around.

"So I see. I'm glad there's plenty of room for all of us. I do hate to be cramped in the shower." With that he grasped the front of Zane's shirt and kissed him. Just like it had before, seeing Sean kiss her husband, and the way that quickly turned passionate sent Sandy's pussy into spasms of delight, especially when Sean reached blindly out to her and pulled her into the embrace. He wrenched his mouth off Zane's and kissed her, while Zane nibbled that spot just under her ear designed to drive her wild, while he grasped her breasts from behind. With the unerring certainty of a man who knew his way around her body, he found her nipples and tugged. Sandy groaned her need into Sean's mouth, while she yanked at his shirt. Her fingers briefly encountered hair-roughened abs, before her wrists were grabbed and held high above her head. Sean continued kissing her, while Zane tortured her nipples through the fabric of her dress. Every pull sent darts of pleasure to her clit, and she moaned her denial when he withdrew his talented fingers.

"We need to get her out of this dress, Sir."

Hearing her husband address Sean like that gave her a secret thrill, the likes of which she wouldn't have thought possible. To know that she was at the mercy of two Doms, one of which was an unknown entity made this whole thing extra exciting. Whether it was the perceived danger Sean represented, the not knowing how far he would take things, her befuddled brain couldn't quite figure out. She stopped thinking altogether when Zane unzipped her dress at the back, followed by the snap on her bra and slid his hands around her ribcage to cup her freed breasts.

"Let her go a minute so we can lose these contraptions." Zane's grumbled command pitched her need even higher.

Sean stopped kissing her, the pressure on her wrists ceased, and in the next instant she was naked, barring her soaked through thong, hold-up stockings, and the heels she still wore.

"Fuck, you're beautiful." Sean's deep voice showed his admiration of her body as much as his perusal of her as he stepped back and let his hot gaze roam all over. "Spread her for me, so that I can look my fill of our sweet cunt."

The dirty words turned her on almost as much as her husband's immediate response.

"Your wish is my command, Sir."

Zane kicked her legs apart and held her wrists firmly behind her back. Sean, in the meantime, shrugged out of his shirt, and kicked his shoes and trousers off with a speed that left her dizzy. As did the size of his erection straining against the damp confines of his boxers. To know she'd done that to him was a heady aphrodisiac indeed, as was her husband's erection pushing against her ass.

Sean divested himself of his boxers, too, and she gasped when his thick shaft bobbed up to his navel. She'd been right. He was huge. While his girth wasn't as thick as Zane's he had a good half inch in length, and Zane wasn't exactly small in that department.

Heavily veined, Sean's magnificent cock looked ready to explode all over again, the broad tip already glistening in pre-cum.

She wanted to taste him so badly, yet Zane's grip on her wrists stopped her from reaching out. As though

Sean had read her thoughts, he groaned and, taking his shaft in his hand, pumped a few times along its length.

"Soon, you get to suck my cock, sweet girl, but for now, I need to taste you properly." With that he got to his knees. As tall as he was that action brought his head level with her breasts, and he wasted no time in taking full advantage of that fact. Sean held each breast in his large hand, and grinning up at her pushed them together, before he took both nipples into his mouth and sucked hard.

Sandy tugged at Zane's restraints, and her knees would have buckled had Zane not pushed his thigh between her legs to keep her upright. Her head fell back against his shoulder, and she gave herself over to the intense sensations Sean's talented tongue subjected her to. Her nipples had always been sensitive, a livewire straight to her clit, and with the dual sensation of Sean's sucks and the gentle friction Zane's leg created between her thighs, she climbed the rungs of arousal in record time. Her hips bucked against her husband's leg as she sought to increase the friction she needed to go over.

A sharp bite to her shoulder coincided with Sean releasing his hold on her nipples with an audible pop.

"No coming without your Sirs' permission, baby girl, or we'll leave you hanging."

Sure enough, Zane withdrew his thigh, while Sean grasped her hips to keep her steady. He kissed his way down her soft belly, interspersing kisses with little bites that left her hovering on the precipice. He bypassed her pussy and, flinging one of her legs over his shoulder, nibbled along the edge of her stocking.

"Hmm, as much as I love these, they need to come off. Look at me, pet."

Sandy's eyes flew open, and the sight of Sean between her legs made another gush of moisture trickle past the elastic of her thong. He licked that trail away, and she groaned.

"Please, I need to, please."

Grinning, Sean blew a stream of hot air across her still covered slit, and her clit contracted in need.

"What do you need, sweet Sandy? Do you need to come?" He nudged his nose along her vulva, inhaling deeply, and Sandy jerked. Not that it got her very far because Zane's hold on her wrists never lessened, and Sean's fingers dug into her hips with so much pressure, she would surely be left with bruises. The thought of carrying his marks made breathing even more difficult, and she groaned her reply.

"Please, so close, I ... God..."

She wasn't entirely sure what pleas were spilling from her lips, and in truth she was far too gone to care. With Zane's harsh breaths in her ear, and Sean's dirty words she was a goner.

"So very eager. I can see your little clit push against this lace. You're close, aren't you, sweet thing? Such a turn-on. What do you think, Zane, should we let her come or torture her some more?"

Sean let go of her hips briefly to tear her thong clean off of her, and then he looked his fill.

"So very wet, and pink. Your hole is clenching, begging to be filled. What do you want in there, pet? My tongue? My fingers? My cock? Or Zane's? Tell me, or I'll leave you hanging and fuck your husband instead."

****

Zane swore, and Sandy gasped, as Zane's cock jerked painfully at Sean's words.

To see the man he loved on his knees between his wife's legs was such a fucking turn-on and that was without Sandy's reply.

"Please, I don't care which. I just need to come."

Sean licked along Sandy's slit, and the appreciative noises he made proved too much for Zane's restraint.

"Make her fucking come and then fuck me already. I need you in me."

Sandy murmured something unintelligible before she went stiff and started to shake in the unmistakable tremors of an orgasm. He let go of her wrists and wrapped his arm around her waist instead to keep her upright, as her knees went from under her, and she writhed against Sean's mouth. Sean kept up his attention to Sandy's glistening cunt, until she slumped against Zane with a small content sigh. Only then did Sean scramble to his feet and kiss Zane. His wife's sweet, familiar musk mixed in with Sean's masculinity as Zane kissed him back, dimly aware of Sandy slipping out from between them. The sounds of the shower came on, and Sandy's hesitant voice broke through the haze of arousal he found himself in, as her hands tugged at the waistband of his trousers.

Sean pulled away from the kiss with a muttered curse, and when Zane opened his eyes it was to see his Sir studying him, while Sandy did her best to get him naked. He tried to push her hands away, but the little minx was having none of it.

"If you two are going to fuck, you need to get naked and into that shower, I reckon … Sir." The added title made him grin, and Sean, too, shook his head. His blue eyes twinkled in both amusement and lust.

"Oh, you'll pay for that sass later, pet, but for now I'll agree with you. I'll want you in the shower, too, though. Tied up so that you can't get yourself off while you watch us."

Sandy's sharp intake of breath matched Zane's as all sorts of deliciously kinky scenarios bombarded his brain.

Sandy's hand faltered mid tugging Zane's trousers down, and he finished the job for her, while kicking his shoes off and yanking his shirt over his head. The buttons went pinging off in all directions in his haste to divest himself of his remaining clothes, and when he at long last stood naked in front of his Sir and his wife, he breathed a sigh of relief.

Through the steam filling up the wet room he could see the flush of arousal on his wife's skin, as well as the marks of Sean's possession.

Seeing the fingerprints, little bites, and the emerging stubble rash on Sandy's delicate, pale skin should have sent him into a frenzy of jealousy. Would have done so in an instant had they been caused by any other man. Now, here, in this moment they only added to the hotness of the situation, not least because Sandy was here to share this moment of reconnection between him and Sean.

He tore his gaze away from her wide-eyed expression and smirked up at Sean.

"I like your thinking, Sir, but if she's coming in there with us, the shoes and stockings will have to go."

"More's the pity, but I agree. Your wife looks fucking hot like that, Zane. I trust you have something in that shower to keep her tied up and helpless for us while I claim your ass."

Sandy's mouth opened in a silent O while Zane laughed and nodded.

"Sure thing. There's a suspension bar in there and a spreader which should work nicely."

Sean nodded while Sandy mumbled her denial and tried to step away from them. *Silly girl.*

Sean was on her before she got very far.

"No is not your safeword, pet. Now be a good girl

and hold still for us while Zane gets you naked and tied up for our mutual pleasure."

Between them they divested Sandy of her remaining clothing, and Zane loved the little mewls of excitement, which she didn't seem to be aware of making. It also gave him pause for thought, as he knelt under the hot stream of water to fasten the spreader bar between his wife's ankles while Sean secured her wrists in the suspension cuffs linked to the bar dangling from the ceiling. When had been the last time he'd heard those sounds? When was the last time they had properly scened like this? Too wrapped up in their work and the nitty-gritty of everyday life they'd—if not *lost* this part of themselves—put it on the back burner. Sandy regularly brought home her work as teacher, and with his business booming, he'd worked longer and longer hours, leaving them both too knackered to be up for anything bar a quick fuck. Even that hadn't happened that often lately, certainly not since Sean had reappeared in his life.

Guilt gripped Zane in a stranglehold, as he looked up his wife's voluptuous body. Rivulets of water cascaded over her amazing rack, drawing attention to the large areolae, and her big, tight nipples begging to be clamped. As though Sean had read his mind, he produced the clamps Zane also kept in his little box of tricks in this room. He ran the cool metal over her buds, while he looked toward Zane for confirmation.

He nodded at the man while straightening up and cupping Sandy's boobs in his hands.

"Give your Sirs a color, baby girl, and breathe in while Sean attaches the clamps."

Sandy gasped and threw her head back, as the first clamp went on easily enough.

"Green, oh God, oh God, it hurts so good."

Sean smiled, adjusted the tightness, and sucked

her other tit into his mouth briefly while maintaining eye contact with Zane.

Such a fucking turn-on.

Zane swallowed hard past his closed-up throat, as emotion swamped him. While Sean and he had shared many a woman back in the day, this meant so much more. He could only hope and pray that Sandy would agree to more than this one time. Zane wanted it all, the three of them together.

Maybe that made him a selfish bastard, though looking at Sandy in the throes of pleasure/pain as Sean attached the other clamp and then kissed her, before he kissed Zane, this just felt right. The slap to his ass stung, and groaning, he allowed Sean to turn him around to face the tiles.

"Now, for you, my sweet boy."

Sandy murmured something unintelligible, not that he had it in him to pay too much attention to his wife right now. It was enough to know she was there with him, watching, her breaths getting heavier in her excitement.

Sean crowded him against the wall, kicked his legs apart, and placed Zane's arms high above his head against the slippery tiles.

"Keep those right there, my boy."

"Yes, Sir."

A bite to his shoulder made him groan, and then he forgot to think altogether because Sean grasped Zane's cock and ran his thumb through Zane's weeping slit.

"So fucking eager, aren't you? Tell me you want me to sink balls deep into your ass while your wife watches us."

"Oh fuck." Sandy's hoarse exclamation matched his own feelings, and he pushed his hips forward to gain more friction from Zane's fist wrapped around his shaft.

"Please, it's been too long."

Sean rested his head between Zane's shoulder blades, and his Sir's breath felt cool against his overheated skin.

"That it has, my sweet boy."

Sean withdrew, and Zane's denial swelled up inside him, until he saw Sir reach down into the box and pull out the lube and condoms. The action treated both Zane and Sandy to the perfect view of Sean's ass, and Zane's cock twitched. One day soon he would claim that delicious butt again, but for now he wanted his Sir inside him, to feel his hole stretched and claimed.

Sandy yanked on her restraints while making the most cock-hardening sounds ever, and when her gaze collided with his, the lust, love, and utter trust that shone back at him made the words tumble out of his mouth.

"I love you, both of you."

Sean froze mid straightening up, while Sandy's eyes went wide and filled with tears.

"I love you, Sir."

Sean swore softly and looked between them as though he was debating something, and it was Sandy who got him to move in the end.

"Please, don't stop, Sir. Zane needs you, and I want to see him happy."

Zane's throat closed up in so much emotion he could barely breathe, especially when Sean closed the distance between Sandy and him and kissed her.

This wasn't just any kiss. The ones they'd shared before had been full of passion, hard, frantic one might say, but this one was tender, tentative, as Sean coaxed Sandy's plump lips with his tongue. When she opened to him, he cradled her nape as though she was as precious to him as she was to Zane. Zane's breaths turned as harsh as the couple's he was watching, and when Sean eventually pulled away with a bite to Sandy's bottom lip, she was whimpering in need.

"You're an amazing woman, pet, and I want us all in this together."

Her lips trembled in unspoken emotion, and it took every ounce of self-control Zane possessed to not take her in his arms and to kiss her senseless. Only Sean's renewed presence at his back kept him anchored, as the other man turned off the shower. Their combined breathing filled the sudden silence. The pop of the lube lid coming off pitched Zane right back into the fevered, anticipatory state he'd been in, ever since Sean had walked into their living room and he'd witnessed the instant chemistry that had sprung up between Sean and Sandy.

While deep down he'd hoped for this, he'd not thought it possible in real life. Was that why Sean and Sandy had never met before now? The temptation to initiate something like this would have been too great, and there should only ever be two people in a marriage, not three. At least, that's what he'd always thought. Now he wasn't too sure on that. This felt too right.

Sean's lubed fingers probed at his asshole, and Zane let out a shaky breath, while Sean murmured encouragement as he added another finger.

"Relax, my boy. Fuck, you're tight. How long has it been?"

"Not since you, Sir."

Sean's probing digits stopped, and the burn ceased. Over the blood rushing in his ears, he just about heard Sandy's croaked words.

"Jesus, don't stop now. He needs you, Sir."

He could feel Sean's smile in the kisses he dropped on Zane's neck, before he slapped his ass with enough force to make him stagger forwards.

"Change of plan, buddy. I'm going to fuck your ass while you sink that big cock of yours into your wife's sweet cunt."

"Oh God!" Sandy's impassioned plea was music to Zane's ears, as he hastened to comply with this plan. Dimly aware of Sean pulling on a condom, he stepped behind his sweet Sandy and grasped her hips.

"I'm going to fuck you so hard, baby girl."

"Please, just do ... oh."

Sandy hissed her approval and popped her butt out as much she could, while he lined his hard dick up with her sopping wet pussy and thrust home.

Her internal muscles gripped him like a warm, wet fist, fluttering around him in a way which told him it wouldn't take much for her to go over. In truth, he wouldn't last long, not with the blunt pressure against his own ass, as Sean pushed slowly past the tight ring of muscle.

"Fuck, I missed you. Relax, let me in. That's it. So fucking good."

Sean reached past them with one arm, grasped hold of Sandy's shoulder, and pulled out of Zane almost all the way only to slam back in again. The action rocked him deeper into his wife, and Sandy started to pant and moan. Zane wasn't far behind her, as Sean repeated that move, and pleasure burst out from the contact, intense, immediate, all-consuming, as the three of them set up a haphazard thrust and retreat system that had his own release boiling to the surface in record time. Sandy's sweet cunt milked his cock in rhythmic ripples as she teetered on the edge of her climax. Sir's possession of his ass awakened every nerve ending he possessed. Sean's growls and grunts in his ear, which matched the animalistic sounds coming out of Zane's mouth... It was all too much.

So much fucking pleasure as his balls drew tight.

"Don't you fucking dare, not until she has." Sean grumbled his instruction in his ear, as he pulled out and then slammed back into him. The action ricocheted Zane so deep inside his wife, she screamed. It all proved too much.

"Fuck, yeah, come for us, Sandy, now. I … argh." Zane just about managed to get those words out, as Sandy's release triggered his own. Zane saw stars as he emptied himself deep inside his wife's body, while Sean stiffened behind him and pulled out.

Chapter Four

Fuck, fuck, fuck.

That one word bounced around Sean's head, as he pulled out of the tight clasp of his lover's ass, yanked off the condom and emptied himself over Zane's delectable buns and his wife's hips. A never-ending stream of cum that marked his subs in the most primitive way possible. Not that either one of them seemed aware of it right now. Zane held onto his wife as though his life depended on it, and Sean braced a hand on the tiled wall to catch his breath.

How he'd managed to stay upright at all was a fucking miracle in itself, because that had been intense, made more so by the emotions which swamped him.

He might have called that fucking, but it was *so* much more. Seeing Zane and his wife still locked together as intimately as two people could be ... fuck, that was such a turn-on. He flicked the shower back on to wash away the evidence of their mutual desire, and Zane groaned as the water hit his back and no doubt sore ass.

Sean hadn't been gentle, had been utterly incapable of being so, not with Zane's ass gripping his cock in a stranglehold, made ten times more potent by Sandy's response to every one of his thrusts into her husband's depth.

He pulled both of them into his arms, mindful of how still Sandy was. Eyes closed, head resting on her husband's shoulder, she looked deliciously disheveled. Strands of her wet hair played peekaboo with her rack, where the still clamped nipples stood proudly erect.

Zane's softening cock slid out of her swollen pussy, and she moaned softly.

"I think we finished her off, Zane. Help me release her out of this get up."

Zane stepped back, held his head briefly into the steam of water and then shook it. Drops of water went flying off the ends of his dark hair, and Sean laughed. It was longer than it had been in the army, but it suited his old buddy.

"Give me a minute. You killed me, too." Zane pulled his head down to kiss him, and as brief as the contact was it grounded Sean like nothing else could.

"You're okay? I wasn't too hard on you?" Sean inwardly grimaced at the hoarse cadence of his voice, but, fuck him, he loved this man, and cared far too much about the soft woman who stirred in his arms. If he wasn't careful he was in real danger of falling for her. The speed with which this was all happening should make him run far away, but his feet were rooted to the spot. Not least, because it was his duty to take care of both his subs.

"Fuck no, mate, I loved it, and it's been a while since I've seen Sandy like this. Let's get her taken care of and into bed."

They worked together, freeing her of her restraints and the clamps, and Sean washed her down while Zane held her in his arms. By the time Sean turned off the shower, and they were all sufficiently dried off, Sandy was more with it. The way she clung to her husband, and the tender looks Zane bestowed on her as he cradled her in his arms and carried her through to their bedroom left a hollow ache in Sean's gut.

What the hell was he doing coming between man and wife? As hot as all of that had been he had no right to be here. Not really. No doubt, come morning Sandy would feel very differently about all of this. At Zane's nudge, he pulled back the bedcovers to enable the man to place his wife on the enormous bed. He had to give it to Zane.

The man had fallen on his feet, and his success in business was echoed in his home. While not ostentatiously big, the four-bed semi-detached Zane and Sandy called home was comfortably furnished with all the modern mod cons in place, never more so in evidence than in this bedroom. The bed was big enough to accommodate four people comfortably—a fact that wasn't lost on him—as Zane slid in next to his wife and quirked an eyebrow in invitation.

"Come on in. I'm fucking exhausted after all that, and even you can't keep going forever. Besides, Sandy is a cuddler. She needs the contact after a scene."

Sure enough, she reached for her husband and almost seemed to want to climb into his skin while he stroked her hair and murmured soothing nonsense into her still damp hair. Seeing her like this, all flushed and rosy and needing Zane, made that hollow ache in his gut widen to the depth of the Grand Canyon.

"Yeah, from you. I'm just a—"

"Stop being a dick and get your ass in here. I know Sandy. She'd never have agreed to any of this if she didn't want you here, so stop the noble crap and help me take care of our girl."

Sean pulled in a sharp breath to ease the instant longing that filled him, but as Zane all but stared him down, and looked ready to punch his lights out, he complied and climbed in the other side. Once there he couldn't have stayed away from them if his life had depended on it, and Zane growled his approval when he spooned around Sandy. As for the warm bundle of curves that fit his hard body as though she was made for him, she sighed, threw one arm back to pull him closer, and then fell asleep.

Zane smiled at him, his even, white teeth just about visible in the darkening room. The lights had to be on a timer or something, and Sean rolled his eyes in silent amusement.

"I'll stay for a while, but I really ought to leave."

"You do that, and she'll never forgive you. Neither will I. We want you here."

Zane shut his eyes, effectively stopping any further protest Sean might have made, and soon his even breathing told Sean he, too, was asleep.

This was his cue to leave, the bedroom, at least. They had a guest room he could use, should use, because Sean never slept easy, but exhaustion pulled at his limbs, too. With Zane's leg curling over his, and Sandy's delectable ass nestled into his hardening cock—*I fucking have turned into a teenage boy*—he gave in. He would just shut his eyes for a moment. Where was the harm in that?

Plenty as he woke up with his hand wrapped around Sandy's throat. Heart galloping and with his sweat in his eyes, he didn't see his buddy's wife. He wasn't in a cozy bed but caught up in the never-ending nightmare that had been his last mission. Bullets pummeled his back, the force of which should mean his death, were it not for his protective armor. From somewhere, Zane's shouts broke through the fever and the noise.

"Fuck, Sean, let her go." The punch to the side of his head mercifully faded everything to black.

****

Sandy had the most delicious dream, one where she was cocooned between two hot, hard male bodies, their even breaths into her ears an echo of her beating heart. Content, happy … until it changed. The comforting warmth turned suffocating, menacing.

I can't breathe.

Panicked, her eyes flew open to see Sean on top

of her. Not only was she pinned by his considerable muscle mass, his fist on her throat closed off her air supply completely. Eyes as hard as steel stared right through her while sweat ran down his face. His usually so sensuous, full lips curled back into a menacing snarl, jaw locked so tight his scar stood out, throbbed in strain, as his fist tightened even more.

Over the thud of her heartbeat in her ears, and the rising panic that meant she saw stars in front of her eyes, she heard Zane's voice. Gruff with sleep, it quickly turned into a full-blown shout as the lights came on, and her husband's face appeared in her peripheral vision. His fists pummeled Sean's back, and then the side light which lived on her night stand made sickening contact with the side of Sean's head. His fist on her loosened, and he slumped on top of her.

Sandy still couldn't breathe, stuck under Sean's bulk and tried in vain to shove his dead weight off of her. Just as she thought she was going to pass out, the heavy pressure lifted and Zane's frantic words in her ear registered, as he pulled her off the bed and into his arms.

"Jesus, baby, breathe. Talk to me. I'll kill him if he hurt you."

Sandy didn't have the strength to reassure him. It took too much effort to fill her lungs with much needed oxygen. Eventually the sickness passed, and the room came into sharp focus, as did the reality of their situation.

Her eyes widened in horror at the bloodstain which appeared under Sean's head and marred the pale carpet. How had he ended up on the floor?

She pushed against Zane's chest, and when that didn't work, she finally found her voice.

"I'm okay. Let me go, dammit. What on earth did you do?"

"What did *I* do? Fuck, girl, he was strangling

you." The hurt in Zane's voice, and the almost desperation in which he ran his hands over her body as though to reassure himself that she really was okay, twisted her insides. She wanted nothing more to snuggle in, to reassure her husband, but, right now, Sean needed her more. The crimson stain on the carpet got wider, and Sean wasn't moving. Was he even breathing?

Her heart twisted anew at the expression on her husband's face when she turned her back on him and scrambled down to the floor to check on his buddy. Putting her hand over his mouth confirmed that he was breathing, even if his respiratory efforts were far too shallow.

"I know that. But he didn't mean it, you of all people should know that." She glanced briefly up at her husband, and the pain in his eyes added to the ache in her chest. However, right now, Sean was her priority, and they had to make sure he was okay. "Jesus, he's barely breathing. Help me move him into recovery and get me a towel to stem that bleeding."

She pushed the night lamp to one side—ignoring the bloody evidence on it—and caught the towel Zane threw her way with one hand, while she probed Sean's skull with the fingers of her free hand. There it was, a spongy mess where the lamp must have made contact and caused the head injury. She pressed the towel to the wound, while Zane carefully maneuvered his buddy into the recovery position.

His hand tightened over the white-knuckled grip she had on the towel pressed to Sean's head.

"Here, I've got this. Ring the ambulance and get some clothes on. We need to get him seen to asap. Fuck, I didn't mean to cause this." Zane's regret and worry showed in the hoarse words. "Hang on in there, Sean, *please*."

Belatedly it dawned on Sandy that they were all stark naked, and she hastily grabbed some knickers, jeans, and a top, while she fumbled for her mobile. It seemed an interminably long time before she got through to ambulance control.

"There's been an accident. We need an ambulance now. It's a head injury, and he's not conscious. … Yes, he's breathing, barely. … We've put him into recovery. … Yes, I will do. … Please hurry. … Okay."

Sandy stopped listening to the controller, and the phone slipped out of her shaking hands, when Sean groaned in pain, and tried to move.

"Whaaa … so … Sand…"

"Easy there, buddy, stay put." Zane pushed Sean back down to the floor and held him there. He shook his head at his buddy and murmured his own apology.

"I'm sorry, man. I didn't mean to hit you this hard, I swear." Zane's voice cracked in emotion while Sean's pain-filled blue gaze connected with Sandy's as he struggled to speak, and she hurried over to the two men.

"It's okay. I'm fine. Don't try to talk. It will all be all right, you'll see."

She took over from Zane in holding the now blood-soaked towel to Sean's head wound so that Zane, too, could throw some clothes on. There was nothing they could do about Sean's naked state, apart from cover his lower half with the woolen blanket that lived on the chair in the corner of their bedroom.

How long she sat there, chatting nonsense to a rapidly fading Sean to keep him awake, while Zane paced the room, she would never know, but, eventually blue lights reflected around the room, and Zane disappeared to open the door to the paramedics. She had never been so relieved to see the green uniform of the two men crew as she was the moment they appeared in the doorway followed by a haggard looking Zane. He seemed to have aged several years since they'd all woken up so rudely, and her heart turned over in her chest. So not how she thought their evening would end.

"Okay then, here, I've got this. My name is Steve, and I'm a paramedic. This here is Ben." The older one of the two guys invading her personal space smiled at her while the other one grasped her shoulders and pulled her away from Sean. He'd slipped back into unconsciousness, and it took every ounce of self-control she had to step away, as directed.

"There, now, we've got this, Miss?"

"Mrs. McLeod, but call me Sandy. Please, will he be all right?"

"Just let us worry over that. What happened here, Sandy?"

Steve's gaze briefly rested on her throat, and Sandy fought the urge to cover up what had to be substantial bruising coming up, if the soreness she experienced when trying to swallow was any indication.

I should have grabbed a Polo neck, dammit.

Some sort of unspoken communication seemed to be going on between the two men, before they turned their attention back to Sean.

"Okay, right, Mr. McLeod, can you hear me?"

Sandy jumped when Zane's large hands landed on her shoulders and pulled her back against him.

"I'm Mr. McLeod. His name is Sean. Sean Manson. He's an old army buddy of mine, and we … well, never mind what we were doing. Just fix him up, will you?"

"I see." Ben, the younger paramedic said, and again that indecipherable look passed between the two men. He got on his radio to update control, and then walked past Sandy and Zane to get a stretcher.

Sandy started to shiver by the time he came back up the stairs, and Zane swore softly and rubbed his hands up and down her arms.

"It's okay, baby girl. We'll get this sorted."

Steve looked up from securing Sean to the stretcher and frowned.

"Looks like your wife is going into shock. We'll take her in the ambulance with us. There won't be room for you, sir, I'm afraid."

"That's okay, I'll follow in our car. Just take good care of them both, will you?"

"That's our job."

Before Sandy knew what was happening, she was bundled into a silvery survival blanket and strapped into one of the pull-down seats in the back of the ambulance. The doors shut on a worried looking Zane, and Steve hooked Sean up to all sorts of equipment while Ben got into the cab and they were off.

Once Steve seemed reassured that Sean was doing okay, he turned his attention to her.

"Warmer now?" he asked.

"Yes, thank you. I don't really know what came over me."

Steve reached out to pat her arm and shrugged.

"You've had a shock. It's only to be expected. Want me to look at that throat of yours?"

"What?" Sandy startled and shook her head. Suddenly his kind smile didn't seem such. More calculating and judgy.

"I'm fine. There's no need. You just look after Sean."

"Nothing more I can do for him now. He's stable, so that's a good thing. Your throat on the other hand…"

He shook his head and sighed. "That looks sore. What happened tonight, Sandy?" When she didn't reply he shrugged. "Okay, tell me to mind my own business, but—"

"Mind your own business. It's nothing."

A short laugh was his response this time.

"Fair enough, but you'll have to tell them at the hospital. I dare say the police will want to have a word as well."

That got Sandy's attention, and she forced her gaze away from a far too still Sean and focused back on Steve.

"Why on earth? You called the police?"

Again, with that infuriating shrug.

"Standard policy when we attend a suspected domestic violence case."

Sandy's ears started ringing, and she tried in vain to swallow down the rising bile. Good lord, what a mess this all was.

"I'm not some battered wife, for fuck's sake. What we did, all three of us, was consensual, and it's nobody's business."

"If you say so, Sandy, but that doesn't explain how Sean ended up in this state, now does it?" He held his hands up in surrender when she opened her mouth to have a go at him and smiled. "Look, I'm not judging here. My first concern is to the patient. Just giving you a heads-up as to what you can expect when we get to the hospital, that's all."

Sandy slumped back in her seat and sighed.

"Fine, I appreciate that, but there really isn't anything to tell. Sean's injury was an accident that's all."

An uncomfortable silence fell between them for the remainder of the journey to the hospital. Once those doors opened all hell broke loose.

Sean was whisked away to be assessed, and Sandy had to endure yet more questioning, first from the doctor in duty, and then the elderly police woman who insisted on taking her statement. By the time Sandy had finished telling her version, her ears were glowing in embarrassment.

"Right, so let me recap that. You're in a consensual BDSM relationship with your husband and tonight you decided to include Sean in that relationship?"

Sandy nodded and forced herself to look the woman in the eyes.

"Yes, that about sums it up. It was *my* decision to agree to that. I was in no way coerced or forced, and if you must know it was fantastic, until… Well, until…" Unbidden the image of Sean on top of her, choking her, sprang to the forefront of her mind, and her hand went to her throat. She'd seen how raw it looked when she'd looked in the mirror after having used the facilities. The WPC's gaze followed her actions and her eyes narrowed.

"So, your bruises aren't due to some form of erotic roleplay then?"

It was on the tip of Sandy's tongue to say erotic asphyxiation was her thing, but that would have been a lie. Besides, knowing Zane, he would tell them exactly what happened, and he would take all the blame on himself. The longing to be back in his arms, to hear him tell her that everything was going to be all right, took her breath away, and she blinked away tears.

"I need to see my husband," she said.

WPC Adderly nodded and smiled. Perfunctory and cold, it didn't reach her eyes, however.

"I'm afraid that's not possible. He has been charged with GBH and is currently at the police station telling his version of events."

"What? But that's insane. I told you what

happened. It was an accident. He didn't mean to. I mean neither one of them did, I mean... oh fuck it."

"I appreciate the stress you're under, Mrs. McLeod, but please refrain from using such language. Tell me again what happened in this supposed *accident,* please."

Sandy didn't appreciate the intonation the woman put on that one word, but she had to get her to believe her, so she swallowed her snarky comeback.

"Fine. I woke up, and Sean was on top of me choking me, only he wasn't himself. He's recently come out of the army—he was in the special forces—like my husband was over ten years ago now, and I guess he has PTSD. Zane did, not that it ever manifested itself like that, but how can they not, you know? The things they see and have to do. Zane has only told me what he can, the unclassified stuff, and that's bad enough." Sandy shuddered and wrapped her arms around herself.

This time WPC Adderly's smile did reach her eyes. She put down her notebook and nodded.

"My brother came out last year, so I know what you mean. Go on, what happened then?" she asked.

Sandy swiped at her eyes and sighed.

"Zane woke up, saw what was happening, and tried to get Sean off of me. When that didn't work he must have gripped the light and hit Sean with it. He wouldn't have meant to cause that injury. He was just worried about me and ... oh hell. I need to see him, please."

Chapter Five

"I know my rights. You can't keep me here any longer. I've told you everything." Zane ran a hand over his face and took a deep breath in to calm his rising temper. He needed to be at the hospital with his wife and Sean, not sitting across this table in an interrogation room, going over the same things over and over. And where the hell was his lawyer? Who cared about it being the crack of freaking dawn. He paid the guy enough to be at his beck and call.

"We just want to make sure we got all of our facts straight and—"

A commotion outside the door interrupted the police officer conducting the interview, and he sighed.

"Interview suspended at 05:03."

The door flung open to reveal Zane's disheveled looking lawyer. Clutching a coffee and looking as though he'd dragged himself out of bed mere moments ago, he nodded at Zane and then addressed the officer.

"You have no right to keep my client here, let alone interrogate him in this fashion without his legal representation present. I demand you stop this charade this instant and let my client go."

He took a sip of his coffee and turned his attention toward Zane.

"Sorry, I got here as soon as I could. The missus wasn't happy with me, I tell you. What's going on?"

Zane shrugged.

"Beats me, they won't tell me anything, other than some nonsense about me being up for a GBH charge." Zane kept his face as neutral as he could, grateful for his years of army training to fall back on.

"It's hardly nonsense. Your actions have put a man into hospital, Mr. McLeod, and your explanation as to why this happened is full of holes. Consensual, my ass."

Zane would have shot out of his chair, had his lawyer's heavy hand on his shoulder not stopped him. He consoled himself with mentally adding up all the various ways he could end this miserable fucker's life, if he chose to. Not that it would achieve anything, but it was tempting in moments like this.

"You don't have to answer that, Zane."

Officer Plod—had there ever been a more fitting name for a copper?—rolled his eyes and leaned across the table in an effort to no doubt intimidate Zane.

"I put it to you, that you changed your mind about this whole threesome thing, and in a fit of jealous rage decided to attack Sean Manson causing his head injury, and it was you who choked your wife. Admit it already."

Oh yes, that pen would look good lodged in that asshole's windpipe.

Zane leaned back and clapped his hands together in a slow clap designed to infuriate the cop. Sure enough, his already ruddy color worsened.

"You should be on stage. On second thoughts, don't. The critics would have a field day. For the last time. I told you what happened, and if that's all, and unless you actually have real grounds to keep me here, I'm going, right, Jack?" He looked up at his lawyer for confirmation, and the man sprang into action.

"Yes, quite right. I assume you have Mrs. McLeod's statement confirming the course of the evening's events?"

PC Plod shuffled his notes around, and the veins on his temple throbbed in his agitation. If he kept this up he would pop his clogs of a heart attack.

"That's not relevant here. A battered wife would say any—"

This time Zane did shoot up. His chair crashed to the floor, Jack sighed, and the clueless ass of a police officer grinned in triumph. A grin that rapidly faded when Zane put his hands on the table and got right in the fucker's face. If he thought he could intimidate Zane and throw this nonsense around he had another fucking think coming.

"How dare you?" Zane's growled words made the weasel swallow repeatedly, and back away as far as his still seated position would allow.

"Zane, *don't*."

Jack's warning rang in his ears, even as he shrugged off the man's hand on his shoulder, too intent to get his point across. No one insulted his wife like this, let alone reduce their D/s relationship to abuse.

"I could have you up for slander. I am *not* a wife beater." Zane took a deep breath in, straightened up and scrubbed a hand over his face. Fuck this shit. He was too fucking tired and worried about the two people he loved to deal with morons like this one.

Clearly sensing to how close Zane was to losing his temper, Jack stepped in.

"Don't worry, Zane. I *will* be lodging an official complaint about Officer Plod and the way you've been treated over this." Jack nodded at him when Zane slowly straightened back up, a silent warning in his eyes.

"Now unless you're actually charging my client, in which case I want to see the evidence you have for this, we are leaving now."

A strained silence fell in the room, only interspersed by Plod's heavy breaths, before he got up and opened the door.

"You're free to go for now." The man looked as though he was sucking a lemon, as he stared up at Zane. "Don't leave town. This isn't over yet, McLeod. I got your number."

Zane gave a short laugh and turned his back on the asshole.

"And I have yours, officer." Jack's voice could have cut glass. "I suggest you get a good solicitor. This is indeed not over yet." He slapped Zane on the back and led the way out of there. It still took far too long for Zane's liking before the doors of the police station spewed them out into the breaking dawn of what promised to be a beautiful day.

"Okay, what the fuck was that all about? Why did you put a man into hospital, and where is Sandy?" Jack asked, as he threw his now empty coffee cup into the nearest bin. "My car is that way. Talk while we walk, man."

Instead of answering him Zane smiled.

"You're not really going to press charges against that idiot, are you?" he asked.

Jack bibbed his car open with his keys and slid behind the steering wheel as Zane got in the other side.

"Fuck no, but he doesn't know that. Let him sweat for a bit. I will, however, lodge a complaint with his superior. They need to update their fucking training. There's no excuse for ignorance. The lifestyle might not be his thing, but he has no right to pre-judge you like this."

Jack started the engine and frowned at Zane.

"He'd have a fit, if he knew my missus was My Lady and the cock and balls torture that'll wait for me at home. Thanks for that, by the way, mate. You owe me big time."

Zane laughed, as had no doubt been Jack's intention.

"Pain slut like you ought to thank me. You know you love that shit. Now shut up and drive. Sandy will be going spare, and I need to find out what happened to Sean. She'll never forgive…" He screwed his eyes shut and shook his head as ice cold fear gripped his spine at the thought of losing her.

Jack sighed, but he did put his foot down.

"Sandy loves you, and whatever you did, you would have done to protect her, right? Not that I know exactly would you did, but if Manson is involved I can guess. You two back on, I assume?"

Zane forced his eyes open and nodded.

"I … fuck, this is all messed up."

Jack gave a short laugh.

"Poly stuff usually is, but if anyone can make it work, it'll be you and Sandy. Now talk. What happened."

It took the rest of the journey to fill Jack in. Give the man his due, he didn't interrupt Zane, even though he could tell that he was dying to. There was a reason Jack was his lawyer. Not only had he known the man since he was knee high, he was also a shark, as well as one of Zane's oldest friends. Back in the day, before Zane had joined the army, they'd both discovered kink at the same time. In Jack's case he was strictly hetero and a sexual submissive through and through. Not that you'd ever guess that unless you saw him with His Lady. Rhonda was a renowned psychologist, and the two of them had met over a case, three years ago now, and never looked back. So, if anyone would get this thing among Sandy, Sean, and Zane it would be Jack.

"Man, I've got to tell you, that sucks," Jack eventually said as they pulled up outside the hospital. "Sandy won't have meant that, you know that. She'll know you did what you had to, and Manson has a hard head. He'll be okay, I'm sure. Now go in there and make that right and give Manson Rhonda's number. He needs help for sure, and you know she specializes in PTSD."

Sean nodded and sighed.

"He does, I just didn't realize how much. Had I known I never would have insisted he stay with us. He did want to sleep in the spare room."

Jack's smile didn't reach his eyes.

"Yeah, maybe that's where he needs to stay until he has a handle on things. Just don't let him run off or refuse the help. I know how stubborn you damn Doms can be. Good luck, man."

Jack's words rang in his ears as Zane negotiated the red tape that stopped him from seeing both Sean and Sandy. Clever girl that she was she'd had Sean moved into a private room, so that she could stay with him. Trying to get through the stern-faced nurse in charge of the ward, however, was another matter. It took all of Zane's charms to get her to relent to let him in, and then she kept wittering on about protocols and visiting hours.

"Look, I appreciate all that, but these are hardly normal circumstances. My wife needs me, and I need to make sure Sean is okay. By your own admission she hasn't left his side. At least let me in briefly so that I can ensure I get a list of things they both might need. I won't stay long." He mentally crossed his fingers at the lie. It didn't sit right with him, but he needed to get in there, before he lost his shit.

"Hmm, I doubt you'll leave once you get in there." The pint-sized woman looked him up and down, and Zane had to fight to keep his amusement under control. "However, your wife has repeatedly asked after you, so I suppose I can make an exception. I warn you though." She rose on her tiptoes and stabbed her index finger repeatedly into his chest. "I'm aware of the circumstances surrounding Mr. Manson's injury, and at the first sign of any trouble, I'll have security escort you off of the premises. Are we clear?"

Sean nodded.

"Crystal, and there won't be any trouble, I assure you."

A long stare through narrowed eyes later, he was finally granted admission, only to freeze at the entrance to Sean's room.

His old buddy looked deathly pale under his tan, and the bandage around his head made him want to puke. At least, he'd been given the all clear by Neuro. Zane had found that much out from questioning Nurse Noreen. A CT-scan had showed there to be no brain damage or swelling, despite his hairline skull fracture, and while he had yet to wake up—and would no doubt have a motherfucking headache for days—he'd been lucky. Or maybe that should be Zane had been lucky. He sure as fuck hadn't intended to inflict permanent damage on the man he'd always been madly in love with. His fear for the other, equally as important, part of his life had spurred him on to act, and he'd grabbed the light in desperation.

Seeing Sandy fast asleep in a chair pulled up next to his buddy's bed, her hand wrapped around Sean's, made that ache in his soul deepen. While it was good to see how much she cared about Sean already, her angry words haunted him.

"What did you do?"

He cleared his throat, and Sandy startled awake. When she saw him, she let go of Sean and literally threw herself into Zane's arms. Never had it felt so good to hold his sweet baby girl in his arms, as he staggered back a step under her frantic onslaught.

"You're here. Oh my God, I was so worried. I—"

Zane slanted his lips over hers, effectively stopping her mid speech and kicked the door shut behind them, as Sandy climbed him like a tree, clung, and kissed him back with all the passion that'd had always existed between them.

By the time they came up for air, and he gently set his precious cargo back on her feet, his world had righted itself, and he smiled down on her while he kissed her nose.

"It's okay, I'm here now. Some asshole policeman at the station wouldn't let me go on a so-called GBH charge, but Jack sorted it out."

"He did?" Her voice sounded so small and lost, Zane wanted to wrap her up and take her away from all this, but she would never leave Sean's side, so that would have to wait.

"Yeah, baby girl, he did. I dare say they'll want to interview Sean when he comes 'round, but he won't press charges." He glanced across at his still sleeping buddy and sighed. "He might want to punch my lights out, but I'll deal with that. Might even let him."

Sandy pushed against his chest, and he reluctantly let her go.

"That's not funny. Don't you think there's been enough knocking people around for one day, if not ever?"

Zane's lips twitched seeing his little Sandy with her arms crossed under her impressive rack, giving him a stare that wouldn't have looked amiss on Jack's Rhonda, before his gaze dropped to the ugly bruising around her throat, and his amusement fled. He gently probed the area, and his gut churned at her wince of pain.

"He'll hate himself for having done that to you, baby, and I hate what I had to do to get him off of you. This is all my fault. I should never have insisted that he stay with us. He did try and tell me he'd be better off not to, but all I could think of was how hurt you would be if you woke up and he wasn't there." He dropped his hand

and ran a hand through his hair. Anything to stop him from crushing her back to him and never letting her go. "I didn't want you to think this was just sex, because it wasn't. At least it wasn't for me."

"Nor me." Sean's cracked voice drew both their attention to the man in the bed. Sandy gasped and rushed to Sean's side. His eyes widened as he no doubt saw the evidence of his actions on her throat and filled with tears, when Sandy grasped his hand, lifted it to her lips and dropped a tender kiss on the back of it.

"Thank God, you're awake. I was so worried."

Zane chose to keep quiet, and rounding the bed took Sean's other hand and squeezed. His buddy's gaze briefly connected with his, and then swung back round to Sandy. The way she looked at Sean. Fuck him six ways 'til next Sunday, he knew that look. If it hadn't been utterly inappropriate in the circumstances he'd have fist pumped the air and shouted *hallelujah*. Instead, he breathed a little easier, and the vise squeezing his chest loosened. They could make this work, if only Sean cooperated. His buddy yanked his hand out of Zane's and lifted it toward Sandy's throat. The amount of effort that took manifested itself in the trembling digits. Sandy took hold of that hand, too, and shook her head when Sean opened to his mouth to speak.

"Don't speak. It's okay really. I know you didn't mean to do that. Just like I know Zane didn't mean to put you into a hospital bed." She offered Zane a wobbly smile, and he nodded his confirmation. When had he gotten so lucky to have such an amazing wife and sub, he would never know. "I'm sorry for what I said back then. I didn't mean that either."

"I know, baby girl. There's nothing to forgive. Like I said earlier, if anyone is to blame here it's me. I was so fucking worried about you, I just reacted. I never meant to put him into the hospital."

Sean struggled to get into more upright position, but Zane pushed him back down, as his monitors kicked off.

"No, you stay right there, buddy, and rest. You'll send the nurses running in otherwise, and that will get me evicted faster than you can say numb-nuts." He smiled at Sean and breathed a sigh of relief when the other man didn't argue. He really had to feel like shit warmed up to acquiesce so easily. "It took all of my charms to get in here in the first place. I'm a supposed danger to both of you according to the cops."

Sean attempted to speak, shook his head, and promptly paled.

"Fucking bull." That croak made them all smile, seconds before the door opened and Nurse Noreen appeared.

"Oh, good, you're awake. You two really need to leave now. Mr. Manson needs his rest. Here." She pushed an oxygen mask on his face and shook her head at Sean. "No, don't try to speak or move." She turned her head to address Zane. "Take your wife home now and come back at visiting time. I'll take good care of him, I promise you, and what he needs more than anything right now is rest, not declarations of whatever. That can wait until he's better and discharged."

Sandy looked all set to argue with the older woman, but Zane knew she was right.

"You heard her, baby, let's get you home. We'll come back in the afternoon, mate."

Sean blinked once to show that he'd heard him, and Zane nodded.

"But, I can't, I—"

"Are you arguing with me, girl?" Zane dropped his voice on purpose. It made Sandy jump and raised

Noreen's eyebrows, but it had the desired effect on his wife's submissive side.

"No, Sir, of course not."

Noreen's eyebrows disappeared into her hairline, and the tiniest of smiles softened her stern expression at Sandy's whispered answer.

"Good girl. Let's get you home."

Chapter Six

Sean shut his eyes and breathed a sigh of relief as the door shut on the police officer sent to take his statement. What a fucking asshole. The wanker was lucky he still couldn't lift his head without feeling as though it was going to explode, or he'd have shoved that self-righteous dick's assumptions down his fat throat and made him choke on them.

Press charges against Zane. What the ever-loving fuck? Sean wouldn't have blamed his buddy if he'd finished him off for having hurt his wife like that, and as for Sandy…

Fuck, those bruises.

He was a fucking liability, and the minute these bloody medics declared him fit enough to leave, he'd walk and never look back. He studiously ignored the ache in his chest the mere thought of walking away from Zane and Sandy caused, and concentrated on breathing instead.

One breath at time. He could do this. They deserved much better than the damaged goods he represented, and fuck … if Zane hadn't stopped him, he could have killed her. The image of sweet little Sandy popped in his mind, and he groaned out loud. At least the hospital had respected his instructions to keep both Sandy and Zane far away from him.

He couldn't cope with another scene like the one he'd woken up to earlier today. Or was that yesterday? Time lost all meaning when you lay in one of these fucking beds, and your brain didn't seem to want to work.

Over the roaring in his ears, he picked up the sound of the door opening again. With it came a waft of expensive perfume, which intrigued him enough to open his eyes.

He didn't recognize the curvy brunette that entered the room, but the steely determination in her eyes set him immediately on alert.

"What is all this nonsense about not allowing Sandy and Zane to see you, Manson? Jeez, I've met a few stubborn Doms in my time, but you take that to a whole new level."

She crossed her arms under her chest, causing the crisp business suit she wore to strain against the buttons and tapped her foot.

"Well, explain yourself, Manson."

Sean pushed himself up into a half sitting position, and cursed under his breath, but he was so not going to be dictated to by a pint-sized bundle of curves with a Mistress complex, it seemed.

"Who the fuck do you think you are?"

"Rhonda Booker, and as of this morning your psychologist, so you better start talking, so we can get this stubborn ass of yours walking in the right direction for once."

Sean shook his head and swallowed a wince as his brain sent shockwaves of pain down his body.

"I don't have a fucking shrink, nor do I need one." His growled reply had absolutely no effect on the damn woman. She simply smiled and fixed him with a stare that would have made a lesser man squirm in his seat, or bed, as the case might be. A grim smile kicked up his lips at his thought processes, and the unwanted intruder narrowed her eyes, and stepped closer.

In another life he'd have thought her beautiful, if far too bossy for his liking, but right now he just wanted to get rid of her.

"Yes, Zane thought you might say that, hence he's paying my exorbitant fees to talk some sense into you."

"Fuck this shit." His shouted expletives hung in the space between them as he saw red. Any other woman would have had the good sense to back away, but not this one. She laughed—laughed for fuck's sake—perched her backside on the side of his bed, and got right in his face.

"Swearing like that in my presence would earn you a sore ass, if I wasn't here in a professional capacity that is."

She winked at his sharp intake of breath to that statement and tapped his nose, as though he wasn't a grown ass man who could lay her flat in one minute, concussion or not.

He chose to ignore that little voice in his ear that he would never lay a hand on a woman without her consent, let alone a fellow dominant. Unless he was out of it in a nightmare flashback of course and that was woman was Sandy.

Fuck!

"Now, that we got this straightened out, care to tell me why you think you don't need a 'shrink'?" She mimed quotation marks around that word. "I'd have thought you could come up with a better insult than that by the way. Then again, Zane did hit you pretty hard. Doesn't seem to have knocked any sense into that thick skull, though, has it? More's the pity."

Sean glared at her as best he could, considering there seemed to be two of her waving around in front of his face at the moment.

"You don't know the first thing about me." He closed his eyes against the wave of dizziness that assaulted him and cursed his weakness all over again.

"I know the type. You ex specials are all the same. Not that I blame you. It comes with the training, I get that, but you're on Civvie street now, and you'll have to adjust. That's why I'm here. To help you do that. Not right now, though. Go and rest." Her cool fingers on his shoulders dug in as he resisted.

"Don't be an idiot, Manson. You want to get out of here, don't you?" she asked, as she pushed harder. He went with the motion, and the dizziness passed as his head connected with the pillow. Horizontal he could do it seemed. Some progress at last.

"I don't need your help," he grumbled.

Again, with one of those irritating laughs.

"Of course not, attempting to choke your lover to death when you wake up is perfectly normal behavior."

Remorse seized Sean the minute she uttered those words, making breathing difficult as his chest tightened in a ball of churning emotion. He screwed his eyes shut. Not that it helped. The sight of the bruises on Sandy's throat would haunt him forever. While he couldn't remember the details, he remembered the nightmare all too well. He'd been back in his last fucking mission, locked in a hand-to-hand combat fight to the death. His team and he had walked right into a fucking trap. A lot of good men had been lost that day, and the few that had made it out…

He shut down that thought process, shoving the associated pain, misery, and guilt back into the box it belonged. That wasn't his life anymore. He was better off being away from that shit, even though it seemed determined to follow him.

"Fuck you, shrink."

"No thank you, you're not my type. Besides, my boy is rather possessive of me, and the only bruises I want to see on his body are mine. Not the ones he would gain trying to knock your beef on the ground."

A laugh bubbled up from Sean's throat, almost against his will. When he opened his eyes, it was to see

Rhonda grin down at him.

"Thought that would get your attention. Seriously, though, I *am* here to help. PTSD is my specialty, and before you balk at that label, what would you say to one of your men who was battling the demons you are, on a daily basis?"

Sean grunted. Dammit, she had him there.

"Exactly. You'd tell him it's nothing to be ashamed of and you'd insist he'd seek help, right?"

Sean didn't bother to answer that, and Rhonda sighed.

"Let me guess, you refused the counselling the army provided on discharge, right?"

He attempted a shrug and swallowed his grunt of pain.

"Thought so. Well, that isn't an option anymore."

"It is, if I simply walk away. I'm not putting Sandy and Zane at risk."

Rhonda sighed and flicked her long hair over her shoulder.

"And that would help, how? Don't you think you hurt them enough? Sandy in particular?"

She let that statement hang in the room and simply stared him down, until he felt like squirming. This bird would do well in an interrogation for sure. Balls of steel, if she had any.

"They're better off without me."

"Bull-crap, and you know that. Look, I've known Sandy and Zane for the last three years. My boy is Zane's oldest friend, Jack." She laughed as recognition no doubt showed in his face. "Yeah, I see you get me now. Know this, soldier, there is no way on God's earth that I'm going to let you walk away from them without fixing this. What happened was an unfortunate by-product of your issues, but we can work on that. Neither

Sandy nor Zane blame you. If anything, Zane blames himself, and—"

"Not his fault at all." Sean interrupted her, earning himself the disapproving arch of one elegant eyebrow.

"Quite. In any case, I've referred him to one of my colleagues to talk this over, if he needs to, but Zane isn't the problem here. You are." She tapped one perfectly manicured red tipped index finger into his chest. "Walking away from the two people who love you would be an insane move, and you know that."

Sean tried to depute that ridiculous notion, but his throat wouldn't work. The nonsensical croak he managed to produce caused Rhonda to hold a glass of water to his lips. He gratefully sucked up a few sips of the tepid liquid through the plastic straw and tried again.

"Who said anything about love? We had sex, that's all." The lie stuck in his throat, and Rhonda fixed him with what undoubtedly was her Domme look. Sweat broke out on his forehead, and it took every ounce of his training to keep his expression neutral.

"Even if that was true for you, and I don't know you well enough to assess the accuracy of that statement, it was certainly much more for Sandy and Zane. Jack told me the tales about you and him. And how he ended it all when he met Sandy. He left the service, you stayed, and that should have been it, but it wasn't, was it? He never stopped loving you."

"He should have forgotten about me. He and Sandy were perfectly happy before I sought him out. I never meant to come between that, and fuck."

"Yes, quite. Well, having spoken to Sandy at length, and having been her friend, I would dispute that. I can say that much without giving away confidences." She smiled grimly at his sharp intake of breath in response to that statement. "It was her idea to invite you to dinner. To meet you, and to see who had her husband so enthralled. What happened after... Well, let me just say that. There is only one other man who causes *that* look in her eyes when she talks about him, and that's Zane."

She got up and put the glass back on the side table.

"Think about that, soldier, and get your head out of your ass. I'll be in touch when you've been released so that we can arrange some sessions to make a start on helping you let go of your other demons. Oh, and one other thing." She looked back at him, one hand poised on the door handle. "If you walk away from this chance at happiness, you're nothing but a gutless coward, despite the recommendations you left the service with." She paused and grinned. "Yeah, I looked you up, soldier. And before you spout any of that love at first sight doesn't exist nonsense." She raised up her left hand, and her engagement ring sparkled in the light. "I knew from the minute Jack walked into the room that he was mine. Took him a few days to accept, but then he *is* a man and you lot tend to think with your gonads." She winked, and before he could even blink she was gone.

It left Sean with a lot to process over the next forty-eight hours the medics insisted on keeping him in for observation, but, eventually he knew what he had to do. Any other option hurt too much.

****

Sandy threw her pen down and rubbed her stinging eyes. Try as she might she simply couldn't concentrate on the notebooks in front of her. Her year two class's handwriting was difficult enough to decipher, especially this particular six-year-old's. What he lacked in skills he made up for in enthusiasm. Unfortunately, it didn't lend itself to being legible. Let alone when her mind was elsewhere. Namely with a stubborn ass of man in a hospital bed across town. She'd been refused entry to his room every time she tried, had only been able to hand over the clothing he'd left at her home that fateful night. Had that really only been five days ago?

She had taken some comfort from washing his stuff and dropping it 'round, even though Zane had told her not to bother. It was one of the rare moments she'd dug her heels in with her husband and Dom.

"I don't care if he doesn't want to see me. I'm still going to try, and you can't stop me."

It was testament to how much that night weighed on her Sir's mind that he'd let her get away with that outburst. Ordinarily speaking, she would have earned herself a sore ass for speaking to him like that. Not this time. Zane had sighed, scrubbed a hand over his face, and gone out the door to work. If she'd thought he'd worked long hours before, she hadn't seen anything yet. He typically left at the crack of dawn and didn't return until late in the evening.

Sandy could have easily resented his actions, had she not understood the reason for them. Work had always been Zane's solace when something bothered him. Deeply hurt by Sean's refusal to see him, and troubled by the guilt he carried over his perceived part of both Sandy and Sean getting hurt, he did the only thing he could do. Bury himself in work.

No matter how many times she told him it wasn't his fault, it made no difference. There was a distance between them. A Sean-shaped hole that only the man himself could fill.

With that unsettling thought she got up to make herself a coffee. The maker was halfway through his process when a taxi pulled up outside the house. She tore her eyes away from Sean's motorbike—a permanent reminder of the man himself—as though they needed that, and the milk carton she'd taken out of the fridge slipped from her hands. Milk splattered over her socks, and up the side of the cabinet, but she hardly noticed the mess, because the man who slowly unfolded his large frame out of the taxi was Sean.

He grimaced as he straightened as though he was still in pain, and then stood regarding the house through narrowed eyes, as though he was debating something with himself. Sandy drank in the sight of him and sighed. The stay in hospital had done nothing to quell his raw sex appeal, and her stomach flipped over when he picked up the duffle bag she'd used to bring in his clothes. He hadn't shaved, the days' old stubble on his strong jaw giving him that dangerous look. Even the white patch still covering his stitches couldn't detract from that.

Lordy me, she was a hopeless case, and, surely, she should rot in hell for having these thoughts about him when Zane wasn't here? Before she could come up with any conclusion to her convoluted thought processes, his loud rap on the door summoned her. Grimacing at the mess at her feet, she hastily pulled off her ruined socks, and hurried to the front door. A quick look at her disheveled appearance in the hallway mirror made her run her hand through her long auburn hair in a vain effort to tame the bird's nest impression she had going on. Nothing at all she could do about the shapeless joggers she was wearing and the equally old but comfortable oversized t-shirt, which tended to slip off her shoulders, or her bra-less state and the make-up free face.

Open the door already before he changes his mind.

With that internal pep talk she yanked the door open and fixed a smile on her face only to see Sean's departing back.

"Wait, I'm here. Don't go."

Her breath stalled in her lungs when he turned slowly and smiled.

"I was just going to get the bike. I—"

"No, you can't." Sandy stormed out of her door and grabbed his arm before she'd even stopped interrupting him. "You can't ride a bike with your head injury. They must have told you that, and, oh for goodness' sakes, come in."

When he didn't respond to her insistent tug, she looked up at him and promptly lost herself in the tender expression in his blue eyes.

"Zane must be slacking if he lets you get away with being this bossy, *little one*."

Oh, my goodness, the intonation he put on those last two words. Every submissive cell in her body sighed, and she dropped her gaze to the floor.

"Please, Sir, come in."

His sharp intake of breath meant she had to look up at him. Conflicting emotions chased each other across his face, before he smiled and nodded.

"As you ask me so nicely." He seemed to notice her bare feet and the milk which was slowly seeping into the bottom of her joggers and frowned. "What on earth happened to you?"

"Oh, it was nothing. I just dropped the milk, that's all. I, erm, best go and clear that up."

Sandy dashed back into the kitchen, all too aware of Sean's gaze on her butt as he followed. Just like that they were back to the sizzling sexual awareness that had existed between them from the minute they'd met. Only this time round it was ten times more potent because she knew what he looked like naked. Remembered all too well what his large, calloused hands felt like sliding over her naked skin, and the skill of his lips and tongue on her sensitive parts.

"Jesus, let me help."

Sean's exclamation as he took in the mess she'd left behind in the kitchen made her turn and bump into him. She hadn't realized he was that close and made a grab for his shoulders to steady herself as her feet slipped on the messy floor. Her breasts made contact with his hard chest, and, groaning, Sean grasped handfuls of her ass and lifted her as effortlessly as though she wasn't far too heavy, and he hadn't just come out of hospital.

"Don't. Put me down. Your head?"

"Will be fine, stop fussing, woman." He deposited her on the kitchen counter and stepped between her splayed legs when she wouldn't let go of him. His gaze dropped to her throats where purple marks remained. It was just as well it was half-term and she wasn't at school or she would have had to wear polo necks all week.

His jaw tightened, and she held her breath when he slid one hand up to her throat and caressed the marks. Her heart rate went into overdrive, as his gaze connected with hers. So much hurt and regret in those amazing blue eyes of his. An echo of her emotions ever since it happened.

"I'm so sorry. That will never happen again. I'm getting help. I've got several sessions scheduled with Rhonda already."

His hoarse promise meant she had to blink away tears, and he swore softly when he noticed.

Sandy had to clear her throat several times to get the words out she needed to say to clear the air.

"I know, she told me, and it's okay, truly. It doesn't hurt anymore."

The slow, almost absent-minded motion of his

thumb across her throat stopped, and he cupped her face instead, and leaned his forehead on hers. So close, they were breathing each other's air, yet so far away at the same time. Sandy wanted nothing more than to breach the distance between them, to show him in the most direct way that it truly was okay. That she trusted him with her body, and her heart. The realization how much she'd missed him hit her hard. It shouldn't be possible to feel this much this quickly, but it had been just the same when she'd met Zane.

Thoughts of her husband meant she couldn't stop her tears, didn't want to in truth. They just had to make this work, because without Sean in their life, Zane and she just wouldn't work. He was the missing piece neither one of them had realized they needed, but if the last couple of months, since Sean had reappeared in Zane's life, told her anything, it was this.

Sean pulled back, and the horrified expression on his face would have been comical in any other circumstance. Now, it just made her cry harder.

"Jesus, baby, don't cry. Not over me. I should go. I never meant to come between you and Zane."

He moved as if to pull away, and Sandy locked her ankles behind his butt and clung onto his shoulders like a monkey. She'd bloody stay like that if she had to.

"No, please, that's the last thing … please, Sir, stay. I want you, and the only way you'll come between us is if you leave now. We both need you, and we can make this work, right?"

Sean's sharp intake of breath reverberated through her, and the instant flash of lust in his darkening eyes caused a sweet ache in her pussy. Her nipples beaded, pushed against the suddenly restrictive fabric of her shirt, and she held her breath when he took her hands off his shoulders, grasped her wrists and held them behind her back with one of his large hands. Sean pulled back more and looked his fill. Judging by the growing bulge behind his zipper he liked what he saw, as confirmed by his next words.

"Yes, we can. There's nothing I want more. You're so fucking beautiful, but we shouldn't. Not without Zane."

Sandy attempted to yank her wrists out of his hold, but she should have known that would be a useless exercise.

"Please, Sir, he won't be back for hours, and I can't wait that long. I need you in me now." Heat rose in her cheeks as she uttered the words. It had never been easy for Sandy to express her wishes verbally, though she knew she had to be clear. There could be no room for misunderstandings, and she was so damn horny, she might just self-combust if Sean didn't make good on the promise in his jeans. She couldn't tear her gaze away from the long, hard imprint of his cock which tested the strength of his jeans.

She licked her lips, and Sean groaned. His free hand slipped in her hair and tugged her head back until she had no choice but to look at him. The heated intensity of his gaze only served to stoke the flames of her arousal even higher.

"Why won't he be back for hours, little one?" Sean asked, his voice thick with need.

"He's buried himself in work ever since, well, you know. He blames himself." She hated talking about this now, but she knew that Sean would want to know. That he would never act on this pull between them, if he thought Zane wouldn't agree to this.

"He has no reason to blame himself. What the fuck?"

Sean's jaw tightened anew, making his scar stand

out, and she ached to run her tongue along the ragged length. One day she would have to ask him how he'd gotten that, but not today.

"I know that, Sir, but you know what he's like and…" Sandy ran her tongue over her dry lips to moisten them, and Sean's hold on her hair, tightened. That delicious sting of pain shot straight to her clit, and she squirmed on the hard counter. "Please, Sir."

Sean smirked and raised an eyebrow.

"A little bit needy there, my sweet girl? Let me guess, the fool has buried himself in work and neglected his little subbie's needs, has he?"

Sandy couldn't get her voice to work, because Sean released his hold on her and tugged at the belt of his jeans. Excitement pooled in her belly, as he slowly pulled it out the loopholes and held it up in front of her.

"Tell me what you need, sweet girl." He wrapped it around his hand several times until a small strip remained. "Answer me, girl, or I shall use this belt on your ass, and not for fun."

Chapter Seven

Fuck it all to hell and back, he hadn't come here for this. Hadn't expected to find sweet little Sandy on her own and so damn responsive. Yet, from the minute he'd seen her, looking deliciously disheveled with her messy hair and tatty clothes, his dick had sprung to life with a speed that left him almost as lightheaded as his head injury had.

He wasn't supposed to do anything strenuous, and fucking Zane's wife would no doubt be classed as a strenuous activity, but he'd never been one to follow the rules.

Besides, looking at her now, her eyes almost black in her arousal, hell, he couldn't resist her, and he didn't want to. What the fuck was Zane playing at, distancing himself from his wife? If Sean was married to this wonderful woman, he sure as hell wouldn't let any opportunity go to show her much he loved her.

That thought hit him in the chest with the full force of a sledgehammer, and he dropped the belt in his hands.

I fucking love her.

Sandy frowned, as though she had picked up on the emotional turmoil he was currently dealing with.

"Sir?" Her whispered question shook him out of his internal soul searching, and he smiled at her.

"I haven't heard your answer, pet. Tell me what you need from me right now." He skimmed his knuckles over the hard nipples poking through the thin fabric of her shirt. Sandy's moan was music to his ears, as was her hesitant reply.

"You, Sir, just you."

He tapped her thighs, and like the good girl she was she released him from the intimate prison she'd had him in, so that he could peel his clothes off. The way she ate him alive with her eyes was such a fucking turn-on. Another one of those breathy moans came from his girl, when he took his hard shaft in his hand and pumped a few times. He swiped his thumb through his wet slit and lifted it up to Sandy's mouth.

"Here, taste what you want, sweet girl."

The way she licked that digit, sucked it into her mouth, made him even harder.

"That's a good girl. Tell me where you want my cock, sweet thing."

He pulled back his thumb and crossed his arms over his chest. Sandy's pout in answer was utterly delightful, and made him want to claim those full lips, bite down on them and mark her in pleasure.

"Everywhere, Sir. Please, just fuck me."

Sean smiled and shook his head.

"Oh, no, my sweet, I don't think so. Show me how much you want me, first. Strip for me and let me see that sweet cunt of yours."

Sandy's sharp intake of breath was utterly delightful, as was the instant blush which appeared across her cheeks and slowly spread down her front.

"Here?" she asked, and he nodded.

"Yes, right here, and do it slowly, my love."

She blinked at that endearment, and he smiled at the rightness of the statement. She *was* his love, and he would show her and Zane, too, when he eventually came home, how much they both meant to him. After he turned his boy's ass red, of course, for neglecting Sandy.

Sandy grasped the hem of her t-shirt with trembling fingers and lifted it slowly. Every inch of skin she revealed made him harder, eager to bury himself in the soft depths of her body. Sandy was all woman with curves to die for, and he groaned when her amazing tits came into view. Heavy and ripe, they hung low, the nipples tight little beacons just begging for his mouth.

He stepped closer, to enable him to grasp the heavy mounds, and Sandy gasped and dropped the shirt on the floor, while her hands went to his shoulders.

"Hands by your side, girl, or I'll have to tie them with my belt." He growled his instructions into the soft flesh of her rack, as he pushed her boobs together and sucked both nipples into his mouth.

"Oh, God, so good, please don't stop."

Sandy squirmed on the work top, but she kept her hands by her side, the white-knuckled grip she had on the edge of the counter testament to how much this cost her. *Such* a good girl. He murmured his approval as he paid homage to her tits and then kissed his way up her throat. He licked across the bruises and made sure to nuzzle along that sensitive spot just under her ear. Sure enough, her heart rate increased, and she started to pant. He caught her moans in the heated kiss they shared as their lips connected. Sean poured all of his emotions into the kiss, delighted with her equally feverish response. By the time he pulled away again, he was in serious danger of shooting his damn load, and that would never do. Sean squeezed the base of his shaft to stop his impending release and issued his next set of instructions with a crack in his voice.

"Now the trousers and panties."

Sandy complied, and he groaned at the peek of pink flesh between her thighs. The sweet musk of aroused woman hit his nostrils, and he squeezed his dick harder. Soon, he would sink into her body, but he was big and he wanted her as ready for him as she could be.

"Good girl. Scoot back a bit, put your feet on the counter, and spread those juicy pussy lips for me. Show me how wet you are, girl."

"Oh, good lord, you're killing me here. Please, Sir, I want … ow." The swat to her thigh left a red handprint behind and his inner caveman roared, especially as her breath hitched, and she immediately complied with his demand.

In this position he could see her cunt open to him, and he licked his lips. Red, puffy, and oh so wet, her lips glistened, her clit an engorged nub sticking out of her hood, as her hole clenched and quivered, expelling more of her arousal. It trickled down toward that other hole he had every intention of claiming, but first things first.

"Good girl. How badly do you want to come, right now?"

An incomprehensible moan was her answer, and he laughed, as her internal muscles expelled more of her cream.

"Please, Sir, please, I need to come."

"Then make yourself come, my sweet. Use your fingers and imagine it's my cock. Smear it around that little clit, fuck yourself with your digits, and look at me while you're doing it."

Sandy's breathing grew labored, and her gaze flew to his, as her fingers started to move. Slowly, hesitantly at first, and then with ever increasing speed as her climax built. *Such* a fucking turn-on. He could feel her gaze on him, as he looked his fill of her sweet cunt. When she came with his name on his lips, it was simply fucking glorious to witness, and Sean couldn't restrain himself any more. Grasping her hips, he pulled her forward, and having lined his dick up with her pussy, thrust into heaven. Her cunt gripped him like a vise, and he swore as he pulled out and rocked back in again. Sandy's hands flew to his shoulders, and her legs locked behind his butt as she matched him thrust for thrust.

In the back of his mind Sean acknowledged the

need for protection, but he was too far gone to care in that moment, and with Sandy's gasps and moans in his ear, echoing his own harsh breaths, he was soon at the point of no return. Sandy came a second time, and Sean pulled out of her, and flipped her, so that her body was facing the kitchen counter. He pushed her torso down with one hand, kicked her legs apart, and gathering the wetness between her legs spread it to her anus. He pushed one slick finger through that tight ring of muscle, and Sandy gasped.

"Tell me I can claim this hole, too, sweet girl." He added another finger, and scissored them to open her up. Sandy clamped down on his digits, and he almost missed her breathless reply.

"God, yes, please. Green, Sir, so fucking green."

Sean closed his eyes and kissed her perspiration covered back, as he withdrew his fingers, wrapped one hand in her long hair, and surged back into her pussy. In this position he went deeper than ever, and Sandy groaned and shook as her pussy muscles rippled around his length, signaling another impending release. He fucked her hard, pushing her hips against the counter, and when she screamed and clamped down on him again, withdrew. Seeing his dick covered in her arousal, he ran the tip of it up to her other hole, and pressed. As wet and prepared as she was he encountered very little resistance. Sean swore when he bottomed out in her delightful ass. The pressure was almost too much as her asshole clenched around him in her release.

"Yes, so fucking good. You're mine now, sweet Sandy. Come for me again."

He started to move, slowly at first, and as his own orgasm built at the base of his spine he pistoned in and out of her. Sandy screamed, lifted up on tiptoes, and bowed her back as he came with a roar, and bit down on her shoulder.

By the time his cock finally stopped twitching, his legs gave way, and he sank to the floor, taking Sandy with him. How long they sat there, with his precious bundle of curves in his arms he would never know, but eventually his softened dick slipped out of the tight clasp of her butt, and Sandy giggled. Her little hands ran up his chest and cupped his jaw.

"We made a right mess, Sir," she whispered and pulled his head down for kiss. It took all of Sean's remaining strength to respond. She must have noticed his lack of response, because Sandy pulled away and frowned at him.

"Are you all right, Sir? Is it your head?" She gently probed at his bandage, and he winced.

"Don't do that, little one. I just need a minute. I think you killed me." He tried to inject some humor into that statement but failed miserably if Sandy's concerned expression was anything to go by.

She scrambled off his lap and frowned. Her own clothes were a soggy mess in the puddle of milk she'd spilled, but his had landed on the kitchen table, so it didn't surprise him when she grabbed his t-shirt and pulled it over her head. It fell to mid-thigh on her, and she looked damn good in it. He would have said as much had a brass band not started up in his head, so he closed his eyes and rested his head on the back of the cabinet.

Fuck, he was tired, and thirsty.

He could hear Sandy move around the kitchen, presumably clearing up the mess, and sure enough, a cool cloth was placed on his forehead moments later. Another, warm one, this time, washed away the stickiness in his groin, and he mumbled his protests. It should be him cleaning her up not the other way 'round, but he didn't have the energy to move.

"Shush, let me do this for you, Sir. Here, drink some water and take these painkillers. They'll help. I found them in your bag."

Sean opened his eyes to find Sandy crouched in front of him, two tiny white pills in her palm, a glass of water in the other.

"Take them, Sir, and then it's bed for you. To rest, I hasten to add. I'll rustle up some food and tell Zane that you're here."

A flicker of unease crawled up his spine at the mention of Sandy's husband.

"He … I shouldn't have…"

Sandy placed her finger over his mouth, effectively stopping his attempt at a protest. "Hush, now, you let me worry over his reaction. I dare say he'll simply be relieved to see you, and if he isn't, well, that's for you two to sort out when you're up for it, which isn't now. Up you get. Can you manage it if you hold onto me?"

Sean would have argued the case that he didn't need any help, had he not felt so rotten. Besides, this was Sandy, and he didn't have to pretend in front of her. She'd seen him at his worst and by some miracle still wanted to be around him. Loved him even, if the open affection with which she looked at him now was any indication.

He cupped her face in his hands and said the words burning a hole in his gut.

"I love you."

Sandy gasped, her eyes filling with tears, but she smiled at him.

"So help me, I love you, too, Sir, but, right now we need to get you into bed. Come on."

Together they somehow managed the laborious trek up the stairs. By the time they reached the guest room, his skin was clammy, and nausea twisted his insides. Fuck this damn head injury and its lingering aftereffects. There was so much he wanted to say to Sandy and Zane, too, when he got here, and his body was letting him down. A soft kiss on his forehead later he slipped into the oblivion of sleep.

****

Sandy watched the even breaths of Sean's chest for ages. It was unbelievably good to have him home where he belonged. This moment would have been ten times better if Zane had been here, too, and Sean was sleeping in the marital bed, but that wouldn't be advisable right now. Rhonda had suggested that Sean should sleep on his own until he had more of a handle on his PTSD.

"After what happened I believe sleep is a trigger for him. It would be safer for everyone if he slept on his own for now."

Sandy had frowned at that, and Rhonda had put down her glass of wine and hugged Sandy. "I know it sucks. I like to cuddle up to my man, too, but you still have Zane. Pretty sure he won't mind having his wife in bed to himself at night, eh?"

When Sandy had grunted at that, Rhonda had pulled back and regarded her though narrowed eyes.

"Okay, spill. I sense all is not well in the McLeod marriage."

Sandy had squirmed under her bestie's Domme stare and sighed.

"It will pass, I'm sure. He just hasn't been here a lot. He blames himself and—"

"And he's being a typical dick of a male and burying himself in work, I bet." Rhonda had taken a sip of her wine and then refilled Sandy's glass. "Want me to speak to him?" she'd asked.

Sandy had shaken her head.

"No, this is just something he needs to work out. We need Sean back here, and then we'll be okay, that's all. He will come back, won't he?"

"If he knows what's good for him, yes." Rhonda had raised her glass and smiled. "Now, let's forget about men and just get drunk, shall we?"

And now, Sean was here, and Zane wasn't. Sandy sighed to herself and moved across the landing to the bedroom she shared with Zane and picked up her mobile. Zane didn't answer, and she refused to leave him a voice mail. Maybe he was just busy with work, and not ignoring her, but, either way, if he couldn't be bothered to speak to her then he didn't deserve to know that Sean was back.

Maybe that made her childish, but right now she didn't care. With Sean's essence slowly trickling out of her, she couldn't regret what they'd done. In the heat of the moment neither one of them had thought about protection. Not that it mattered, anyway. Zane would never have let Sean near her if he'd had any concerns about that side of things.

She was on the pill, so no harm done, and she didn't want any barriers between herself and her men. *Her men.* That had such a lovely ring to it.

Sandy fired off a text message—**Phone me, we need to talk**—poured herself a much-needed glass of wine, and ran a bath.

One long soak later, Zane still hadn't rung her, and Sandy scowled at the phone. Checking in on Sean showed him to still be sleeping. Peacefully, thank God. She wasn't sure she'd want to go near him if he was caught up in one of his nightmares. Sean would never forgive himself if he hurt her again. Her hand went up to her throat, and she shuddered. No, that had been way too close to be ever repeated.

She padded down to the kitchen and having tossed together a salad and grilled some steaks, picked at her food. She'd never liked eating on her own, and tonight was no exception. She covered up the remains, put them in the fridge, and settled down in the living room to get on with her school work. Those books wouldn't mark themselves, after all.

Chapter Eight

Zane nodded to his replacement and rolled his shoulders. He'd been on this job for twelve hours straight and needed the break. In truth what he really needed was to go home to his wife and lose himself in the sweet delights of her body. He was well aware that he'd neglected her, had been somewhat of an ass in truth, and she deserved better. Much better. She had to be hurting as much as he was over Sean's refusal to see either one of them.

Knowing Sean, he felt it was the right thing to do. He would distance himself rather than put either Zane or Sandy in harm's way, but fuck that shit.

It wasn't fair. Maybe Zane was just a selfish bastard, but he wanted both Sean and Sandy in his life. They *could* make this work, despite everything, if that blasted man would just let them help.

He scowled up the swanky apartment building he'd been watching and waited until Zachary was in position to tap his earpiece.

"They've been in there for hours. Knowing her she'll come out just after midnight. Persuade her to go home, if you can. Her Daddy will blow his nut as it is, knowing she's back with Montague."

"Sure thing, boss. Now go home. You look done in. The rest of us can handle this. And don't worry. You can leave our spoiled heiress to me. Not averse to putting her over my knee and spanking some sense into her."

Zane gave a short laugh.

"I pretend I didn't hear that, Zach."

"Pretend away, but we both know that's what she needs, and I'd be only too happy to oblige. She's a spoiled bitch, but she's damned hot."

"If you say so. I'm outta here."

Zane clicked off the communicator and switched his personal phone back on. He groaned under his breath when he saw the missed calls and message from Sandy.

Trying to ring her back achieved nothing. Then again, she was probably asleep already. It was almost eleven PM after all.

With a sigh, Zane started the engine, and made his way across town to his place. Traffic was light, and he breathed a sigh of relief when he pulled up on his driveway. Soft lighting came through the front windows. She hadn't drawn the blinds, and he could see movement in the shadows. Too fucking tall to be Sandy and those moves belonged to a male.

What the fuck?

Zane reached for the Glock in the glove box and clicked the safety. He let himself in the house as silently as he could, cursing inwardly at her having not set the alarm. So help him, once he'd dealt with the intruder her ass would be so sore she wouldn't be able to sit down for at least a week. He crept down the hall and swept the living room. Sandy was in there, fast asleep on the couch surrounded by her class papers. A least she was safe, but who the fuck was in his house? Whoever it was moved as silently as he did. Army training for sure, then.

He brought his gun higher and spun around as he felt the slight air displacement warning him of approaching danger.

"Jesus, stand down, Zane, it's me. What the fuck?"

Sean flattened himself against the wall, hands up in surrender as he looked straight down the barrel of Zane's firearm. "Put that thing down before you hurt someone. Since when are you carrying at home?"

Relief swamped him, and he lowered his gun slowly. Sean took it off him, made sure the safety was on, and then put it on the side table in the hall, before he gave Zane the full Dom glare.

"What the fuck, man?"

With the adrenaline still pumping through his system, Zane wasn't sure whether he wanted to deck the man, or kiss him, especially as the sight of his bare chest proved rather distracting.

"I could ask you the same. What the hell are you doing in my house and half naked to boot?" He ran his gaze over the other man's physique and fought against the immediate pull of attraction, the need to wrap Sean up in a bear hug and never let him go. "And are those my joggers?" Belatedly he registered that little nugget of information, and his gaze swung back 'round to the living room and his peacefully sleeping wife. At least she had clothes on...

"What the hell has been going on, Sean?"

He fixed his attention back on Sean and noticed the blanket at the guy's feet.

"Calm down and I'll explain it. I was just going to cover her up to make sure she doesn't get cold." Sean bent down to snatch up the blanket he must have dropped when Zane confronted him, weapon in hand.

Shit, I could have killed him.

He scrubbed a hand over his face and shook his head. He was so fucking tired.

"Don't bother. I'll take her up to our bedroom. She'll be more comfortable there."

Sean nodded and sighed.

"Yes, she would be. I'd have done that, but I didn't want to disturb her, in case she woke up. She needs her sleep."

Zane swung back round to glare at Sean, even as his heart leaped in his chest at the care and concern he read in the other man's voice. Plus, he was here. That had to mean something, right?

"Why would she need her sleep? What did you do?"

"Exactly what you're imagining, Zane." Sean ducked the punch Zane aimed his way, and in a move he shouldn't have been able to make considering he was still recovering from his head injury, Sean twisted Zane's arm back up his back and pushed him against the wall.

"Enough, boy. Remember who the fuck I am and calm down." The growled words in his ear had the desired effect, and Zane took a deep breath in.

"All right, get the fuck off of me, so that I can see to my wife."

Sean swore softly and let go of him. Zane forced himself to not look at his buddy. He didn't want to see the effect his words had on Sean, and he knew he wasn't being fair. This was what he'd wanted, wasn't it? Sean in their life and connecting with Sandy. Only he hadn't been here to see it, and that bothered him more than it ought.

They had to get this out in the open once he'd deposited his baby girl in their bed, where she ought to be.

"I'm going to make us some coffee, and warm up the steaks she left in the fridge," Sean said.

Zane ignored him and picked up his sleeping wife. Sandy stirred slightly. Sleepy eyes sought his, and she smiled in recognition.

"Zane?"

"Shush, baby. Go back to sleep. Just taking you up to make sure you don't get a crick in your neck." Her hands went 'round his neck, and she sighed and snuggled into his chest.

"Love you."

That mumbled declaration soothed away the last

remnants of the anxiety that churned his guts. He straightened up and turned only to find Sean in his way.

"She does you know, love you, I mean. I would never get in the way of that, buddy."

There went another punch to his gut, because the way Sean looked at Sandy all snuggled up in Zane's arms told its own story, and it made his heart beat faster. Sean looked like he cared, truly cared, and when their gazes connected, the raw emotion in the man's eyes confirmed the truth.

"I love her, too. I love both of you, buddy, but if you don't want me here, I'll leave." His voice cracked on the last few words, and he scrubbed a hand over his face in a move so achingly familiar it hurt to see.

"Don't talk fucking nonsense. Of course, I want you here. Now get out of my way so that I can put her down, and then we can talk, okay?"

Sean didn't move, however, searching Zane's expression instead, and Zane sighed.

"Sir, with all due respect." Sean's eyes heated, and his full lips kicked up in that sinful smirk he knew too well. The one which meant trouble and a very sore ass were in Zane's immediate future. "Move, please."

Sean laughed and finally moved his large frame out of Zane's way.

"As you ask me so nicely, boy, I will. Don't be too long. I'm fucking starving, and those steaks looks delicious."

Sean reached out to brush a strand of hair off Sandy's face and then dropped a lingering kiss on her forehead. Witnessing that tenderness made Zane long to be alone with his Sir. As if he read his mind, Sean smiled, grasped the back of Zane's neck, and slanted his lips over his, coaxing Zane to submit. When he kissed Sean back, time ceased to exist, as Zane lost himself in the tender, yet passionate onslaught on his senses. Eventually his screaming biceps reminded him that he still had Sandy in his arms, and he pulled away.

"Fuck, I want you so much, but if I don't put our girl down, I'll drop her."

Sean laughed, his blue eyes twinkling in amusement, as he put his arms under Sandy too, to help support her weight.

"I hope you're not suggesting *our girl* is too heavy, boy." He winked at Zane, and Zane loved the intonation his Sir had put on those two words. Not least, because she was now cushioned between them, like she ought to be. The three of them in this together "'Cause, I gotta tell you, I love her curves."

"Hell, no, I love them, too." He paused and took a deep breath in. "And I love you. I'm glad you're here with us."

Sean sobered and nodded.

"As am I, but we need to talk this through, and eat." His stomach rumbled loudly at that moment, and they both laughed. It broke the tension of the moment.

"Yes, agreed. Just give me a minute."

By the time Zane had carried his wife up the stairs and deposited her safely in the middle of their bed, the smell of food wafting up the stairs made his stomach growl, too.

Seeing Sean in full domestic mode in his kitchen soothed that hollow space in his soul which had been there ever since that nurse at the hospital had told him Sean refused to see him. Sean grinned at him, when he looked up from setting the table.

"There you are, tuck in. I'm starving, and I fucking love your wife's cooking."

Zane had to agree, and silence fell between them as they ate. Bellies filled, they regarded each other over the intimate setting the small table provided.

Sean reached across and took Zane's hand in his and squeezed. A zap of electricity charged up Zane's arm at the innocent contact, and the fine hair on his neck rose in response.

"I missed you, Sir." He inwardly grimaced at the hoarse tone of his voice but soldiered on. "When did they discharge you? And you are okay, right? Your head, I mean not the other thing. That will take time. I should fucking know."

The circular movement of Sean's thumb on the back of Zane's hand stopped abruptly, and he almost wished he hadn't opened his mouth.

Sean's shoulders tightened, and the scar on his face stood out as he clenched his jaw.

"That will never happen again." Sean raised his gaze to Zane's, and the pain in the other man's eyes was hard to take. An echo of his own demons when he'd left the service. Some things you never forgot, no matter how much time had passed. He gave a tight nod to show his understanding. There was no need to belabor that point.

"That's why the spare bed was messed up, right?"

It was Sean's turn to nod.

"Rhonda's suggestion. Sleep is my trigger, and it's just safer for everyone if I sleep on my own."

"For now, anyway."

A grim smile kicked up the corners of Sean's sensuous mouth at Zane's words.

"For now. Look, I need to say this to get it off my chest." He took Zane's hands in both of his. "Sandy told me you blame yourself, and that you've been distant. I mean, what the fuck, man? If anyone is to blame. it's me. No, let me speak." He stopped the protest Zane was going to make with a shake of his head, and Zane slammed his mouth shut. "I should have taken myself off to the spare room that night, regardless of what you said. Regardless of how much I wanted to stay with both of you, and I didn't want to hurt Sandy's feelings. Turns out I hurt her far more by staying, but—"

"Sandy forgave you for that almost instantly." Zane did interrupt his buddy then, and Sean's eyebrow rose, signaling his disapproval. Well to hell with that. If he earned himself a sore ass for that it was worth it. Besides, the thought of his Sir's hand on his backside made him hard. It would be a relief to cede control for a few precious hours and to know that this man *got* him. "It took me marginally longer, and for what it's worth, I'm sorry I caused that. I'm even more sorry, I froze like I did. *Fuck*, if Sandy hadn't been there to help you, you could have bled out before..." He reached across the table to touch the bandage on the side of Sean's head.

Sean smiled.

"You did what you had to do, and I've got a hard head. Takes a lot to crack my skull, and you came damn close, but the damage is mostly superficial. Hairline fracture if you must know and soft tissue damage, hence the bandage. I'd say you knocked some sense into me, but that would be lying." He winked at Zane, and a weight lifted off Zane's shoulders. "They kept me in mainly because I said I had no one to look after me. Didn't want to burden you and Sandy. Still wouldn't have had it not been for that Rottweiler you sent to see me."

Zane smirked and shook his head.

"Quite an apt description for Rhonda when she's in full Domme mood, I guess. She'd like that, I reckon, just don't let Jack hear you say that. He'll go for your throat. No one disses His Lady and gets away with it."

"Possessive, is he?" Sean asked.

"Just a tad, but, then so is Rhonda. Aren't we all

over the people we love, whether that is one person or two."

Sean's gaze heated at Zane's answer, and he wished there wasn't a damn table between them. Zane couldn't stand the physical distance between them anymore. He wanted, needed to reconnect with Sean, just him and his Sir.

"I guess we are. I want you, boy." Sean's voice dropped on those last few words, and Zane shot to his feet, rounded the table, and got to his knees in front of his Sir. He fixed his gaze on Sean's bare feet and murmured his answer.

"Then have me, Sir."

Sean's sharp intake of breath was music to his ears, as were his Sir's next words.

"Be careful what you wish for, boy, because if we're doing this, then know you've earned yourself a sore ass for having neglected our girl."

Sean grasped Zane's chin and tilted his head up until their gazes met. Silent determination greeted Zane, as well as so much emotion it made Zane swallow hard to get rid of the lump in his throat.

"I know, and I'm sorry, Sir. I won't let that happen again. I was just…" He couldn't bring himself to continue, but he should have known his Sir wouldn't let him get away with that. The hold on his chin grew painful, and Sean positively glared at him.

"You were just what? Say it out loud, boy. If this is going to work, all three of us we need to talk about everything that bothers us. You know that."

Zane shut his eyes and nodded.

"You hurt my feelings when you cut yourself off." The hold on his chin turned into a caress as Sean stroked his fingers along Zane's jaw, and then kissed him. It was the briefest of touches, so gentle, he might have imagined it, had he not heard the whispered words.

"I know, my love, and I'm sorry. It was a dick move on my part. I won't cut you out like that again."

Sean opened his eyes and lost himself in his Sir's gaze all over again.

"Promise?" he asked, not at all ashamed at the tears he was fighting to not give into.

"I promise, and you must promise me something, too."

"Anything, Sir."

"If I ever do that again, pull me up on it."

Zane didn't even try to hold his emotions in this time, and he knew he didn't have to. This was his Sir, and he could deal with his tears, just as he could deal with the burdens Sean carried with him.

"I will, if you promise to do the same for me. We need to be our best for our girl."

Sean nodded, and swiped the tears off Zane's face with his fingertips.

"That we do, but right here and now I don't want to talk about her. I want to redden my boy's ass to wipe the slate clean and then fuck him senseless until neither one of us can move."

The words hung in the air between them, and Zane gave his consent.

"God, yes, Sir."

How they made it up the stairs and into the spare room, Zane would never know. They left a trail of his clothes behind, as he frantically pulled them off, in between kisses, which turned ever more passionate. Teeth clashed, mouths devoured, but, finally, mercifully, he was naked, bent over the end of the bed, and ready to take whatever his Sir had in store.

"Always so eager, my boy."

Sean's guttural voice pitched his own need

higher, and he rubbed his rock-hard dick along the edge of the bed to gain some much-needed relief.

A red-hot strip of pain exploded across his butt cheeks, and Zane grunted. Fuck, that stung. Not that he had much time to process it, because another, just as hard strike happened, followed by several more in quick succession, which left him panting for breath.

"That's for trying to get yourself off without me, boy." Sean's hands dug into the painful welts he'd just laid across Zane's ass, and Zane hissed through his teeth at the rough sensation.

"That was my belt, and there's more of that to come if you don't behave, are we clear?"

"Yes, Sir. I'm sorry."

"Good, now these are for your treatment of Sandy."

More pain exploded across his butt, as Sean's hand connected with his flesh this time. Every few painful swats, Sean stopped and massaged the fiery globes, while murmuring words that Zane's fuzzy brain couldn't compute. He was fast slipping into that happy place where time ceased to matter, and pain didn't exist anymore. While he still felt the swats, the pain morphed into pleasure. Intense, all-consuming, until it all stopped.

Over the blood rushing into his ears he heard Sir's insistent voice.

"Give me a color, buddy, now."

"Green, Sir, don't stop. I want you."

A bite to his shoulder made him wince, brought him back a little into the here and now, as did Sir's reassuring weight on his back, as he straddled his legs and then proceeded to massage the tight knots out of his shoulders. Long, firm strokes, down to the hot mess that was his ass cheeks, until his whole body was a mass of fevered anticipation. The heat in his ass was only surpassed by the pain in his cock. He couldn't, wouldn't, come without his Sir's permission, but, fuck him, he needed to. How he'd missed *this* though. This complete surrender to his Sir and the peace it brought.

A different kind of peace from the one he gained from the Dom headspace he got from a scene with his wife. He so fucking needed *this*.

"That's my very good boy. Roll over for me now."

Zane struggled to obey and eagerly swallowed Sir's cock when Sean knelt next to his head.

"That's it, buddy, work me good."

Mouth full of Sean's cock, he was dimly aware of the other man shifting position again and then his Sir's full lips closed over his dick. Zane grunted and stepped up his efforts to make Sean come.

He hadn't counted on Sean's skillful mouth, which took him to the edge in record time, and gagging, he came up for air.

"Fuck, please, Sir, I can't … fuck."

Sean released Zane's straining cock, squeezed his balls to stave off Zane's orgasm, and grinned up at him.

When had he moved again? Not that it mattered, because Sean shifted his hands from Zane's groin and cupped his ass. That sweet sting of pain made his cock jerk and leak yet more pre-cum.

"Put your legs over my shoulders, buddy."

Zane didn't need to be told twice, and Sean grunted his approval, as he rimmed Sean's tight hole, repeatedly, and then thrust his tongue inside.

"Fuck, please, I need you in me, Sir."

Sean raised his head from between Zane's splayed legs, and the lust and love that shone out of his heated gaze meant Zane lost any control he might have had. He reached for Sean's head and tugged, desperate to kiss his lover, his Sir, to reconnect on the most basic level possible.

Sean locked his arms and hovered over him, seemingly determined to not be rushed. Had it not been for the fire in his eyes, and the tight set of his shoulders, his harsh breaths and the erratic pulse thundering at the base of his throat, Zane might have thought that Sean wasn't as desperate to fuck him, as he was to be fucked by his Sir.

"We need lube."

Zane closed his eyes and fought for control. It was on the tip of his tongue to say, "fuck the lube," but Sean would never do that. So, instead he gestured to the chest of drawers next to the bed.

Sean lifted off of him with a smirk, and Zane counted backwards in his head. Anything to stop himself from coming too soon, as he watched Sean rummage through the drawer.

For the love of God, please let there be lube in there.

Zane didn't even care whether it was in date or not. Odds were against that, as he very rarely needed to use any extra lubrication with Sandy. Thoughts of his wife made him groan and grasp his cock, just as Sean held up a tube in the air triumphantly.

"We're in luck. Now where were we, my boy?"

Zane held his breath as Sean slathered his cock in a generous amount of lube, and then crawled back up the bed and over him. Two slick digits probed at his back passage, while Sean kissed a path of heated awareness up Zane's abs. By the time he withdrew his fingers and kissed him, Zane was so revved up and ready he was seeing stars. Their hard cocks rubbed against each other, and both men groaned at the resulting friction.

"Please, for the love of God, I'm ready. Just fuck

me already."

Sean withdrew, lifted himself off of Zane and shook his head.

"No, I won't fuck you. I'll love you instead."

Zane couldn't breathe, couldn't think, as their gazes locked, and Sean took the base of his huge cock in his hand and teased the broad tip along Zane's butt crack. Zane dug his heels into the bed, lifted his hips, and impaled himself on his Sir's cock on the down stroke.

"Fuck, take it easy, I don't want to… You feel so damn good, boy."

Instinct and need took over, and soon thought, let alone speech was impossible. Zane clung to his Sir, meeting him thrust for thrust, as his orgasm built and built. Sean growled low in his throat, and stiffened, signaling his own release, as surely as his panted instruction for Zane to come.

Never-ending streams of his cum exploded over Zane's abs as he let go, dimly aware of Sean reaching his own peak before his Sir collapsed on top of him.

Eventually, as their breathing slowed, and the room came back into focus, Sean rolled off him and flung his arm over his eyes.

"Jesus, you fucking killed me, buddy."

Zane rolled with him and rested his head on his lover's chest.

"Great way to go, though, right?"

Sean's tired laugh alerted Zane to the fact that he'd better leave. He frowned at his thought processes, even as he swung his legs out of bed, and saw Sean watching him with a tender smile.

"I'm just gonna go and clean up."

"You do that, and then go join your wife. I'm too fucking tired to move right now."

Zane sighed, not wanting to leave.

"You sure you're going to be all right? Your head okay?" he asked, which earned him a half-hearted punch to the shoulder.

"Stop fussing over me. Go."

Zane stood up on wobbly legs and bent down to kiss Sean goodnight. The other man's eyes remained closed, and his even breaths told Zane he was fast slipping into sleep.

Which left only one thing to do. Clean up and join his wife.

Chapter Nine

The delicious smell of brewing coffee tickled Sandy's senses, as she opened her eyes to the familiar surroundings of her bedroom. How had she ended up here, and naked to boot? She'd been marking papers, after Sean had fallen asleep and...

Her heart beat faster as last evening's happenings came back to her in glorious technicolor details. She sat up and froze when she saw the messed-up sheets on Zane's side.

He had come home then, but what had he made of Sean's arrival? The urgent demands of her bladder stopped further ruminations, and she hot footed it over to the en-suite to relieve herself. Having taken care of business, washed up a little, and got rid of her cotton mouth by brushing her teeth, she felt much more refreshed and ready to take on whatever might await her downstairs.

Male laughter traveled up the stairs, and Sandy released the breath she hadn't been aware of holding, as she sat back down on the bed. Okay, they weren't arguing or fighting, so that had to be a good thing. She couldn't make out what they were saying to each other, but they seemed to be getting along just fine. From the sound of it they were in the kitchen.

Her pussy ached in remembered pleasure, and a spike of arousal coursed through her veins. She would never be able to look at that kitchen counter without blushing again.

A door opened and shut, and the smell of sizzling bacon that wafted up the stairs made her stomach grumble. Jeez, she was hungry. Then again, she hadn't eaten much last night, and...

Whatever thought processes she might have been

capable of in her caffeine deprived brain fled like a flock of birds when her husband appeared in the doorway. Dressed in nothing but low riding, faded jeans, he looked good enough to eat. Zane smiled at her as he held onto the top of the doorframe, elongating his muscular torso and drawing her gaze to the treasure trail which arrowed down to the unsnapped waistband of his jeans.

"A man could get used to seeing his wife undress him like that with her eyes." He laughed, when she hastily yanked her gaze up to his face. "Morning, sweetheart. I was coming to check on you, and wake you up if need be, but I should have known you'd sniff the coffee out even in your sleep."

A door opened again, and Sean's gruff voice hollered up the stairs.

"What's taking so long? Get your asses down here, or I'll eat breakfast all by myself."

"Over my dead body. Least you can do is feed us. Besides, can't a man enjoy his wife first thing?" He winked at Sandy, and her mouth fell open at Sean's laughing response.

"You best not be enjoying her too much, boy. I want in on that. *After* breakfast. Don't make me come and get you."

Everything south clenched in need at that hidden promise, and Zane's smile grew sinful, as he stalked across the room, pulled her to standing and kissed her. Not just any kiss either, but one so full of passion and need that Sandy could only cling to her Sir and surrender. His erection pressed against her belly, and she whimpered in need as her nipples grew stiff and her pussy slick with her juices.

Zane eventually released her, his breaths harsh and demanding as he grasped her butt cheeks and growled into her neck.

"Fuck breakfast, I need in you *now*. Hold onto me."

Sandy locked her hands between his neck, and brought her legs around his waist, as Zane took the few steps required to push her up against the wall.

She flexed her hips, rubbing her needy pussy all over his groin, and Zane swore and fumbled with his jeans with one hand.

"Fuck, stop that, or I won't last five minutes."

Sandy's giggle in response earned her a mock stern look from Zane.

"She laughs. *Laughs.*" He flexed his knees, and in the next instant his freed cock slid into her up to the hilt. They groaned in unison, and Sandy flung her head back and gasped for breath at the rough intrusion. Zane stilled and kissed her neck, his breaths harsh and erratic against her ears.

"Fuck, yeah, you're so tight. Relax, baby, that's it. Fuck, I missed you."

Sandy made a conscious effort to relax her muscles, and Zane started to move. Slowly at first, while he kissed her, tongue-fucked her in a way that made her forget anything but the building pleasure as he grew bigger inside of her still. Stretched her so damn good, she was going to come in record time.

"Tell me you're close, baby. I can't hold out much longer." Zane's guttural words as he wrenched his mouth off her, and pumped into her like a madman, forced an incoherent moan from her, as the first trembles of her own release consumed her. Her back hit the wall repeatedly, and her fingernails dug into her Sir's neck as she screamed her release. Zane, too, growled low in his throat, stiffened, pushed in deep and stayed there, as his cock twitched deep inside of her.

"I love you." That grumbled declaration into her

perspiration damp neck meant she had to blink away tears, as his softening dick slipped out of her and he ever so gently put her back on her feet. "And I'm sorry about having been such an ass with work and what not."

Sandy smiled up at him, but before she could respond to that, Sean's somewhat hoarse voice interrupted the intimate moment between them.

"As touching and hot as this all is, I made a full English, and I would appreciate it if my subbies could do as they're told for once and get their delectable asses downstairs. I'm too hungry to tan your backsides red on an empty fucking stomach."

Sandy gasped. Zane laughed and stepped away from her, so that she could see the other man. She swallowed hard when she saw the impressive erection tenting Sean's joggers. Arms crossed over his massive chest, he watched the two of them. While his words had held a hidden threat, his eyes twinkled in amusement. Amusement which turned to molten heat as he ran his gaze over Sandy's naked body.

Despite the orgasm she'd just had at her husband's cock, her pussy tingled anew. Lord, she'd turned into a right hussy, but if he touched her now she'd come again in an instant.

"You're so fucking beautiful, little one, especially when you're all rosy and flushed after sex like this." He stepped closer, skimmed his knuckles over her nipples, and then turned to kiss Zane. Sandy clenched her thighs together to relieve the immediate sweet ache in her cunt. It was just so damn hot to see the men kiss. Sean deepened the kiss, pushed Zane up against the wall next to Sandy, and pinned his arms high above his head. Sandy wasn't at all surprised to see Zane's cock semi harden in response to Sean's kisses.

When he finally stopped kissing her husband, she

was so aroused her juices trickled down the inside of her thigh and joined the wetness created by Zane's cum.

Sean noticed. Of course, he did. He was clearly in full Dom mode right now, and neither man ever missed any of her responses when they were in that headspace.

He smirked and without relinquishing his hold on Zane leaned across to kiss her. Zane's familiar taste mixed in with the dark, virile scent that was Sean. He tasted of Zane, coffee, and bacon, and she couldn't get enough of his kisses.

Sean must have felt the same way, because he swore softly when he broke the kiss, released Zane, and got to his knees in front of her.

"Then again, who needs breakfast when a man can feast on his girl's sweet cunt? Hold her up for me, buddy." Sean grinned up at her, as he kissed each breast and then worked his way south to where she was already throbbing in need. Her hands flailed wildly only to be grasped by Zane.

"I've got you, baby girl. You just feel." Zane started kissing her at the same time that Sean flung one of her legs over his shoulder and licked along her slit.

Oh. My. God.

She bucked against his oh so talented mouth and moaned into the kisses her other Sir gave her. Sean murmured his approval as she gushed for him. When he pushed two fingers into her pussy and curled them in just the right way, while sucking her clit into his mouth, Sandy flew over that delicious edge into another orgasm so intense she could do nothing but lean on her men.

Sean kept up his suckling and licking until the worst of her tremors had subsided, and then kissed his way back up her body. Zane moved out of his way, and Sean's hands replaced her husband's on her wrists as he pinned her against the wall and kissed her. Tasting herself on his lips was the biggest turn-on yet. His erection dug into her belly, and she squirmed against it as much as she could. His cock jerked, and Sean groaned into her mouth before he released her and bit down on her bottom lip. That sting of pain shot straight to her clit, and she gasped.

"Minx, not had enough attention for one morning, yet?"

She shook her head, and both of her Sirs laughed.

"Well, what are we going to do about that, buddy?" Sean asked Zane.

"I think we should let the lady have what she wants."

Sean released her, and the sight of her husband fully aroused again and stroking his large shaft sent a tingle of excitement down Sandy's spine. Not least, because Sean pulled off his joggers and his cock sprang up to almost his navel. He, too, grasped his cock and faced Sandy.

"I think you're right there, buddy. Tell your Sirs what you want, little one."

Sandy couldn't tear her gaze away from her two men stroking themselves as they watched her through hooded lids. To know that she had the power to make them be this aroused, that these two really were hers, was almost too much to take in.

"Are you, truly?" she asked. "My Sirs, I mean."

Both men frowned at her, but it was Zane who spoke, his voice rough and raspy and such a turn-on.

"Yes, baby girl, and doubting subbies will not get what they want, will they, Sean?"

He turned to face Sean, pushed his dick up against Sean's, and kissed him.

Sean responded in kind, and Sandy groaned at the sight they made as they devoured each other's mouth and flexed their hips against each other. Their cocks grew harder, both broad tips leaking copious amounts of pre-cum, and Sandy sank to her knees in front of them.

"Please, Sirs."

She wasn't exactly sure what she was pleading for, only that she would self-combust if she didn't somehow get in on that action.

Eventually the two men broke apart and cock in each hand approached her.

"Now isn't that a wonderful sight. Our subbie all naked and eager waiting for us."

Sean nudged the inside of her thigh with his foot.

"Open wider so that we can see how wet that sweet little cunt is. That's it. Now use your hands and spread those lips. "

"Fuck!" Zane's guttural response to her complying with that demand made her pant. More of her juices slid over her fingers, soaked her hand, and trickled down toward her butt. Would they both take her, she wondered?

"Please, Sirs."

"She begs so nicely, too, doesn't she, Zane?"

"That she does. Which of her holes shall we claim *this* time?"

Sandy shivered at hearing herself discussed like that. It should have been demeaning, but in this moment right here, with the men she loved, it just added to her arousal. Not least because she knew that her Sirs would only give her immeasurable pleasure.

"Hmm, we'll work that out as we go along, buddy." Sean held his hand out to her and when she placed hers in his pulled her up to standing. Zane closed in on her rear and kissed her neck, his cock a hard ridge against her ass.

"I'm inclined to stay right here. Been a while

since I tapped that sweet ass." He ran his large hands down her back until he could grab hold of large handfuls of her butt. Sandy gasped and went on her tiptoes, because Sean repeated the same moves on her front and cupped her pussy. He slipped his index finger inside of her at the same time as Zane pushed his thumb through her butthole, and she groaned.

"Our little subbie likes that, I see." Sean's breathy words into her neck as he added another finger to her cunt, forcing her higher on her tiptoes, made her head fall back against Zane's chest. She screwed her eyes shut against the onslaught on her senses and squirmed between her men as much as she could.

She was hot and cold all at the same time as shivers wrecked her body.

"Please, please…"

Sean added a third finger to her pussy, and her internal muscles clenched down on the long, thick digits. Zane stepped closer, withdrew his thumb from her butt and lifted her legs around Sean's lean hips. Sean's large hands replaced her husband's as he grasped her butt to keep her steady, stretching her tiny hole at the same time. She only had moments to mourn the loss of the men's fingers in her body, before Zane's hot breath ghosted across her butt crack. He slipped his fingers through her wetness and took her arousal all the way back to her anus.

"So fucking wet for us." His tongue replaced his fingers, and she cried out when he pushed past the ring of muscle and murmured his approval. He thrust his tongue in and out of her ass repeatedly, until she wanted to scream at him. She needed more, so much more, as her clit ached and her vaginal muscles clenched in desperate need to be filled. Sean's biceps trembled with the strain of holding her up, and then he flexed his knees while he pushed her up higher. That move meant the loss of her husband's tongue in her ass, and she moaned her denial. One of Zane's hands joined Sean's on her butt, as he leaned against her back, while the other slid through her slit.

"Relax for us, baby. I'm just gonna help Sean's cock to slide in that sweet pussy. Look how hot you look in that mirror sandwiched between us."

Sure enough, when Sandy glanced to the side she could see their reflection in the full-length mirror on the wall. She'd all but forgotten it was there, and Zane was right. Seeing him grasp Sean's cock and guiding it inside her waiting pussy was insanely hot.

The velvety tip slid inside, and she groaned as she was filled inch by delicious inch of cock.

Seeing his thick shaft disappear inside her body made this extra hot, as was the expression on her Sirs' faces. Their gazes locked in the mirror as Sean bottomed out inside of her, and her heart threatened to beat itself out of her chest.

"That's it. Hurry up, buddy, and claim that ass. I won't last long at this rate."

"On it."

Zane nuzzled into her neck, and having fisted his cock a few times, leaving streaks of her cream behind on it, he delved back between her legs to take more of her arousal back to her nether hole.

"Please, I'm ready, just … oh *fuck*." Sandy's words turned into a long, drawn out moan, as Zane pushed steadily against her butthole and slid in slowly. It was too much, and not enough as muscles stretched to accommodate both her Sirs' cocks. Sandy closed her eyes and concentrated on pulling air into her lungs, and then the men began to move. Exquisite pleasure erupted with every coordinated thrust and retreat of the two men's cocks in her body. Slowly at first, and then with increasing speed, they claimed her, made her theirs, pitched her higher and higher into the maelstrom of sensations that assaulted her.

The first of her orgasms left her breathless and trembling between her men as she clenched down on both their cocks. Her Sirs swore in unison and then stepped up their efforts, all the while murmuring encouragement and calling her their *good girl.*

Sandy lost all sense of time, as their sweat-slicked bodies rubbed against each other and she rode the waves of pleasure, until she was nothing more than a mass of fevered sensation. She was dimly aware of first Zane and then Sean reaching their climax before the world went dark for a while.

When she came back to the here and now, she was on the bed safely cocooned between her two men, and she sighed in contentment. Both men's hair was wet as though they'd showered, and a pang of regret assaulted her at having missed it.

"Ah, sleeping beauty is back with us, buddy." Sean kissed her nose, and Zane's deep chuckle to her right made her grin.

"I was getting a bit worried there," he said.

Sandy looked between them and pouted.

"You two showered without me? That's not fair."

Zane laughed, and Sean shook his head in amusement.

"I was knackered enough from making love to you on an empty stomach, let alone trying to hold you up in the shower while you were out of it, sweet thing. We took turns in watching you and cleaned you up as best we could here." He winked at her, and promptly sobered when she blinked away tears. "Hey, we didn't hurt you, did we?

Zane, too, swore under his breath and then propped himself up on his elbow to study her expression.

"No, it's not that." Sandy grimaced at the choked whisper she managed to produce.

"Then what is it, baby girl?" Zane asked. His concerned gaze scanned her face, before it settled on Sean briefly.

"It's just you called it…" She couldn't get the word out, so she stopped trying, and understanding slowly dawned on her men's faces.

"He called it making love, because that's what it was, baby." Zane nuzzled into one side of her neck as he spoke and Sean followed suit on the other.

"Indeed, we love you, so to call it fucking seemed inappropriate, not that I'm against a good fuck, you understand." He nibbled on her earlobe, and Sandy sighed in pleasure.

"I love you, too, both of you."

Both men raised their heads and grinned down on her.

"Good, now that we got that settled, I'm starving, so I'm gonna start again with that damn breakfast." Sean swung his long legs off the bed, and Sandy couldn't tear her gaze away from the side of his taut ass, before it disappeared in his joggers. More was the pity.

Zane chuckled next to her.

"Our guy does have a fine butt, doesn't he?"

Sean wriggled it at the two of them before he turned around and fixed them both with his best Dom glare.

"This time, when I call you get your sweet asses down for breakfast, understood?"

"Yes, Sir," they replied in unison, and Sandy got the giggles.

When she eventually got her merriment under

control it was to find her husband watching her. The silent intensity of his gaze meant she sobered instantly, and she whispered her question.

"Sir?"

Zane smiled, lighting up his stern features, and she released the breath she hadn't even been aware of holding.

"Thank you for this." He waved his hand around to encompass the room. "I swear, when we married I never envisaged that we would end up like this."

"Like what, Sir?" Sandy asked. "In love with the same man?"

Zane skimmed his finger along the fading bruising on her throat and nodded.

"Yes, but we can make this work, right? Even with his…" He paused, sat up, and ran a hand through his hair. It made all the strands stick up all over the place, and Sandy reached across to tidy them up for him.

"Yes, of course we can. Rhonda will help him as much as she can, and if we just keep on loving him then it will all work out, you'll see."

Zane nodded and laughed as his stomach chose that moment to rumble loudly.

Sandy, too, smiled, and nudged him.

"You heard the man. He's making breakfast, so let's go and eat."

"He makes the best freaking full English ever, I tell you," Zane said.

"Oh, better than mine, is it, Sir?" Sandy picked up the cushion and threw it at his departing back as he struggled to get his jeans on. He straightened and raised an eyebrow.

God, how much she loved him.

"Watch it, girl."

Sandy stuck her tongue out at him and then ran

from the room screaming as he lunged for her. Not that she got very far, because she collided with Sean's broad chest.

The spanking she earned herself for that meant that breakfast turned into brunch, and she found sitting most uncomfortable for the next few days.

Then again, it had been *so* worth it.

Epilogue

Two years later

"Mrs. McLeod?" The crisp voice called Sandy in for her appointment, and she sighed.

"I'm here, but my husband hasn't made it in yet. He's on his way, so can you see someone else first? I really want them here."

The young woman frowned as she no doubt processed that slip of the tongue and Sandy raised her head a bit higher, as the woman next to her whispered something to her partner and laughed.

Two years into their relationship she was used to the looks they garnered. The whispers behind their backs when it dawned on folks that Sandy was in a relationship with two men. While she didn't make it a habit to flaunt her private life—especially not at work—her school had eventually found out. After an awkward meeting with the head teacher, during which Sandy had told the woman in no uncertain terms that her private life was just that and had nothing to do with her ability to teach, the rumors had only just stopped and then this had happened.

Sandy put one hand on her tummy and smiled as their child turned somersaults or something. He or she was certainly an active little thing, and today they would find out the sex. No way on earth would she do that without both the Daddies here.

"Well, okay, but if he's not here after the sonographer has seen the next couple, we really need to get on with it."

Sandy nodded to show her understanding, and the couple who had been sniggering at her were called in.

Which left only the young girl snapping gum and her disapproving mother in the waiting room with her.

Lord knew what the old hag was glaring at her for. Sandy was a responsible adult in her late thirties, at least, and while this pregnancy hadn't been planned and she had no idea who the actual father was, at least she was old enough to have a baby. Unlike the girl whose huge stomach dwarfed her small frame. She didn't look a day over fourteen, for pity's sake.

Sandy lifted her hand to the collar Sean had placed on her a year into their relationship and encountered her wedding and engagement ring which now lived on the platinum band. As her fingers tended to swell by the end of the day in the summer heat, her Sirs had decided the rings were better off there. Touching that visible reminder of her Sirs always grounded her. Sod what everyone else said. They knew what they had, and that's all that mattered. Far from being sordid, they were in love, and their baby would be truly blessed by having two devoted fathers rather than just one.

Both men had been adamant that they didn't want to find out who the biological father was.

"What the fuck does that matter? We're having a baby." Sean and Zane had both twirled her around the living room until she'd been dizzy.

A loud commotion in the corridor alerted her to her men's presence, and sure enough, moments later Zane burst through the door, closely followed by Sean. The sheer masculinity and presence of her men took Sandy's breath away, like it always did when they first entered a room.

"Hey, baby, we didn't miss it, did we?" Zane asked and planted a kiss on her lips. "We would have been here sooner, had our Lord and Master not driven like an old granny." He winked at her, and the fine chain he wore around his neck to show Sean's commitment to him twinkled in the rays of the late afternoon sun coming through the broken slats of the NHS blinds on the window.

"I was merely following the speed limits like a responsible citizen, buddy. If we got ourselves arrested on the way here we definitely would have missed seeing our son."

Sean, too, kissed her, and then sat down on her opposite side. Both men grasped one of her hands each, and Sandy sighed.

"Your *daughter* and I are still waiting."

Old hag across the room looked about ready to have kittens, while her daughter had seemingly forgotten to chew her gum and stared at them, openmouthed.

Sean looked around the room and frowned.

"I really wish you'd allow us to pay for you to go private. We can afford it after all."

It was an old and frequent argument between them.

"If I have told you once, I told you a thousand times, there is no need. This is one of the best maternity units in London. Save your money for a private midwife if they give me grief over the homebirth."

Sean grunted a dismissal, and Zane's hold on her hand grew painful. The men exchanged a look, and Sandy sighed. She knew they didn't agree with that decision, but she also knew they would support her in whatever she decided. And her mind was made up. If this scan showed everything to be still okay, she would have that home birth. She was pregnant, not ill.

"Mrs. McLeod, we're ready for you now."

The same nurse as before popped her head around the corner, and her eyes grew wide when she noticed Sean and Zane.

Her men tugged Sandy to her feet and grinned. The joint excitement pouring off of them was simply delightful.

"Let's do this, little one. I'm so ready to meet our son," Sean said.

"Or daughter, doesn't matter to me." Zane said, and Sandy fought the urge to kiss him senseless. That really would put the cat amongst the pigeons as the saying went.

"Right, well, we have a problem here. Only the father is allowed in the room, I'm afraid, so Mr. McLeod?" The nurse addressed Sean and Zane laughed.

"I'm Mr. McLeod."

"Right then, if you and your wife would follow me." She made to move, but Zane stopped her with a smirk toward Sean.

"However, we're both the fathers, so we'll both be attending, right, baby?" Zane squeezed her hand, and she looked up at Sean. He looked pensive, so she did the only thing she could do. Got on her tiptoes and kissed him. His hands immediately went in her hair as he took control of the kiss, while Zane nuzzled into her neck. When they broke apart to the sounds of repeated throat-clearing the young nurse had turned a nice shade of beetroot, while Sandy grinned at her.

"Like my husband said. They're both the fathers, so they will be coming in with me or I'll simply refuse the scan."

"Right, that is…" Clearly flustered, she looked between them all and then shrugged. "I suppose we can make an exception this once."

When they entered the room, the actual sonographer could not have been nicer. Then again, both Zane and Sean turned on their charm, and there wasn't a woman alive who could resist them when they did that.

"Right, that all checks out. You have a perfectly healthy…." She paused for dramatic effect as she froze the image and looked up.

"Yes?" Zane asked while Sean looked ready to pop a blood vessel. His scar stood out against his tanned face, a sure tell of his emotional state. He'd come a long way in his sessions with Rhonda, but some things remained the same.

"A daughter. Congratulations again."

Sean released a breath, and Sandy was stunned to see the tears in his eyes.

"Heaven help us, buddy. That'll be another sassy female in the house." Sean scrubbed a hand over his face and placed a tender kiss on her belly, not caring a jot that he got the ultrasound gel over himself in the process.

Zane kissed her forehead, and he, too, had tears in his eyes.

"Thank you, baby girl."

The sonographer cleared her throat, and once all the formalities were completed and clutching a set of grainy photos in their hands they emerged into the carpark with goofy grins.

Their daughter chose that moment to kick in earnest, and Sandy grabbed her Sirs' hands and placed them on her belly.

"Emma says hello."

Sean and Zane both grinned and exchanged a look over her head.

"You owe me fifty, Sean. Told you she'd call her that if the baby was a girl."

Sean threw a mock punch at Zane and laughed when Zane ducked it easily enough.

"As if I care about the money or the sex. We're having a baby."

Sandy laughed and tried to glare up her

impossible men, but it was hard to do when she was blinking away tears of happiness.

The End

MCLEOD SECURITY

DEDICATION

To all my readers who've embraced this series so enthusiastically. Thank you, and I hope you enjoy Gabe's and Lissa's story.

MCLEOD SECURITY

GABE'S REVENGE

McLeod Security, 2

Doris O'Connor

Copyright © 2018

Chapter One

"Boss, you might wanna check this out." Gabriel Henshaw's earpiece crackled, and frowning, he looked up at the monitors, which made up one side of his office. A quick scan of them didn't show anything unusual. Business as usual in his various establishments. He smirked at Ange's grinding down on her latest conquest. The fucker was too far gone to notice she'd just relieved him of his wallet.

Bad, bad *girl.*

Angela, though no one ever called her that, was getting on a bit—at almost forty her days as a stripper were numbered—but she was a professional and Gabe could respect that. His amusement grew, when he saw her take out several notes out of the police commissioner's wallet before she stuffed the thing back in his pocket. That right there was why he hadn't sacked her yet, even though some of his staff had expressed worrying concerns about her lately. He'd have to run a fresh background check on her soon to be on the safe side, but for now she'd stay. As far as he knew, she never took advantage, just helped herself, and the men were never the wiser.

Besides, Gabe enjoyed taking her tight little cunt for a ride himself. Ange knew the score, never clung, unlike some of the younger bimbos who crossed his path and thought they could keep him. Or worse still, reform him. Gabe chuckled to himself. He hadn't met a bit of pussy yet, which would have convinced him to settle down, and he'd lost count how many he'd known intimately over the last forty-nine years of his leaving his mark in London's shady underbelly.

No one messed with Gabe and lived to tell the tale, let alone someone who owed him money like … what the fuck was Andrini doing now?

Gabe's sip of whisky went down the wrong way when he switched views to his casino. Not only was Andrini at the roulette table, he appeared to be causing a ruckus of some sort, *and* he'd brought his daughter.

It had been years since he'd last seen Lissandra Andrini in person, and his gut twisted in unwanted emotion. The pictures in the folder he had on her didn't do her justice. The girl was stunning. Her long black hair was piled on top of her head in some form of complicated updo, designed to look messy. Several long strands were left loose. They framed her heart-shaped face and whispered across the top of her breasts. And what a rack she had. A man could lose himself in that bounty. Surrounded by Gabe's men, she looked far too young and innocent to be anywhere near his establishment, let alone in a dress that hugged every one of her amazing curves. What the hell was Andrini thinking bringing her here dressed like *that*?

Fuck me. The little girl he used to bounce on his

knees—back in the days when Gabe cared about such things—long before her father had tried to sell him out to the fucking competition—was all grown up.

"I'll be right down."

Laughter came through his earpiece, and, irritated beyond measure, Gabe slammed his office door shut behind him, nodded at Luca, who stood to attention when he saw Gabe, and stabbed the button for the service elevator.

"What the fuck is Andrini doing here?" More laughter came through his earpiece, and Gabe scowled at the doors. Why could this thing not go any faster?

"Boss, you wouldn't believe me, if I told you. He's gonna pay his debts, he says…"

The odd intonation in his second in command's voice made the fine hair on Gabe's neck stand up. Andrini was broke. Even the house he lived in with his daughter was mortgaged to the hilt. Gabe knew because he held the deeds and had been waiting for the right moment to pounce. That only left one asset the bastard could sell… Revenge was best served cold, but *this* left a foul taste in Gabe's mouth.

Not for the first time he cursed the promise made to Lissandra's mother, before she died from the bullet meant for Andrini.

"Look after my little girl, please, Gabe. Kill him if you have to but spare her. She's an innocent in all this."

Ghosts of a past when he actually had a beating heart in his chest. Was capable of emotions and listened to his conscience.

The doors finally slid open, and Gabe entered through the kitchens.

"Keep him there. Where's the girl now?" he tapped his ear to ask the question.

After a moment of static, he got his answer.

"See you figured out his method of payment then. Stowed her by the kitchens for you, boss. What do you want me to do with *him*?"

"Let him gamble, for now. He brought me what I wanted."

A low whistle came through, before Gabe clicked off the communicator and slowed his steps as he rounded the corner. This side room was used by the kitchen staff for their breaks, but it was empty now, apart from one lone figure.

Revenge was in his grasp in the form of one luscious bundle of curves. Her light, flowery scent wrapped itself around him, and Lissandra gasped when he stepped up right behind her.

"What are you doing here, girl?"

She spun around at the sound of his voice, hands held up in a defensive move. Her eyes widened, and her breathing sped up, when she appeared to recognize him. Sure enough, her next words confirmed his assessment.

"You're Gabe." She closed her eyes and shook her head. "Of course, you are, but I don't understand."

Gabe smirked, and she took a step back and another when he slowly advanced on her. Her back hit the wall, and a whimper escaped her when he put his hands either side of her shoulders and caged her in. Even with her killer heels on, she barely reached his chin. So small, and curvy, and downright delicious. Fear poured off her in waves, and so help him, that turned him on, even as a small, long forgotten and buried deep part of his conscience brought out his protective streak.

"Please, I don't know what's going on. I just want to go home, *please*."

Blue eyes, the color of the deepest ocean, pleaded with him, as she looked up at him. She was the picture of youthful innocence, but Gabe knew better than to fall for the oldest trick in the book. She *was* Andrini's daughter, and until he knew for certain what game the fucking asshole was playing he would keep his guard up around this sweet young thing.

"There'll be no going home, little girl. Your father owes me a lot of money, and until I get it, you will be staying with me."

Those baby blues of hers pulled together in a deep frown, and she shook her head.

"You're insane. I'm not staying with anyone, let alone you. I demand you let me go this instant." She pushed against him, and Gabe laughed. While she was surprisingly strong for someone so little, she was no match for him. He grasped her wrists, and lifting her arms, held them high above her head, while he pinned her to the wall with his body. Fuck him, this close to her, her soft curves fit against him in all the right places, as though she was made just for him. A ridiculous notion, but he hardened anyway. He knew the minute it dawned on her, because heat rose in her cheeks, and she stopped struggling.

Indulging himself, Gabe bent his head and inhaled deeply next to her ear. Her pulse jumped. He grinned and growled in her ear.

"Nice try, little girl, but you don't get a say in this, at all. You're mine now." A shocked gasp reached his ears, and she resumed her struggles. When it didn't get anywhere, she hissed at him through clenched teeth.

"I'll never be yours, you … you bastard."

Gabe threw his head back and laughed. Her knee came up in an attempt to emasculate him, but Gabe blocked that easily enough by shifting out of the way. Transferring her delicate wrists into just one of his hands, he ran his free one down her arm slowly.

"Now, now, little girl, that wasn't very nice. Here we are just having a pleasant conversation and you try and do that."

Lissandra glared up at him, her full, kissable lips pressed into a thin line of disapproval. "Let me go, damn you. You have no right to manhandle me like this. I'll scream for help."

"Go ahead. Be my guest. Do you honestly think it would get you anywhere? This is *my* casino, sweet thing." She groaned but opened her mouth as though she was indeed about to launch into a screaming fit. "Know this, little girl, you start screeching, and I'll put you over my knee." He smiled grimly at her sharp intake of breath. "I'll also find something to occupy your mouth and it won't be a gag."

He flexed his hips to prove his point, and another one of those cock-hardening moans came from his captive.

"You wouldn't dare." That breathy denial served to make him harder, and he smirked down on her.

"Try me, little girl."

Her mouth opened and closed, but no sound emerged other than her rapid breaths, and satisfied he'd made his point, Gabe released her and stepped away. She immediately wrapped her arms around herself and shook her head.

"Good girl, see, we'll get along just fine."

"You can't do this. Papa won't let you." You had to admire the girl's spunk, as she dropped her arms and jutted her chin up and out in defiance.

"Your dear Papa won't get a choice, but by all means let's ask him." Gabe tapped his communicator. "Bring in Andrini, will you?"

"Sure thing, boss."

Hope flared in her expressive eyes, and he almost

felt sorry for her, until Andrini's slurred voice grated on his nerves.

"Tell your buffoons to get your hands off me, Henshaw."

Gabe turned slowly and let his gaze wander over his nemesis. The man looked a mess. Years of drinking and gambling had taken its toll, and from the looks of it he was half cut again. Sure enough, Lissandra's sigh confirmed it.

"Really, Papa, you promised."

Andrini shook off the hold Gabe's men still had on him and ignored his daughter.

"What do you want from me, Henshaw? You got your payment."

Lissandra's sharp intake of breath spoke volumes, as did her strangled exclamation.

"Papa, no, you *didn't*."

Again, the man ignored his only child, stuffed his hands into his trouser pockets, and pushed his chest out in a vain attempt to make himself appear bigger than he was. Gabe swallowed down his disgust at the fucking weasel. Andrini reeked of stale cigars, alcohol, and desperation.

"Tell me one good reason why I should accept this *payment*." He glanced toward Lissandra, and a twinge of unease settled in his gut. She'd gone so pale, she looked as though she might faint, and her perfectly manicured hands would leave gouges in her soft skin, so hard was her grip on her forearms. "I can take any pussy I want. What makes this one so special? You do know how *much* you owe me, right? I could destroy your miserable little existence in a second."

He deliberately turned his back on the girl, but he heard her shocked gasp loud and clear. No doubt she now thought him a monster.

"She's my daughter." Andrini's voice rose to a falsetto screech that hurt Gabe's ears. The man's double chin wobbled, and sweat broke out on his upper lip.

"So?" Gabe asked. He turned and made a big show of studying the terrified girl. At least he had his answer. She wasn't in league with her father on this. She was too still, too utterly shocked, for this to be an act, and her father was a cock-sucking asshole to put her through this. "That makes her tainted goods as far as I'm concerned."

Lissandra opened her mouth as though to protest, but one shake of his head stopped her. She dropped her head instead, and that twitch of unease turned into a lump of stone at the bottom of his stomach.

"How dare you? She's a virgin and fertile. I had her doctor confirm it. She would fetch a grand price in Ollivanti's auctions. She's … fuck."

Gabe planted his fist in the vile asshole's face and stopped the man's tirade. The sound of the fucker's nose breaking under his knuckles, blood spurting everywhere, followed by the coward's howl of pain masked the girl's whispered exclamation.

"Papa." One word, which held a word of pain and betrayal and made Gabe want to wrap his hands around her so-called father's meaty neck and strangle him with his bare hands.

"Quit that sniveling, Andrini. Boys, take her back to the house. She doesn't need to hear any more."

Like the well-oiled team his men were, they sprang into action and surrounded Lissandra, but she resisted.

"No, I want to stay. What auctions? What the hell did you do, Papa? Why? I told you I'll find a job. We can get out of this, we—"

"Don't be so fucking naïve." Andrini's snarl

interrupted her, as he spat blood on the floor in front of her. "You're so like your useless mother. She couldn't have given me a son, could she? Someone to be proud of, to carry on the business. No, she gave me *you*. Utterly fucking worthless, but at least you're good for *this*. Count yourself lucky I'm giving you to him." He spat more blood and fixed his bloodshot eyes on Gabe.

"You need an heir to carry on your business. She'll give you one. I figured you didn't want to impregnate one of your whores, and this makes us even." He sneered and puffed out his chest again. "I took her mother off you, so now you get the daughter. Fair is fair and all that, right."

Gabe had heard enough. One well-placed uppercut snapped the fucker's head back, and another one to the gut made him hunch over and fall to his knees.

"Get her the fuck out of here now."

His men swung into action, and Gabe vented his frustration on the asshole by beating the shit out of him. By the time he was done the fucker was a bleeding, unmoving mess on his floor, and Gabe flexed his bruised knuckles.

"Go and dump him in an alley somewhere, boys." Without waiting to see if his instructions were followed, he turned and stalked back up to his office. Every instinct in him screamed at him to go after Lissandra, but if he went near her now, he would be utterly incapable of being gentle, and the girl had been through enough for one day. He wasn't a complete asshole, and he wouldn't force himself on her. Gabe had never forced a woman in his life, and he wasn't about to start now.

Besides, none of this made sense. That fucker Andrini was up to something. He could have easily sold her off to Ollivanti. The crime lord's territory bordered on Gabe's with the Thames separating their businesses.

The mere thought of Lissandra in the cruel hands of that bastard made Gabe see red again, as he pushed open the door to his office, and shed his dirty clothes on the way to the adjacent bathroom. He held his hands under the cold tap and stared at his reflection as the water washed away the foul stench of his enemy.

Fuck it, he needed to kill, or fuck.

He turned off the water, stalked over to his desk, and picked up the phone.

"Find Ange and bring her up here, will you. I don't fucking care if her shift is over."

He slammed the phone down and adjusted his still-hard dick away from his zipper. Ange would take care of that, and once he could think straight, he'd come up with a plan.

One thing was certain. Lissandra was his responsibility now. Scowling, he picked up the phone again and hit the speed dial to his housekeeper.

Mavis had worked for him for as long as he could remember and was loyal to a fault.

"Yes, Gabe, what's the problem?"

"No problem, more of a situation. The boys are dropping off Andrini's daughter." He smiled grimly at the sharp intake of breath down the line. "Make her feel welcome, will you? She'll need clothes and all that feminine crap. Can you sort that, please?"

"Right, she's staying then? How long?"

"For the foreseeable future."

Chapter Two

Lissandra held it together until Gabe's men had deposited her in the back of a black SUV and slammed the door shut. She barely had time to appreciate the sleek, modern interior, before the glass partition slid up, separating her from the driver, and the car sped off. The locks clicked shut, and Lissandra burst into tears. Once she started she couldn't stop. What the hell had just happened to her? Her father's betrayal left an aching gap where her heart ought to be. While they'd never been close, and she knew he was in deep with seriously nasty people, he'd always protected her from that side.

Or rather, thanks to her dear Mama's trust fund, which she'd inherited on her mother's untimely and violent death fifteen years ago now—she sobbed harder as she tried to summon her mother's voice in her mind and couldn't—she'd been safely away at first boarding school and then taking her art degree in Paris.

While she'd known her father was on a downward decline, she hadn't fully appreciated how bad it had become since she made the permanent move back home. Had been summoned to return to do her *duty*.

Lissandra had been shocked to the core to see not only the state of her father, but also the house. The once proud Victorian building had fallen into disrepair. The roof leaked, rendering two of the five upstairs rooms unlivable. A mold infestation threatened to overtake the entire building. Peeling wallpaper, missing doors, and a general air of neglect made her former home a gloomy place to be.

She'd immediately offered what was left of Mama's trust fund to help with repairs, but her inebriated father had laughed in her face.

"You think that will help? Live in the real world,

girl. You couldn't even come home with a proper degree, could you? Waste of time taking an art degree."

His dismissal of a subject so dear to her heart had hurt at the time. Mama had been a talented artist, and all her tutors had said she'd inherited her late mother's talent. She'd stupidly thought Papa would be proud of her, but the man who stared her down through red-rimmed eyes held little resemblance to the vibrant, strong man he'd been when Mama had been alive.

People said grief affected everyone in a different way, and she supposed that was true, but her father had lost himself to gambling and drink. No matter how much she pleaded with him to stop—and in his rare lucid moments he promised to seek help—he didn't.

How could I have been so stupid?

She should have known something was up when he'd asked her to dress up. Her birthday was tomorrow, and she'd stupidly thought he'd wanted to treat her. That little girl inside of her, the one desperate to gain back her beloved Papa's approval, had squeed for joy when he'd smiled at seeing her come down in her finery.

"Oh, you'll do just fine."

Her heart had sunk when the cab had taken them to the casino. Still, she'd hoped. Casinos weren't just for gambling. Henshaw's was also known for the first-class entertainment Gabe put on, and the fine dining. What little hope she'd held for this to be a celebratory dinner had evaporated the minute they'd entered to a decidedly frosty reception. Gabe's goons had surrounded them, and amidst noisy demands from her father to be allowed entry, they'd been escorted to the roulette table. She hadn't caught what Papa had said to the croupier, but the assessing gaze and the way the men around her had sprung into action had given her a very bad feeling.

Never in a million years would she have thought

her own father would sell her like a piece of meat, however. How could he?

Anger won over her despair, and she swiped the useless tears off her face. If Gabe thought she was just going to lie down and think of England while he used her as his personal broodmare then he was in for a surprise.

Not that Gabe had said that exactly. In fact, he'd seemed outraged at her father's suggestion, and her stomach churned recalling that moment he'd broken her father's nose as effortlessly as other men broke bread.

Her belly flipped anew for entirely different reasons this time, because Gabe Henshaw was everything her father wasn't. Strength, virility, dominance, and danger literally oozed out of every one of his pores. He had to be at least six and half feet of muscles—prime male meat, her incorrigible roommate Chantelle would have said. Despite him having to be at least twenty years older than she was, he didn't look his age. The gray strands in his dark hair and neatly trimmed beard suited him, added to the whole vibe of experienced man, and lord help her, one of the many reasons why Lissandra had yet to use her V card was because men her age never did it for her. Her celebrity crushes were Sean Connery and Sam Elliott, for pity's sake. Chantelle used to tease her mercilessly about that.

If only she was here to talk her off the ledge. Chantelle would know how to handle a man like Gabe. Chantelle would no doubt also tell her, to stop protesting and to enjoy the ride.

Lissandra was all too painfully aware that being in effect sold off to Gabe didn't bother her half as much as it ought to. When he'd crowded her against that wall, imprisoning her with his large body … every feminine cell in her body had sighed in submission, especially when he'd threatened to put her over his knee.

The car stopped as abruptly as it had driven off, and Lissandra had barely a moment to school her features into a mask of indifference before the door was yanked open, and a brawny hand reached into the interior to grasp her arm.

"I can get out by myself, dammit. Stop manhandling me."

Soft laughter reached her ears. Naturally the suited muscle that hand and laugh belonged to, took no notice of her protests, and giving into the inevitable, Lissandra let him haul her out of her car. She swallowed hard when she realized where they were. An impressive, tall luxury apartment complex rose before her. The Thames was right in front of her, and Lots Road Power Station with its imposing twin towers was behind her. Chelsea Riverside meant serious money, not that she got a chance to fully take in her surroundings, as flanked by several of Gabe's men, she was ushered into the stunning marble, chrome, and glass foyer. The concierge behind the desk looked up and nodded at them.

No help was going to be forthcoming from that quarter. Then again, what did she expect? No doubt Gabe owned the entire building, and even if he didn't, who in their right mind would take on four, clearly armed bodyguards? This close to them she recognized the slight bulges under their tailored suits.

Thoughts of bullets brought her mother back to mind. Lissandra had sat frozen in the back of the car, seeing her mother take a bullet that had clearly been aimed at her father. Their driver had spirited Lissandra away to safety, and Mama had died in the hospital later that day.

Thoughts like that were not helping to slow down her breathing. If she kept going like that, she'd be in danger of going into a full-blown panic attack. There was no way on earth she would let that happen, so Lissandra forced herself to take deep breaths in through her nose and out through her mouth, while she watched the leader of the group guarding her insert a key into the lift panel. It popped open to reveal an electronic keypad. He was too fast for her to memorize the code he used, and besides, she highly doubted they would leave the key for the panel lying about. The lift ascended with quiet, deadly precision. Lissandra kept her gaze on the floor levels lighting up, and when the lift continued on its journey for several more seconds after the last floor lit up, she had her answer.

Naturally, Gabe would be in the penthouse, and one that didn't advertise its presence to mere plebs like her, who might also live in these luxury apartments.

When they finally stopped, and the door slid open, Lissandra couldn't help her gasp. They stepped out into a carpeted entry, which opened up into a huge, open plan living area. A kitchen was to her right, doors opening up to what she presumed must be bedrooms on her left. The lights of the city were a sparkling display through the floor to ceiling windows that made up most of the walls in the space.

Lissandra knew she had to look like a buffoon, standing there dumbfounded. No doubt her mouth was open, and she couldn't be entirely sure she wasn't drooling. How much was Gabe worth to afford this? With her luxury surroundings came the heart-sinking realization that she was trapped. There was no way on this earth she would be able to escape from this luxury prison, and she blinked back more tears threatening to erupt.

"Ah, there you are. Welcome, my dear."

The kindly voice belonged to a little old lady with silver hair, who appeared from the kitchen area, and smiled at Lissandra. Her smile slipped when she seemed to notice Lissandra's anxiety, and she clapped her hands together.

"Right, off with you. I've got her now."

"Oh, come on, Mavis. Don't we get a drink or something? One of your cherry pies?" The big guy standing next to her shifted from foot to foot, looking more like a little boy then the menacing presence he had been. Mavis took no notice of him, just waved him away and made shooing noises, while she turned her attention on Lissandra.

"Go away. You made the girl cry. That's no way to treat a lady. Be off with you before I get my frying pan and bash some sense into your heads."

The way all four of them stepped back, hands in the air, would have been comical in any other circumstance. Now, it just added to the anxiety which clogged up Lissandra's throat and threatened to make the contents of her stomach appear.

"As for you, my dear, come and sit down before you fall down. What has that boy done to you, eh?" Gentle hands guided her into the open plan area, and onto one of the plush seats in the living area. Lissandra gratefully slid onto the leather couch before her wobbly legs gave up on her. "There, now, let me fetch you a cup of tea. Nothing is that bad that it can't be fixed with a cuppa, and I've got some ginger biscuits, too. That'll help settle your stomach."

The kind words made Lissandra burst into renewed tears, which only got worse, when the other woman clucked her tongue, sat down next to her, and enveloped her in a bear hug.

"Oh, you poor wee thing. There, there now. It will be all right you see, Lissa."

By the time Lissandra finally had her emotions

under control, she'd soaked the starched front of Mavis's apron with her tears, and she murmured her apology.

"I'm sorry, I'm not normally such a watering pot."

Mavis tucked her hair behind her ears and smiled.

"That's quite all right, my dear. These are hardly ordinary circumstances for you. I dare say it's not every day that Lissa Andrini finds herself ensnared by her father's enemy."

Lissandra jerked, and Mavis brows drew together in a frown at her reaction.

"I'm sorry. My mouth tends to run away with me. If I overstepped the mark, then, please forgive me. I shouldn't be having this conversation with you, anyway, but with Gabe. Lord knows what he was thinking. Let me get you that tea, Lissa."

Mavis rose, and Lissandra put her hand out to stop her.

"No, it's not that. It's just, you called me Lissa."

Mavis turned, hands on her ample hips, and frowned.

"Would you rather I call you Lissandra? We don't stand on ceremony on here, and I only use the boys' full names when they're in trouble."

Lissandra smiled through her tears and shook her head.

"They're hardly boys, Mavis, and no, it's not that. No one has called me Lissa since my mother died, that's all."

"Ah, I see, you were very young when she passed, weren't you?" Mavis asked.

Lissandra swallowed hard to dislodge the lump of emotion in her throat and nodded.

"I was eight, yes. How do you know all this? I mean, you know who I am and…"

Mavis shrugged.

"I've known Gabe for a long time, and I know the whole sorry tale. What happened to your mother was such a waste. That bullet was meant for Andrini, not her. Anyway, let me get that tea." With that she bustled and reappeared moments later with a tray holding not only a cup, saucer, and a teapot, but also milk, sugar, biscuits, and an assortment of mini sandwiches. Seeing them made Lissandra's stomach rumble, and Mavis laughed.

"Ah, thought you might be hungry. You just go and help yourself, and eat something, while I go and make sure your room is ready."

Again, she hurried off, leaving Lissandra to her own devices. By the time she drank her second cup of tea and had eaten nearly all of the tuna and cucumber sarnies, she didn't feel as though she was either going to faint or throw up any minute. She hadn't even realized how hungry she was until she started eating. Taking her cup with her, she walked over to the plate glass window and took in the views. This would be stunning in the daylight, no doubt.

"Ah, there you are. There's a wee balcony out there to sit on when the weather is nice as long as you don't mind heights. The views are better from the bedrooms though, and the terrace is enclosed. Always makes me feel a tottie better. Come, I'll give you the tour, and show you your room, so you can freshen up."

True to her word, Mavis gave Lissandra the tour of Gabe's apartment. Just as she'd expected, four bedrooms led from the carpeted entrance hall. All of them had en-suite bathrooms, with the master bedroom being the last one along. Lissandra's stomach fluttered in something suspiciously like anticipation when she took in the huge bed dominating the middle of the room. Surely, that ought to fill her with disgust, not tendrils of arousal. Gabe's scent clung to this room. Nothing too ostentatious, just hints of the dark, spicy musk of his cologne, and Lissandra hastily turned her back to the room.

"And this here is your room. Gabe asked for you to have the one next to his."

Mavis swung the door open and flipped the lights on, and Lissandra gasped. The room was almost identical to Gabe's, if slightly smaller. While Gabe's room had been decorated in darker colors, this one was done up in soothing pastels and had an altogether more feminine feel to it.

The reason made anger rise in her belly, and Lissandra ground her response out through gritted teeth.

"This where he keeps all the women he kidnaps?"

Mavis sucked in a sharp breath and shook her head.

"Oh, my dear, you have him all wrong." At Lissandra's snort in answer Mavis's wise old gray eyes narrowed, and she crossed her arms under her impressive bosom. "Oh, that boy is no angel, but he's never raised a hand to a woman, or kidnapped one. Trust me, I brought him up better than that. Had it been up to his good for nothing mother, I…" Mavis slammed her lips shut, as though she said more than she ought to have done and sighed.

"Anyway, I've put some toiletries in the en-suite for you, and there's one of my nighties under the pillow on the bed. No doubt, it'll swamp you, but it's better than sleeping in the buff." She winked at her when she said that. "I figured you wouldn't be comfortable enough to do that. There's also several bathrobes in the wardrobe, which will do, until we can get you some clothes, or the boys bring over your belongings. Size sixteen, right, in dresses? And I'd say…" She walked around Lissandra, studying her as though she was an insect under a microscope. "Thirty-four double D in bra size, am I right?"

Lissandra couldn't get her voice to work at all, so she simply nodded.

"Thought so. Well, make yourself at home. I'll be off now. There's more food ready to heat up in the fridge, and if you need anything else, just pick up the phone. Someone will answer it and help you. Same goes for any emergency. There's an alarm button right next to the lift, which will send security straight up to get you." She paused and smiled when Lissandra couldn't help her hopeful jerk. "Gabe's security, Lissa, so don't get any ideas. You're perfectly safe here, and I'll be on the floor just below if you need me for anything. Sleep tight now."

With that, Mavis left her to her own devices, and seconds later the ding of the lift doors signaled her departure.

Despite Mavis's instructions, Lissandra approached the lift. Sure enough, there was a red button to press, but she couldn't see any other mode of opening the doors. When she stepped close enough to touch the doors slid open on their own.

Stunned, Lissandra stepped into the lift and pressed the button for downstairs. Nothing happened, and none of the other floor buttons worked either. She glared at her reflection in the mirrored walls.

Face it, there's no way out, so you might as well enjoy the place.

With that thought in mind, Lissandra ran herself a nice hot bath. When her toes and fingers turned wrinkly she got out, and by the time she'd dried her hair with the state of the art hair dryer she found in her nightstand drawer, she was yawning.

The last thought she had before sleep overtook

her, was if her father was still alive. Gabe had been so very angry at him, and why did that make her heart miss a beat? She hated Gabe Henshaw, didn't she?

Chapter Three

"Get the fuck off me. I'm not in the mood after all." Gabe scowled at the woman kneeling between his legs, trying her best to get him hard. What the fuck was that all about? Gabe never had a problem getting it up, yet from the minute Ange had paraded into his office, smiled and tried to kiss him, his previous hard-on had turned into the equivalent of a limp noodle. Even now, with one of her hands caressing his balls, the other rubbing up and down his shaft and her painted lips around his tip, he didn't manage a twitch.

His mind briefly conjured up a young dark-haired woman, and his dick semi-hardened instantly.

"There you are, it's all right, you're getting there."

Ange's voice broke the spell, and Gabe pushed her off him.

"I said get off me, woman, and get the fuck out of my office." Ange sprawled backward on the floor, legs splayed, giving him the perfect, if brief, glimpse of her shaved cunt before she scrambled upward. Did fuck all for him, and his mood darkened. He got to his feet and turned his back on her wanton display. By the time he'd tucked himself back in his jeans and pulled several notes out of his wallet, she was back on her feet, and pouting.

"Jeez, what the hell is wrong with you, boss? *You* asked for *me*, remember."

Gabe threw several hundred at her and scowled.

"I know. That should be more than enough for your troubles. Now get out."

Ange looked all set to flounce out, but common sense won out, and she picked up the notes, stuffed them in her cleavage and then paused, hand on the door handle.

"I won't tell anyone, you know. It happens. Nothing to get upset about. I—"

She blanched at his growl of sheer outrage and made herself scarce.

How fucking dare she assume he had a problem? He didn't fucking have one, or rather he didn't until Lissandra walked back into his life.

He poured himself a double measure of whisky and yanked open her folder. On the top of it were the latest reports he'd had about her. He hadn't had a chance to look at them yet, but, *fuck him.* She looked even more edible in casual jeans, with her hair tied back into a ponytail and not a scrap of make up on her face. These pictures had been taken last week at Heathrow. So, she hadn't been in the country long then? The sense of unease he'd had ever since the interlude with her father grew bigger and killed dead any lecherous thoughts he might have had right there and then.

The girl needed protection, and after tonight's debacle that fell squarely on his shoulders. The up to date reports on Andrini only added to that damn itch down his spine. Especially that pic of Andrini getting into a blacked-out limo, registered to Ollivanti's company two days ago. Ollivanti kept his cards close to his chest, and getting intel on the crime lord was notoriously difficult. No one liked to talk for fear of ending up as fish food, and the guy had someone on his payroll in the Met Police.

Which made him almost untouchable. Almost... Gabe scowled into the distance. This thing with Lissa would force things to a head, because if her father was plotting something with Ollivanti, protecting Gabe's territory lines wouldn't be enough anymore. While he would love to take that fucker out for good once and for all, the inevitable loss of life of innocent bystanders such a turf war would cause made his guts churn.

Gabe picked up the phone.

"Increase security at my place and step up surveillance on Ollivanti and Andrini, will you? ... Yes, I know I said dump him, but scum like him will always crawl back out of the gutter. ... Wake up my attorney, too. ... I want him at my place in the morning. ... Yeah, carry on with that. ... No, the girl stays with me."

He absentmindedly listened to his second in command and froze when he noticed the day.

"Fuck, forget what I said. I need you to get the girl's stuff from her place. Yes, all of it. ... Also..."

By the time he listed all of his instructions he'd drunk himself through half the bottle. He also had the beginnings of a plan. She would hate him, for sure, but, better that than the alternative.

He tapped his earpiece.

"Bring the car 'round. I'm going home."

Hearing the affirmative, he switched the thing off and slipped it in his pocket. His team could take care of the rest. The car ride over to his place, achieved in minimum time, thanks to the time—even in London traffic was light at three in the morning—he stepped out of the lift and froze.

The faint scent of her perfume was still in the air. The whole place felt different, and it wasn't just the washed-up dishes in the sink.

He smiled grimly as he traced the items. That had to have been Lissandra. Mavis would use the dishwasher, and no one else was here. Her high heels were left by the leather seating arrangement in the living area, and Gabe felt himself harden, as he recalled how those shoes had looked on her slender feet.

Not a sound could be heard in the apartment, so she had to be sleeping. She would never know...

Gabe crossed the hall and carefully opened the door to the bedroom next to his.

She'd left the sidelight on, had fallen asleep where she stood from the looks of it, and his cock gave up any pretense of not being able to work. The speed with which he rose to the occasion left him lightheaded and grasping the doorframe. Not only for support but also to stop himself from marching up to her and taking what she so inadvertently offered.

She must have had a shower or bath because she was still wrapped up in one of the fluffy towels, and fast asleep on the bed. The knot on the towel had come undone, which made the fabric slip, exposing one of her full breasts. The nipple was pebbled in response to the cool air, and his mouth watered with the need to taste. Would she like it rough or gentle, he mused? And why on earth was a woman this sexy still a virgin?

Gabe ought to rot in hell for the erotic images that were now bombarding his brain. That girl was young enough to be his daughter. He'd known her mother, for fuck's sake, had introduced her to the older Andrini, and tenderhearted Valentina Johnson had fallen head over heels in love with Andrini at first sight.

And here he was, twenty-five years later, lusting after the daughter of that ill-fated union. No wonder Mavis had chewed his ear out once she'd left Lissandra up to her own devices. What the hell was he doing?

Lissandra stirred in her sleep, and he froze. She didn't wake up however, just turned, obscuring his view of her rack. Unfortunately, or fortunately as the case might be, that side roll made the towel hitch higher on her ample thighs. When she brought her knees up to her chest, Gabe got an eyeful of her sweet pussy. Covered in fine downy dark hair, it was temptation personified. Groaning, he adjusted his now rock-hard dick away from the zipper of the jeans he'd changed into, after his suit had gotten covered in her father's blood.

Thoughts of that asshole was the equivalent of an ice-cold shower. Not that the reprieve lasted long. He couldn't leave her like that, so he yanked out the duvet, the edges of which were tucked under the mattress, and pulled it over her to cover her up. Ideally, he'd have lifted her to tuck her in properly, but there was only so much restraint he was capable of. Lifting her up, actually feeling the touch of her soft skin, would send him over the edge for sure.

Why her, and why now, he had no idea, but this woman had gotten under his skin with a speed that left him breathless and his cock only interested in her, it seemed. The interlude with Ange had driven that point home rather forcefully.

Much to his disgust his hand shook as he brushed a strand of hair out of her face, and he forced himself to step away. He could do this. He could beat this, right?

Once he'd had her, this strange spell he was under would be broken. Gabe scowled at his reflection when he was in his own bathroom and stripped for a much-needed shower. Ange's perfume still clung to him, made him gag, and it was suddenly imperative to wash the other woman off of him. Not that they'd done anything. Not that he owed the woman sleeping in his guest bedroom any loyalty, but fuck him…

Turning the hot water to cold achieved sweet fuck all at getting his erection to subside, so Gabe did the only thing he could do. One hand braced on the tiled wall, he jerked himself off. He came in record time, images of sweet little Lissandra in his mind, her name on his lips as he spurted thick ropes of cum, which disappeared down the drain with the swirling water.

When the last twitch of his dick had subsided, he

turned off the water, and dried himself off. His blasted cock was still at half mast, as his thoughts turned back to Lissandra.

Fuck him six ways from next Sunday. He wanted her, and he hadn't this much problem controlling that part of his anatomy since his teenage years. It was going to be a long three weeks until he could rectify this situation.

****

A brass band seemed to have taken up residence in Lissandra's head, as she struggled to a state of consciousness. God, she hated mornings, especially when she woke in a strange place, and … what the hell was going on out there? Struggling to rid herself of the fog for brains she always woke with, the events of the previous night broke through the haze and she froze.

She was in Gabe's apartment, and the noise she heard wasn't a brass band, but heavy footsteps and clanging, as though someone was erecting scaffolding or something.

Male curses traveled through the shut door and then Gabe's authoritative voice.

"Will you keep the noise down? You'll wake the girl up."

Somehow being referred to as *the girl* stung. Then again, what did she expect from him? She was his to do with as he pleased. There was no need to lower himself to using her name. That's if he kept her, of course. Hot tears streaked down her face, and she angrily swiped them away, disentangled herself out of the duvet, and padded across to the marble bathroom to freshen up. Having relieved herself, and with her hands and face washed, teeth brushed, and wrapped up in one of the soft fluffy robes she'd found in the walk-in wardrobe she felt marginally ready to face the world out there.

Everything was ominously quiet now, and she jumped at the soft knock on her door. Before she could bid or deny entry, the door opened, and Mavis's silver head appeared.

"Oh, good, you're awake. I brought you some coffee, and breakfast among other things."

She pushed the door all the way open, and Lissandra could have kissed her when the full-flavored scent of strong, freshly brewed coffee hit her nostrils.

"Here, take this and I'll bring the rest in."

Lissandra closed her eyes, inhaled deeply of the elixir of life, and downed that first cup almost in one go.

"Figured you'd be just like your mother. Never did work out how she didn't burn her mouth, inhaling hot coffee like that." The deep, amused tones could only belong to Gabriel Henshaw, and Lissandra gasped when she saw him standing in the entrance to her bedroom. The mug clattered out of her hand, only saved from shattering into a gazillion pieces by the luxurious rug that covered the wooden floor.

"What the hell are you doing here?" She spat the words out at him, while making a grab for her robe to ensure she was covered up.

"I live here, little girl, and don't bother covering up on my account. I saw it all last night."

"Gabe, really, behave. Lissa is your guest." Mavis's admonishment saved her from responding. Not that she could have got her vocal cords to respond to the demands of her brain if her life depended on it, because Gabe chose that moment to step closer. His presence filled the room, and she swallowed hard when he sat down on the opposite side of the bed and reached over her to snare one of the buttered croissants on the tray. He popped the whole thing in his mouth. His Adam's apple bopped up and down as he swallowed. Gabe licked his lips and smirked at her, when she couldn't seem to stop staring at his lips.

"Happy Birthday, Lissa."

His voice dropped to a low sexy growl, which settled straight in every one of her erogenous zones, and she was extremely glad she was sitting. Even if she was in far too close proximity to this man. He'd been devastating in his tailored suit last night, but this morning, with his hair still damp from a shower, and sticking up all over the place, he was ... well, she didn't know *what* he was, other than too close to her. His proximity made breathing difficult. Especially, as every inhale brought his scent into her lungs. It should be illegal for any man to smell *so* good. The hint of dark, spicy cologne, mixed in with the scent of virile and aroused man, if that long hard ridge she glimpsed in his jeans was any indication.

Not that that was due to her. It couldn't be. Lissandra might never have had sex, but she knew enough to know that men woke up like that in the morning, and...

"What time is it?" She blurted out the question, and one of Gabe's dark eyebrows rose in response.

"That's what you're leading with?" he asked and shook his head. He swung both of his legs on the bed next to her, scooted up, until he could rest his back against the headboard, and crossed his arms over his chest. That action only served to emphasize the width of his chest and the biceps straining against the sleeves of the t-shirt he wore this morning. Fine, dark hair covered his strong forearms, and Lissandra followed the veins down to his large hands. Strong, and slightly calloused, they were the hands of a man not afraid to use them. The hands of a killer.

That thought sent a shiver of unease down her

spine, and her next words came out as a mere whisper.

"What have you done to Papa?" she asked.

"Why do you care?" Gabe uncrossed his arms and nudged her chin up with his index finger, leaving her no choice but to look at him. The heated intensity in his amber gaze made breathing even more difficult, because she didn't know what to make of it. He was angry, that much was clear, but whether that anger was directed at her or her father she couldn't determine. Drawers opened and shut while they were in their silent stare down, and Lissa jumped when Mavis spoke.

"There, I've put all your clothes away, my dear."

Clothes? What clothes? She tried to turn her head, but Gabe's hold on her chin tightened.

"Thank you, Mavis, that's all for now. Let me know the minute Parkinson gets here, will you?" He didn't look at Mavis while he spoke, his attention entirely focused on Lissandra.

"I mean it, behave yourself, Gabe."

This time the faintest smile kicked up the corners of his sinful mouth, as he replied.

"Haven't you got something to bake, Mavis?"

"Hah, I do, and fine, I'm going. I'll be around, my dear, if you need me for anything. And Happy Birthday from me, too."

With that the door clicked shut behind her, and Gabe finally released his hold on her chin. She felt curiously bereft without it. Pulling her legs up her to her chest, she hugged them to herself in a vain effort to restore some of her equilibrium.

Easier said than done with Gabe sprawled out next to her, as though it was his God-given right to lie in her bed. She couldn't help herself. Her gaze traveled down his muscular legs and snared on his bare feet. Dammit, why couldn't he be old and puffy and unattractive?

"How do you know it's my birthday?" she finally asked when the silence between them grew uncomfortable.

"I know everything there is to know about you, little girl. Besides, I was there when you were born." He smirked at her sharp intake of breath.

"Eat something, birthday girl. Mavis made the croissants fresh this morning, just for you. She'll be offended if you don't at least try and eat them. They're still your favorite, right?" This time he winked, shut her open mouth with his index finger, and then mercifully got off the bed. Not that her reprieve lasted for long, because he only walked around it, picked up her abandoned mug and then refilled it from the pot, added cream and held it out to her.

Their fingertips touched as she took it off him, and a jolt of awareness shot up her arm.

"Damn." That muttered curse, as though he'd felt that, too, meant she *had* to look at him. Brows drawn together in a frown, he didn't look angry however, more like he wanted to eat her alive. Her breath caught, and her nipples pebbled against the soft terry of her robe, and, much to her internal horror, her pussy grew wet. This was all so very wrong, but it seemed this man revved up her libido without even trying. Heaven help her if he chose to touch her. His gaze dropped, lingering on her throat, where her heart was trying to beat out an uneven staccato rhythm and lower still into the V of her robe. If it hadn't given away how much his silent perusal of her affected her, she'd have been tempted to pull the lapels together. Instead she held onto the coffee cup as though her life depended on it.

Gabe shook his head, scrubbed a hand over his beard-roughened jaw, and walked over to the glass wall.

He yanked the blinds open, and Lissandra gasped anew, this time at the view. The Thames was winding its way underneath them, and they seemed very high up. The wall slid open at the flick of a switch to the side, and Gabe stepped out on what looked like a terrace. Belatedly, Lissandra recalled Mavis telling her about it. The weather was kind for once, and a warm breeze blew in. When it became clear that Gabe had no intention of stepping back in her room, Lissandra followed him. Not before she snared the two remaining croissants, however. She bit into one as she stepped onto the terrace, and she couldn't help her moan of delight, as the warm buttery breakfast delight melted on her tongue. Crumbs fell into her exposed cleavage, making her all too aware of the fact that she was buck naked under the robe. *So, why the hell have I followed him out here?*

He turned at that moment, and her heart all but stopped at the way he looked at her. *Jesus*. For the first time Lissandra truly appreciated what Chantelle meant when she talked about eye fucking. The way Gabe looked at her, she might as well not be wearing anything.

He didn't say anything, and, having washed that bite down with a swig of coffee, she cleared her throat repeatedly before she managed to speak.

"You're right, these are delicious."

Gabe nodded, and his slow, dangerous smile nudged her core temperature up a few more degrees. To hide her reaction, she turned and walked up to the glass balustrade. It reached mid chest on her, and while it was still a little scary being this high up, it also gave her the courage to peer down. She took a step back, straight into the hard wall of muscle that made up Gabe's tall frame.

She jumped, and his large hand came to rest on her shoulders.

"Relax, you're perfectly safe here." A shiver went

up her spine at the feel of his thumbs stroking along her neck. It was the lightest of caresses, yet it sent her hormones into overdrive. With her hands full she had no choice but to let him. Oh, it would be so easy to simply give in, to lean back into his body and to accept the protection he offered. Instead she stiffened her spine and held herself away from him as much as she could.

"Am I? Safe, I mean?" she asked, and the far too arousing circles he drew on the sensitive skin under her ears, stopped. His fingers tightened on her shoulders, and then he released her with a sigh. Stepping around her, he took the mug and remaining croissant out her hands and placed both items on the little table and chairs she belatedly noticed.

He held out his hand for her to take.

"Come, I want to show you something," he said.

Lissandra shook her head and wrapped her arms around herself.

"I'm not going anywhere with you, especially not like this." She looked down on herself. Gabe's laughter caught her by surprise.

"By all means, get dressed, if it makes you feel better. My boys collected all your stuff from that hovel you've been living in."

Hearing him refer to her family home in such derogatory terms made her see red, and she gritted her teeth.

"How dare you? That's my home, and you—"

A low, menacing and animalistic growl rumbled from his big chest, and Lissandra froze. Oh, no, she'd pissed him off for sure, and yesterday's threat to put her over his knee slammed into the forefront of her mind. What in the hell was wrong with her to think about that now?

"*This* is now your home, and you'd do well to

remember that, little girl." She couldn't help her sharp inhale, and he nodded once. "You asked me earlier what I'd done to the asshole who fathered you." He paused, and she swallowed hard at the grim expression on his face. Right now, seeing the quiet fury which locked his jaw, made his nostrils flare with the sheer force of his breathing, she believed every rumor she'd ever heard about this man.

"Did you kill him?" His amber gaze flashed in something akin to fury, intensified as he cocked his head to one side and studied her.

"Would it bother you, if I had?"

Horrified at the quiet menace behind Gabe's words, made ten times more potent because he'd dropped his voice to a controlled, flat, emotionless cadence, she stepped back. He didn't follow her, simply smiled and raised one eyebrow.

"Of course, it would. He's my father. He's the only family I've got left." Her voice caught on the last few words, and much to her horror she blinked away tears.

"And you love him."

That statement sat between them like the big elephant in the room. She opened her mouth to confirm that she did, but nothing came out. She stared up at Gabe, horrified at the realization that she didn't. Oh, she craved his acceptance, had loved him once, but lately? What she felt for the old man he'd become, was more pity than anything. The need to do her duty by the man she owed her very existence to, but love? Whatever love she might felt for him had died with those hateful words he'd flung her way when he'd all but sold her to this man.

"He's my father," she said, and repeated it as though to convince herself that this meant anything. "Mama would have—"

"You mother, may she rest in peace, wouldn't have wanted you to waste one tear on that scum," Gabe interrupted her. The absolute conviction behind those clipped words meant they lodged in her belly like poisoned darts. Lissandra shook her head and bit her lips so hard she tasted her own blood.

"How dare you? You have no idea what my mother would have wanted."

Cruel laughter filled the space between them, made those arrows take root, as a million questions popped up in her brain.

"Don't I, Lissa? Why do you think I know how your mother drank her coffee? She woke up with me a long time before she ever graced Andrini's bed."

"No, you're lying." Lissandra wrapped her arms around herself and shut her eyes. Anything to ward off those images threatening to make her sick.

"You're wrong. Mama loved Papa. She never would have. You're wrong. You're a damn fucking liar." A sob escaped with the last words, and she slammed her hand over her mouth to stop anymore from escaping.

Before she even knew what was happening, she was in his arms. Held tight against his hard body, she fought against him, but she was no match for his superior strength. No matter how hard she pummeled against his chest, he wouldn't let her go, just murmured words in her hair she couldn't catch over the ugly crying she was now doing.

When she eventually got herself under control, she realized she was sitting in his lap on one of the recliners dotted around the terrace. It seemed to wrap 'round this side of the apartment with various plot pants and garden furniture dotted around and what looked like a covered hot tub outside the next wall of windows, which had to belong to Gabe's bedroom. He was next to hers, after all.

She struggled to sit up, and his hold on her loosened. Gabe produced a starched, white handkerchief from nowhere, and accepting it, she noisily blew her nose. He nudged her chin up to make her look at him, and this time his brown gaze held none of its predatory nature. A genuine smile lit up his ragged features, and he swiped the remaining moisture off of her face with his thumbs. For one heart-stopping moment she thought he would kiss her, found herself leaning forward to meet his full lips, in fact, before he blinked and released her.

"I'm not lying, Lissa." He put his index finger over her mouth when she opened it to voice her protests and shook his head. "No, hear me out. You're right, your mother loved your father to distraction, and she never cheated on him. The same can't be said for Andrini, of course." Gabe smiled grimly at her sharp intake of breath. "She knew, of course she knew, but she always forgave him, always hoped he'd mend his ways." He pulled back further, seemingly lost in thought, and shook his head. "As if a leopard ever changes his spots. Power went to his head, made him hungry for more, and he didn't give a shit about who he stepped on to reach that goal, including me." His thigh muscles tensed under her, and she held her breath. She knew some of the history between Andrini and Henshaw, but it was one-sided and only what she'd picked up in snatched, overheard conversations as a child, which hadn't made sense back then.

Out of nowhere, another memory rose to the surface. Of her, as a child, sitting on this man's lap with her sweet Mama looking on and laughing. The remembered happiness of that moment took her breath away. She wanted to hold onto it, but as quickly as that memory had appeared it drifted back into the recesses of her brain.

She looked up at him and frowned. The man whose lap she sat on had definitely been him. A much younger version, without the grooves on his face, and the gray streaks in his hair, less menacing and dangerous, as he'd joked with her mother.

"You used to come and visit." Those words blurted out before she could take them back, and Gabe grew even tenser. His hand clenched into a white knuckled fist, and when he looked down on her his amber eyes had darkened, held a wealth of emotion before he blinked, and the moment was lost.

"You remember that? You were very young back then."

Lissandra tried for a smile, but failed miserably, if the expression on his face was anything to go by.

"Not really, just snatches. I know Mama was happy when you came. She laughed a lot, then."

Gabe swore under his breath, and in the next instant she was off his lap and sitting on the recliner by herself, while Gabe prowled the space in front of her like a caged tiger. After minutes of simply sitting there and watching him, she had to break the tense silence.

"What happened? I mean, you stopped coming and Mama cried a lot, I remember that much."

Gabe froze, scrubbed a hand over his face, and shook his head.

"You don't know? Can't believe for one minute Andrini didn't brag about his hand in that."

When she shook her head, he frowned.

"Really, I don't. I mean, I heard rumors since, but he never told me anything about … well, about that side of his business. Why would he? I'm only a girl, after, all, a complete disappointment, and women don't count as anything other than arm candy."

She swallowed hard at another memory. This time of dear Mama in tears, as her so-called husband berated her.

"The one thing I need from you, and you can't even do that. Why can't you be nice to him? It would get me this fucking deal."

Seeing that scene play out in her mind sent a shiver down her spine, and she hugged her arms around herself, as she saw it through adult eyes now.

She blinked when Gabe's hands settled on her thighs. On his haunches in front of her, he studied her.

"What is it? What have you remembered now?"

"I'm not sure, I mean he wouldn't have used Mama like that, would he?"

Gabe's eyebrow rose, and his smirk said it all.

"Andrini is capable of most things, and even back then he was desperate man. Making me take the fall for the drug deal gone wrong wasn't enough for him." She pulled back, and he nodded. "That's why I disappeared. I did a few years at Her Majesty's pleasure. Got let out early for good behavior, if you can believe that."

His short laugh rang hollow, and her stomach cramped.

"When did you get out?" she asked.

"Three days before your mother got killed in the crossfire." A muscle ticked in his jaw, and Lissa wanted to scream as the terrifying possibility occurred to her.

"Did you kill my mother?"

Chapter Four

Fuck. Gabe's immediate denial stuck in his throat, as the talons of grief and remorse pulled him under. Thoughts and feelings which he'd thought himself immune to sat on his chest and threatened to swamp him, making the simple act of breathing difficult.

To give himself time and to hide his reaction to her words, he straightened slowly and turned his back on her.

"Why would you ask me that?" He ground the question out through gritted teeth. He sensed her get up and step closer. The briefest of gentle touches on his arm, and then she stood in front of him. Arms wrapped around herself, she worried her plump bottom lip with her teeth, and Gabe swore softly. She looked so much like her mother had at her age, it was unreal.

"Just answer the question, please. I was there in the car. I saw her being shot."

He flinched when her expressive eyes filled with tears.

"I know, Lissa, I'm sorry."

She gasped, shook her head, and stepped away from him, until the glass balustrade stopped her.

"Oh my God, you did do it, didn't you? I heard rumors, even out in Switzerland, but … no, don't you dare touch me, you *bastard*, you." She put her hands up to ward him off when he took a step toward her and shook her head. "How could you? What did my mother ever do to deserve this?"

"Nothing, sweet girl. The bullet wasn't intended for her, believe me. That asshole used her a shield, when the first shot went wide. Neither you nor your mother should have been there."

Like a spring released from its box, Lissandra

shot forward and slapped his face with surprising force for someone so small. He blocked the next move easily enough, grabbed her wrists, and spun her around so that her back was resting against his chest. She still fought him, kicking and snarling like a feral kitten, while he held her pinned against him, feet dangling off the ground with her calling him all the names under the sun. He took it for a while—she needed to vent—until she started to sag against him, and he put her back on her feet.

"Have you quite finished, girl?" He growled the question into her ear and was rewarded with another backward kick by her left foot. Thank heavens she wasn't wearing shoes, or his shins would be black and blue, come morning.

"No, let me go, you murdering scum." The words, while brave, came out on a hoarse whisper, and Gabe sighed and relaxed his hold on her a little more.

"That would only be an insult if it was true, little girl." She stiffened in his arms. "Now, promise to behave yourself and I'll let you go. Hit me again, and so help me, your delectable ass will be red raw, are we clear?"

He didn't miss her sharp intake of breath, but she did murmur her acquiescence.

"I can't hear you, little girl."

"Yes, damn you."

He transferred both of her wrists in one of his and delivered a sharp swat to her ass.

She jumped and yelped, and her startled gaze collided with his.

"That's 'yes, damn you, Sir', at least, girl."

Her eyes widened, and she looked all set to argue before she offered him a tight smile.

"Fuck you, *Sir*."

The snarky intonation she put on that title, while she yanked her chin up and did her best to stare him down, should have made him do good on his promise to put her over his knee. However, the slight wobble in her bottom lip, coupled with the way every delectable curve of her body was pressed into his frame, meant any such action would be a very bad idea indeed. He wouldn't be able to keep his hands off of her, and he didn't want her first time to be angry sex. She deserved better than that.

"Oh, fuck we will, my dear, but not now and not here."

Her eyes grew wide, her already fast breaths sped up even more, and Gabe swallowed a groan. He let go of her and stepped back for some much-needed breathing space. As it was his cock was trying his hardest to break out the confines of the denim surrounding it. Gabe couldn't even remember the last time he wanted a woman this damn much.

"So, you're going to add rape to your rap sheet. Murdering innocent women wasn't enough for you?"

A gasp from behind them alerted Gabe to Mavis's presence, and sure enough when he turned his head it was to see her standing there. Hands pushed into the pockets of her ever-present apron her lips were pressed into a fine line, signaling her disapproval.

"Parkinson is here, Gabe," she said.

"Thank you, Mavis, I'll be there in a minute."

She nodded, glanced at Lissandra and shook her head.

"Tell her the truth, Gabe, all of it. Or this will never work."

With that, she turned and left them alone on the terrace.

"Oh my God, she knows, doesn't she? I thought she was nice and I could trust her. Oh, I'm such a fool."

Lissandra tried to get past him, but he stepped in her way.

"Lissa, don't." She pushed against his chest in a vain effort to make him move and then glared up at him.

"Don't you dare call me that. Only Mama ever called me that. Don't you fucking dare…" She slammed her hand over her mouth and shook her head. Misery and despair rolled off of her in waves, and Gabe had to fight the urge to take her in his arms. She wouldn't welcome that move right now, if ever, and now was not the time.

Instead he crossed his arms over his chest, widened his stance, and simply looked at her.

"I'll call you anything I damn well, please, little girl, and you *will* lose the attitude. I told you last night, you're mine now, so you better get used to it. As for Mavis, she is the most loyal person I ever met. Without her, I doubt I would have survived my childhood, so you be nice to her, do you hear me?"

"Or what? You'll kill me, too?" The mumbled reply grated, and he took several deep breaths to calm himself.

"If I wanted you dead, you'd be six feet under already, girl. After the hit on your father went wrong, I've never trusted anyone else to do the killing for me ever again." He waited for that to sink in, and sure enough her head came up, and she stared wide-eyed, confusion evident on her face.

"I thought… it wasn't…"

"No, little girl. I'm not such a bastard that I would rob a child of its mother, especially when that mother's only crime was falling in love and staying with that fucker, Andrini. Besides, I prefer to kill with my hands. Much more satisfying." He uncrossed his arms and wrapped his hands around her slender throat. Her heartbeat jumped under his palms, and he squeezed just once before he released her. "To feel the life draining out a piece of scum that crossed me … that's sweet."

"You're a monster." Her whispered reply made him grin.

"Yes, I suppose I am. You better get used to it, little girl, and don't get any silly ideas of crossing me. You behave and do as you're told, and we'll get along just fine."

She swallowed hard, but gave the tiniest nod, and that would have to do for now.

"Good girl, that wasn't so hard now, was it?"

"So, you'll kill me if I don't *behave*?" She mimed quotation marks around that one word and nudged her chin up in a move of defiance that simply served to make him harder. It would be fun to tame all that passion, indeed, and knowing that he would be the first man ever to touch her, to teach her … *fuck,* what a turn-on that was. Gabe had never cared much about being the first. He wasn't possessive over the women he fucked. That would mean he cared about them to be anything more than a convenient set of holes to sink his dick into, but this was Lissandra Andrini. His revenge and he was fast beginning to realize his destiny, too. Whether she'd also prove to be his downfall remained to be seen.

"Killing is too easy an out. That's the only reason Andrini still lives. I want him to suffer, to wallow in his own filth. Death is too good for the likes of him. As for you…" He paused and smiled. "I've already told you what I'll do to you. And once that ass of yours is red raw I *will* fuck it, so, maybe I'll kill you after all with the *petit mort*, at least."

Her sharp intake of breath almost sounded like a moan, and acting on instinct, he stepped closer, and shoved his hand under her robe to cup her mound. Wet heat greeted his palm, and he smirked, while a blush suffused her pale skin.

"What are you? You can't … oh…" She tried to clamp her legs together, but one shake of his head stopped her. He forced himself to remove his hand, looked at the glistening evidence of her arousal on his palm and held it up for her to see.

"Protest all you want, Lissa. Hate me if you must, but your body doesn't lie." He licked the wetness off his hands and immediately regretted that, as her feminine musk hit his nostrils. Damn, she smelled good.

"I do, I hate you." Her denial was too breathy to be truly effective, and Gabe laughed.

"No problem, my sweet. You don't have to like me to enjoy fucking me. Now, go and get dressed, and meet me in the living room in ten minutes. Don't make me wait, or so help me I drag you out there like this or maybe naked." He grinned at her simmering outrage. "I'm sure my men would enjoy the view."

"You wouldn't dare?"

Gabe threw his head back and laughed.

"Oh, my sweet, never dare the monster."

****

Oh, that man. Dumbfounded, Lissandra stared after his departing back. He had to be lying. Her father wouldn't have used Mama as a shield…

Even as she thought that, desperately tried to think back to that awful day, those frightful moments observed through the glass of the limo, she knew Gabe had spoken the truth. She'd known it then, in that awful moment, when her mother had screamed, and the red stain had appeared on her chest.

Lissandra closed her eyes and took deep breaths to quieten her rioting emotions. At least Gabe hadn't been the one to kill Mama. She knew instinctively that he wouldn't lie about that. In fact, she was as sure as she could be that everything he'd said to her had been the truth, which also meant he would make good on his threat to parade her stark naked if she didn't get dressed.

Her pussy clenched at that thought, and Lissandra rolled her eyes and put her hands on her hot cheeks. She couldn't be turned on by that notion, could she? Yet, as she hastened back to her room to pull on some clothes, the wetness between her legs called her a liar.

How fucked up in the head was she that she lusted after her captor? Stockholm syndrome, eat your heart out, only, she was painfully aware that she hadn't been his captive for long enough to attribute this raging attraction she felt to the man to any sort of syndrome.

Had she met him in any other circumstances, she would have lusted after him just as much. So, what did that make her? Not frigid, as her last disastrous attempt at going out with someone her own age had suggested.

While she'd known deep down that the *boy*, who'd called her that, after his kisses had left her cold had been wrong—if you could call a twenty-five-year old scientist a boy—she laughed out loud. Compared to Gabe he *had* been a boy. Even men closer to Gabe's age seemed mere imitations, compared to Gabriel Henshaw's overwhelming presence. The truth of the matter was she simply melted under Gabe's dominance. That damn online test, which Chantelle and she giggled over when they'd both been worse for wear just before she'd left to return to London, had been spot on.

Lissandra was a natural submissive that thing had claimed. Chantelle had hooted in laughter. "There, you go, that explains everything. You need whips and chains and all that shit to get off, right. Damn, had I known that, I'd have hooked you up with Pierre. He's into all that stuff."

At that thought they'd both dissolved into flood of giggles. Pierre might be into all things kinky, but he was also ugly as fuck and even shorter than Lissandra.

"More like he should be at the receiving end of it," Lissandra had said once she could talk again, which had caused another bout of hysterics.

God, she missed her friend. What she wouldn't give to have her here, but Chantelle had taken herself off for some fun with her newest boyfriend, backpacking around the world. According to the latest update she'd received—a garbled one via someone's satellite phone—they were somewhere in the Himalayas right now.

Gabe's raised voice coming through the shut door of her bedroom made her jump. She couldn't make out what he was saying, but he sounded pissed, so Lissandra hurriedly pulled on some underwear, leggings and long t-shirt, bundled her hair up in a messy bun, and yanked open the door.

"I just don't think this is necessarily the best course of action, Mr. Henshaw. I would be failing in my duties as your solicitor if I didn't point this out to you."

Gabe's short, somewhat cruel laugh sent shivers down her spine. She wasn't going to like whatever those two had concocted, that much was clear.

"Duly noted, Parkinson. However, I pay you the big bucks for your expertise at getting things done, not your opinion."

"But, sir, the girl is so much younger, and marriage is a big step."

Lissandra gasped, and both men turned as one to watch her approach. She was dimly aware of a middle-aged man in a suit bowing his head in greeting to her, before all her attention was taken up by Gabe. He looked equal parts pissed and determined, while the lazy way he gave her attire the once-over made her toes curl in her sandals.

"You're late, girl." He made a big show of

studying the Rolex on his wrist, and tutted. "At a swat a second, I make that a tally of thirty-nine I need to inflict on that backside of yours. Come here."

He pulled out one of the chairs around the dining table, covered in official looking documents, and Lissandra froze.

"You wouldn't. No, I won't."

"You, girl, will do as you're told and get yourself over here now, before I add to that. You really must like pain."

The solicitor made a rough sound at the back of his throat, and adjusted his tie, while he looked anywhere but at her. Gabe had no such compunctions. The intensity of his stare on her pinned her in place, bent her to his will, and she'd taken several steps toward him before she even realized what she was doing.

"You're not going to spank my behind. You have no damn right … err … Sir." She added the title, to soften her denial somewhat, all too aware that she was literally pulling the tiger by the tail, and she had *some* self-preservation left.

Much to her surprise and utter relief, Gabe laughed. His eyes softened as he looked toward her, and he shook his head.

"As tempting as that thought is, I pulled out this chair for you to sit and sign these papers, so sit, *now*."

This time she didn't hesitate, and her throat went dry when Gabe pulled out the chair next to her and sat down, too. Parkinson also seated himself, offered her a tight smile, and held out a fountain pen for her.

"If you'd like to read through the papers and sign where I marked them, both of you, and all the documents, please."

Lissandra took the pen off him, saw him pass an identical one to Gabe and then promptly dropped hers when she saw the titles on the documents.

Marriage agreement
Non-disclosure contract
Limits list

"Is everything all right, Miss Andrini?" Parkinson's voice sounded tinny, far away, and then Gabe's heavy hand on her shoulder pulled her back in from the brink.

"Breathe, Lissa. Helps with the whole being alive thing."

She dutifully pulled air into her lungs, and that strange buzzing sound in her ears faded.

"What is this? Why do you want me to sign these?" She grimaced at the high-pitched squeal she managed to produce, and Gabe shrugged and pulled his hand away. Strange though it seemed, she immediately missed the contact. He was the only somewhat familiar presence in this alternative universe she seemed to have been dumped in.

"Read and sign, especially this one."

He pushed the limits list toward her, and Lissandra knew she resembled a beetroot right now. Her cheeks sure felt hot enough to fry an egg on.

"Perhaps we should give the girl a minute, sir." The solicitor's somewhat strained voice broke through her paralysis, and she looked up.

"She's had all the time she needs. Read and sign, girl. I haven't got all day."

Gabe's voice right next to her ear held an edge of steel she couldn't help but respond to, and she made a hasty grab for the pen.

Her head hurt just looking down the limits lists. How on earth was she supposed to know what half of this meant, let alone if she liked it?

Parkinson sighed and looked most uncomfortable

while Gabe laughed.

"That's why there's several boxes, sweetheart. Just tick don't know if you're not sure." She jumped and wanted the ground to swallow her whole when it dawned on her that she must have uttered her thoughts out loud.

"What if I don't want to do any of this? Are you really into all of this stuff?"

Lissandra inwardly groaned at the needy, breathy whisper she managed to produce. Gabe put his large hand over her trembling one.

"Most, but not all, no. Would it help if I crossed out the things I won't do and starred my favorites?" he asked.

Lissandra swallowed hard. Gabe nudged her chin up, and the concern she read in his dark gaze made her feel slightly better.

"Breathe, little one. This doesn't need to be scary, but it helps to clarify these things beforehand. Also," he glanced at the documents on the table, and smirked. "I find it somewhat telling that you freak out at this list, and not the marriage contract or the pre-nup."

She couldn't help her jerk in reaction, and he nodded.

"Okay, freaking out at all of it then."

"I'm not freaking, I just…" She cleared her throat, disgusted at that squeak she managed to produce. Gabe's smile deepened, and the hold he had on her chin turned into a caress. His thumb traced the outline of her lips, and she leaned into his touch, craving the reassurance right now, his gentleness so at odds with this whole fucked up situation.

"Just what, little Lissa? Tell me."

"I don't understand any of this? You've got me. My father all but sold me to you, so why do you want to marry me?"

Gabe's eyes flashed in silent fury when she mentioned her father, and for that one second, she saw the ruthless killer before he smiled. It didn't reach his eyes, and it made her insides clench in fear and arousal. Why the danger he presented turned her on so much, she had no idea. His hand slid down to her throat and stayed there. An obvious claim of ownership, which helped calm her. She couldn't do anything but submit to his will, and with that knowledge came peace.

None of this made sense, but as his whole focus shifted to her, she knew deep down that he wouldn't hurt her, even though he could. After all, she'd half expected him to force himself on her, yet here they were, discussing marriage, and limits, and she was so out of her depth it wasn't even real.

"I made a promise to your mother before she died, girl." She gasped at that revelation, and he nodded. "I promised to make sure you're safe. To keep you away from your father's machinations, and while you were out of the country you were safe. You're not anymore. Andrini is up to something, and until I know what that is, your place is by my side. As my wife you have protection. Should anything happen to me, the boys will take care of you." He paused and tightened his hold on her throat just long enough for her to get worried. She gulped in air when he let go. "Also, locking you in marriage to me means there'll be consequences if you betray me. Your father's blood runs in your veins, and I'm not stupid enough to trust an Andrini, no matter how much I want to claim that curvy body of yours. I'm not proposing marriage out of love, sweetheart, but like I said before, we don't even need to like each other to fuck."

"Mr. Henshaw, really."

Parkinson's exasperated voice interrupted Gabe,

and he looked over the table to where the solicitor looked as though he wanted to be anywhere but here. Lissandra almost felt sorry for the man. Sweat dotted his upper lip, and his eyes shifted left to right behind their steel-rimmed glasses.

"You're here to witness the signatures, that's all, Parkinson. Leave your moral compass at home, but if it makes you feel any better, I can assure you that anything my *wife* and I will be doing will be entirely consensual."

He leaned back in his chair, crossed his big arms over his chest, and smiled.

"In fact, sweet little Lissa can walk out of here right now, if that's what she chooses to do. I'll expect Ollivanti will pounce on her the minute she does, but, hey, maybe she'd prefer his hands all over her before he puts her to work in one of his brothels. Andrini owes him money, too, I understand." He tipped his chair back on its back legs and regarded his solicitor through narrowed eyes. "Perhaps that will work better for your morals, Parkinson?"

Parkinson opened his mouth to say something, but nothing came out, and Gabe's chair came crashing back down onto the wooden flooring with so much force Lissandra felt the vibration under her soles. Oh lordy, he was pissed.

"I wasn't suggesting that, sir, at all." Parkinson dropped his gaze, and Gabe's short laugh broke the tension.

"Good to know." He picked up the pen, snatched up the limits list, and started to star and cross out various items on the list before he passed it back over to Lissandra.

"Over to you. What will it be?"

Chapter Five

She really had the most expressive face and Gabe felt like the worst asshole for scaring her with the Ollivanti threat, but, dammit all to hell and back he wanted her submission freely given. Not forced on her by circumstances. Not because she was sold to him by that fucker Andrini, but because deep down she wanted him. Gabe, the man, not the crime lord, not the man who owned her.

He scowled when she hesitated, half rose out of her chair and then sat back down again. Her brows drew together in a frown, as she read down the limits list. It was always telling how a submissive reacted to this part of the negotiations. Not that Gabe had allowed himself to indulge in that side of him lately. If he was going to marry Lissandra, however, then he wanted to start this marriage off on the right foot, with him as her Dom as well as her husband.

He daren't examine why this was so important to him. Why he felt the need to put all this in writing, other than the need to have all this negotiations above board for her protection as much as his own.

Gabe ignored the little voice of reason, which argued he didn't need to do any of this. He could just ship her off to a safe house, out of the country even, but the thought of any other man's hands on her pale skin, made him see red. Bound to him like this, he would know where she was at all times. It was the only way to keep her truly safe, if not from him and all the wicked, perverted things he wanted to do to her, but safe from the rest of this fucked up world.

"What does this mean?" she asked, and he followed the line of her pen to his starring of Shibari.

"Ah, ropes in short. Shibari is an ancient form of

Japanese rope bondage. Ropes are my preferred method of restraining a submissive."

"Oh." Her breathing sped up, and after a short glance up at him from under her eyelashes, she ticked the box to give her consent. Her reactions going down that list were as insightful as they were torturous. His damn dick would have zip marks along its length.

She ticked yes to spanking with his hands, maybe to impact toys. Anal received a maybe, which surprised him. He'd have expected her to put that as a hard limit. Clamps received another maybe, and she breathed an audible relief when she reached the more extreme facets of the lifestyle, namely blood, scat, water, and needle play, all of which he'd crossed out.

He had listed knife play as favorite, and her hand shook as the pen hovered over the no box.

"What does that mean?" she asked.

Gabe put his hand over hers, and she jumped.

"I like the mind fuck, Lissa. I don't cut, ever, and I don't leave permanent marks, but fear increases the pleasure." She looked doubtful, and he could almost see the wheels turn in her head as she mulled this over. "It's all about trust, little girl. If you trust me enough to do as I say. Then again, the whole lifestyle is built on trust, negotiation, and communication."

Lissa blinked and nodded, and he released her hand.

She focused her attention back on the list. "What about age play? You're not going to dress me in nappies, are you?"

Gabe laughed and shook his head.

"No, little girl. There are many facets to that. I'm not averse to adopting the role of *Daddy* if my little girl needs a firm hand, however." He let that statement sit in the room, and Lissa squirmed on her seat.

"Would you expect me to call you that? Daddy, I mean?"

Something inside of him shifted at that breathless question, brought out his protective instincts kicking and screaming. "That depends, if my little girl would need to call me that. I prefer Sir, myself."

The telltale blush which stained her pale cheeks, and the way her breathing sped up made his chest tighten in unwanted emotion. Fuck him sideways. He hadn't expected *this*. Then again, with the lack of proper father figure in her life, perhaps he shouldn't have been surprised at her reaction.

"I don't … that is … it would feel weird to call you that … Sir."

Gabe cupped her face, and a shudder went through her.

"It's just a title, baby, no big deal."

"Okay." She ticked yes, and after a moment of hesitation she also ticked yes to knife play before she signed the form next to his signature.

"Good girl." His murmured praise made her smile, and the invisible boulder of worry he'd been carrying on his shoulders lightened considerably.

The marriage contract and non-disclosure were next under her perusal, and she signed both without any hesitation, and far too quickly if Parkinson's twitching was any indication. Sure enough, the solicitor cleared his throat repeatedly.

"You really ought to read those thoroughly, Miss Andrini."

She raised her eyes from the pre-nuptial agreement she was perusing, and her shoulders straightened.

"I'm well aware of that, and I can assure you I am. I'm a fast reader, and besides, there isn't much in these. One I have to sign to agree to marry him, and the non-disclosure is a non-starter anyway. I would never discuss my private life with anyone, and I certainly wouldn't go to the police. They weren't exactly in favor in my house, growing up, and damn useless when Mama…" Her shoulders dropped, and Gabe swore softly under his breath.

"Anyway, let me read this … this thing." She looked at Gabe, and the fine sheen of tears in her eyes slammed in his gut as though she'd used a sledgehammer to drive her point home. "I don't want any of your money, so this should be easy, too." She offered Gabe a wobbly smile and turned her attention back to the document in front of her.

"Nonetheless you're entitled to certain things," Parkinson said. "As you can see my client has been more than fair should you decide to terminate the marriage down the line. How much you will be entitled to, will depend on the length of your marriage and whether there are any children."

Lissa gasped as she reached the settlement figures and shook her head.

"I can't sign this."

"Not enough for you?" Gabe asked. Try as he might he couldn't keep the snarl out his voice, and Lissandra jumped.

"No, it's not that. It's too much." She looked up at him. "What exactly do you expect me to do for all this?" The wobble in her voice got to him, and Gabe shrugged.

"Be my wife, my submissive, mother of my children, the usual stuff."

"You want children then, but I thought…" She bit her lip and dropped he gaze.

"One thing Andrini did get right is this. I *do* need

an heir. If I'm going to get married, then, yes, I'll expect children. Besides, it's the usual consequence of sex unless we use birth control, and I have no intention of doing that with my *wife*." He dropped his voice on the last word, and her head shot up. He caught the brief look of longing and hope in her expressive eyes, before she gave a tight nod, picked up the pen and hesitated next to his signature.

"What about my career? I was hoping to carry on painting, maybe sell some like Mama did?"

Gabe put his hand on her shoulder and squeezed.

"You can do both, Lissa. I would never stand in the way of your talent. In fact, when you've signed those, I've got something to show you."

Still, she hesitated, but eventually she did sign it.

The rest of the formalities passed in a blur. She was far too quiet during the whole countersigning procedure, which involved Mavis and his second in command, Stone. Eventually, though they were left on their own, and Gabe held out his hand.

"Come on, let me show you what I wanted to earlier."

This time, Lissa did take his hand, and followed him out into the hall and down the corridor until they reached the first bedroom. He flung open the door and stepped by to let her through.

"Happy Birthday."

Seeing her face light up in wonder was worth the hassle and expense of this rush job. The previously unused guest bedroom had been stripped of all its trappings. The walls were now a brilliant white. Without the curtains and blinds, it was a sun-filled, light, airy room, perfect for any artist to work her magic. The boys had brought over her artwork, and meagre supplies, which Gabe had matched and doubled up with brand new equipment.

"Oh, this is? You did this for me?"

Arms outstretched, Lissa twirled around, a huge smile spreading across her face.

"No big deal." He shrugged for good measure, and she advanced on him hands on hips.

"Maybe not to you, but to me it is. How did you even do this so quickly?" she asked.

Gabe pushed his hands into his jeans pockets to stop himself from reaching out to her. He grumbled his answer.

"You can achieve most things with the right amount of cash. Be careful with the walls. The paint is still wet."

Something in his expression halted her forward progress, and she frowned.

"I guess so, but that doesn't explain why you did this. Any of this?"

"Don't read too much into it, girl. It is your birthday, so this seemed a fitting present. I'm glad you like it. Also." He pulled out the velvet box, which Parkinson had picked up from the jewelers on the way over here and held it out to her.

Another one of those gasps came from his girl, when he flipped it open to reveal the diamond engagement ring. The turquoise stone had reminded him of the color of her eyes, when they darkened in thought, like they did now, while the simplicity of the design had appealed to him. It didn't look as expensive as it had been—damn thing had cost a fortune— but he'd known, the minute he'd found it online, this was the ring he wanted to see on her hand. The fact it was ready for pick up straight away and in her size, had been an added bonus.

"Marry me?" he asked when she did nothing but

stare at the ring in seeming shock. He couldn't tell whether she was pleased or not, but when she eventually tore her expressive eyes away from the box and looked up at him, the sheen of tears did him in—again.

"You really didn't have to do that. I didn't expect…"

Gabe had heard enough. He took the ring out of his box, discarded it on the floor, and pushed the engagement ring on her left finger.

"There, now you look the part." The tender emotions swamping him at the sight of his ring on her finger were an unwanted complication, which made him push her away when she looked as though she was going to hug him.

"I've got stuff to do, so enjoy your new studio." He stepped away from her. "Let Mavis know if you need anything else."

Lissandra blinked and wrapped her arms around herself.

"Right, okay … you're not staying?"

"No, I told you this isn't a love match. I'll see you at our wedding. Until then, you have the run of this apartment. Stone will stay here to keep an eye on things and will accompany you if you feel the need to go out anywhere. I would strongly suggest you stay put, however, at least until I know what the deal is with Ollivanti and Andrini. Can you do that for me, little girl?"

A nod was his only answer, and Gabe forced himself to leave.

****

For the second time that day, Lissandra stared at his departing back. What on earth had just happened? The ring on her finger sparkled in the light, and she held it up to truly appreciate it.

Lissandra was no expert in jewelry, but she knew deep down that it must have cost a fortune. It felt heavy on her finger, an all too visible sign to what she'd agreed to.

Oh my God, I'm getting married.

Suddenly, she couldn't get enough air in her lungs, and pushing open the sliding doors which made up the wall of the bedroom, she hurried onto the terrace. Not that it really helped. Without Gabe's comforting presence next to her the drop down seemed menacing, the glass balustrade too feeble to stop her from plummeting to her death in the murky waters of the Thames so far down below.

She fell rather than sat into the swing seat which made up this corner of the terrace. The rocking motion soothed her roiling stomach, and pulling her feet up, she closed her eyes and concentrated on breathing. Eventually the panic attack ceased to hold her in its grip, and she opened her eyes. Grief, she hadn't had one of these in a long time.

They'd been a constant companion of her childhood and teenage years, following on from witnessing her mother being gunned down, but she hadn't had one in ages. Clearly, coming back to the UK and finding herself in the precarious position of being engaged to the man responsible for hiring the bullet that had killed her mother, had pitched her back into that nightmare.

Lissandra stopped the swing and shot to her feet. There was only one thing for it. She had to get rid of these emotions threatening to crush her, and there was one foolproof way of doing that. Paint.

She stalked into her new studio and set to work, pouring out her emotions onto the canvas with bold strokes of her brush. She sent Mavis away with a flea in her ear, when she popped her head round the door, asking her to come for lunch, and kept on painting.

Eventually, she was done. Her fingers cramped from holding the brush, and her back hurt from standing up for hours, but the brooding man who stared back at her from the easel was Gabe. Dark, menacing, his hands covered in blood, which dripped onto his boots, he looked like the killer he was, and yet... Her breathing sped up at the expression she caught in his eyes. Thoughtful, piercing, tortured, they called to her just like they did in real life.

The door opened and shut, and Mavis inhaled sharply.

"Oh, my goodness. Is that how you see him?"

Lissandra blinked, tore her gaze away from the painting she created, and nodded.

"That's what he is, isn't he?" She took a step away from the painting and winced when she caught sight of her hands. Like Gabe's, they were covered in red paint, a far too symbolic sight. Her stomach roiled, and she blinked back tears. "Mummy."

Before she'd even stopped her anguished whisper, Lissandra was engulfed in a bear hug. The comforting smells of starch and a myriad of cooking scents enveloped her, and Lissandra hugged the other woman back, grateful for the human contact.

"How can I marry him when he ... he..." She couldn't bring herself to say it out loud, and Mavis hugged her harder.

"Oh, you poor bairn. You're overwhelmed, and I don't blame you. He could have handled this much better, but Gabe isn't a monster, you know."

Lissandra snorted her disbelief and pushed the old woman away.

"He was responsible for my mother's death, and

yes, I know the bullet wasn't aimed at her but Papa, but that still makes him a murderer. He might not have wanted Mama dead, but he certainly intended to kill my…" Lissandra took a deep breath in to calm her rioting nerves and continued. "He still wanted Andrini dead, wants him dead, and yes, I know that man is bad news, maybe even worse news than Gabe, but he's the only family I have left, and fuck it."

She wrapped her arms around herself and shook her head.

"I've no one."

Mavis regarded her through narrowed eyes, and Lissandra could positively feel the disapproval radiating off the older woman.

"I'm going to forget most of what you said, because you're not yourself and it's been a very trying twenty-four hours for you, but…" She grasped hold of Lissandra's left hand and using her ever-present apron wiped the paint off the ring. "This means you're one of us. I know Gabe, have known him since he was knee high and living in the roughest council estate our dear city has to offer, and I do know this. He looks after the people he cares about. It might not seem like it to an outsider, and from what I can gather Andrini's operation never ran like this, but here in this place, you're safe. We're all safe. Hells bells, that boy found me and gave me a job, because he knew I would never accept charity, and besides, he has powerful enemies. Anyone associated with him becomes a target, and by keeping you here, by keeping all of us close to him here in this building, he keeps us safe, so think about that before you condemn him. He's no innocent choir boy, but he's also not the monster others make him out to be. Now, Ollivanti, there's a true monster. My own niece…" Mavis let go of Lissandra's hand and closed her eyes briefly. Dread crawled down Lissandra's spine, and she reached out to lightly touch the other woman's arm, to offer comfort, to reassure in any way she could.

"You don't have to tell me any of this. Clearly, it's very painful for you."

Mavis nodded, opened her eyes, and the raw pain in her wise eyes took Lissandra's breath away.

"She was only fifteen, got lured in by his goons, and we never saw her again. She died of an overdose, some three days before her eighteenth birthday. I went with my brother to identify her body, and … God. It was the worst thing I ever had to do. Sean couldn't stand it. He died a month later, heart attack, but I think he just gave up. No reason to carry on living, not when his only daughter found such a terrible end." She pulled a much-needed breath into her lungs and shook her head. "Whatever Gabe is, whatever he does, whatever he may do in the future, he has never, nor will he ever prey on young girls. Does he run brothels and lord knows what else? Of course, he does, but he looks after the girls, and without him they'd be on the street, so don't. Just *don't*!"

She pointed to the painting and shook her head. "Yes, that's one side of him, but it's not the only one, and if you'll only let him in, you'll see that." She paused and studied Lissandra for a second. "But then, I think deep down you already know that, don't you? And you hate yourself for feeling anything but disgust for him." She smiled and held her hand up when Lissandra shook her head and opened her mouth to refute that notion. "It's okay, you're young and impressionable, which is why he's giving you space."

Lissandra blinked and tried to speak, but nothing but a rough sound came from the back of her throat, as though she was drowning in phlegm.

She tried again, and this time she managed a

squeak.

"Space, is that what you call it? He announces we're to be married and then just leaves me here? Why does he even bother? He clearly doesn't want to be around me."

Lissandra hated how needy that last sentence sounded, but for heaven's sake. She couldn't sort out her emotions, not even in her head. She was all over the place.

"Oh, sweetie, don't you know why he's staying away?" Mavis smiled and patted Lissandra's arm. "That man has had about five cold showers since you arrived. Think on why he would feel the need for those and count yourself lucky. Your wedding night..." She smiled knowingly, and Lissandra fought and lost the heat creeping into her cheeks.

"Let's just say, it will no doubt be a night to remember. Now, you haven't eaten all day, so freshen up and come out and smell your cake."

"Cake?" Lissandra echoed, and Mavis grinned.

"Of course, cake. It's your birthday, so layered chocolate cake it is. Your favorite, Gabe tells me, and Stone is itching to snare a piece. There's only so long I can hold that man off. He has the sweetest tooth of all of Gabe's men, so hustle, girl."

That conversation set the ground rules for the next three weeks of frantic activity in preparation for her wedding. Stone, a brooding hulk of a man, was her ever present companion when a seeming never ending litany of people came to the apartment to get Lissandra ready for her wedding. They plucked and preened Lissandra, until she barely recognized herself.

She was waxed in places she didn't even know you could wax, quite frankly, and, perhaps far more mortifying was the fact that she *liked* it.

Without any hair on her pussy everything felt far more sensitive, not helped by the tons of expensive, and sexy as all out, lingerie she was sent. Her stomach fluttered at the thought of Gabe having picked those out for her to wear. First off, she'd ignored them, like she had ignored the note that had come with a little, innocent enough looking brown box. She'd dropped it upon opening when it had revealed its contents.

A set of butt plugs.

You may want to make good use of these.

In the end curiosity had won out, however.

What would it feel like to wear lace and satin next to her skin, and to have that forbidden place stuffed full?

Downright decadent and arousing was the answer, and for the first time ever Lissandra felt like a desirable woman when she looked at her herself in the mirror. It might be all kinds of wrong to get excited at the prospect of Gabe seeing her in these, but she couldn't help it. While she might not have seen him around, his presence was everywhere.

Lissandra lost count how many times she'd woken up with a start in the middle of the night, heart pounding in dread at some nightmare which still held her in its emotional grip, some unforeseen danger, which had sent her out of bed and into Gabe's bedroom.

There, surrounded by his things, breathing in the scent of his cologne which clung to his bed sheets, she'd felt safe. It made no sense to her, this need to surround herself with him, but there it was. No doubt a psychologist would have a field day for her simmering attraction to a man old enough to be her father, her *Daddy*.

She hugged that word to herself, recalling the intense flash of emotion in his amber eyes, when she'd called him that during their discussion of her limits list. While she highly doubted she could bring herself to call him that during any kind of scene they might be involved in—there went her panties again—what was that saying? Never say never.

After all, when she stepped off the plane at Heathrow a few weeks ago, she could never have foreseen the turn her life would take. And now she was here, the morning of her wedding, staring at her reflection in the mirror.

"You look stunning, my dear." Mavis dabbed at her eyes with her apron, and Lissandra smiled at her. This wedding dress had been another surprise. Lissandra had wanted to hate it, when it had arrived, had railed and cursed at the poor woman who'd delivered it.

"Take it back. I'll choose my own damn wedding dress."

Stone had interfered with a smirk on his scarred face. Not for the first time Lissandra wondered what on earth had happened to the man to cause such a jagged scar. It ran along the left side of his face, down into the side of his bottom lip and gave his mouth a lopsided appearance. With his shaven head and the myriad of tats on his beefy arms, shoulders, and neck, he looked the part of the bad guy, all right. Even if he didn't act like that around her and Mavis. Her opinion of the big guy had been changed forever, when she'd caught him crying at *The Notebook*, especially after all the grumbling about having to watch it with her in the first place.

And then there had been the whole episode of the lost kitten that had somehow found its way onto the balcony. To this day it remained a mystery how that tiny scrap of feline had made it this high up. Stone had vowed to find its owner, which had turned out to be a three-year-old little boy with special educational needs who lived on the third floor of the apartment building. He'd taken the kitten with him into the lift when he was not supposed to. The tiny feline had jumped out of his jacket pocket unseen and must have somehow come up in the lift to Gabe's apartment, and eventually the balcony.

"I dare say he jumped into a delivery box. Boss will be furious if that happened. If a kitten can get through, then who knows what else might."

The entire overhaul of Gabe's security that had followed that incident had been overkill as far as Lissandra was concerned, but she would always remember the careful way Stone had held that tiny life in his hands, and the way Gabe's voice had softened over the phone when she'd tried to plead with him to let her keep it. Oh, deary me, her fiancé's voice alone did strange things to her insides.

"Lissa, you can't. That kitten must belong to someone, and Stone will find out who. Also, when you find out how that animal got up to my apartment, ensure that leak is dealt with, Stone."

She shivered recalling the ice in his voice on those last few words. Gabe was not a man to be crossed, as Stone had reminded her when she'd thrown that hissy fit over the dress.

"I'll take that, and you may go," he'd said to the white-eyed, pale young woman who'd tried to give her the dress. Addressing Lissandra, he'd continued. "If the boss sent this, then he wants you to wear it, simple as. No point taking your foul mood on the messenger, Miss Lissa." He'd tempered the grumbled words with a wink.

"Boss got great taste, so, at least look at it. No point in cutting your pert nose off to spite your pretty face now."

Lissandra had looked at the damn dress in a huff, wanting to hate it, but, instead had fallen instantly in love with the shimmering creation of white lace. Long sleeved with a modest neckline, it left her back bare, skimmed her hips and ended in a train. It was elegant, sophisticated, and sexy all at the same time. With her make-up and hair professionally done by the small team that had turned up at the crack of dawn, the woman who stared back at her from the mirror seemed older, somehow.

"Here, before I forget, this will cover something old, borrowed, and blue all in one." Mavis produced a delicate, blue, and antique looking garter and held it up for Lissandra. "This was my grandmother's. She wore it her wedding, and every woman in my family has worn it since on her big day. I never thought I'd get the chance to pass it on, being that my dear John and I didn't have any children of our own, so, please take it."

Lissandra's instant denial died in her throat, seeing the shimmer of tears in the dear old lady's eyes. She didn't trust herself to speak, so simply nodded, and with a grin on her lined face, Mavis got to her knees and disappeared under Lissandra's skirt to slide the delicate fabric onto her thigh.

"There, now you're ready." Red faced from her exertion, Mavis straightened and smiled at Lissandra. "You are ready, right? Because it's a bit of a drive, and that boy will lose his shit if we're too late."

Lissandra laughed at the unexpected cuss word coming from Mavis, and the older woman winked. "Oh, I know, but sometimes bad language is warranted." She held out her arm, grasped Lissandra's stunning bouquet of wildflowers, and led her out of the bedroom.

Stone's low whistle of appreciation made Lissandra's cheeks heat, and the big guy winked at her.

"Well, Miss Lissa, told you the boss got good taste. With that, I'll be off to let him know you're on your way. Luca here will ride with you in the limo."

Another one of Gabe's security stepped up and nodded at her. He was even taller than Stone, if less wide with not as much muscle mass, but the grim determination around his blue eyes left Lissandra in no doubt that he was just as deadly. All of Gabe's men had that quiet air of danger which surrounded them like an invisible cloak. Strangely enough, Lissandra didn't find that strange anymore. Far from making her uneasy, it made her feel protected, cared for, and if that wasn't a sure sign that she'd lost the plot once and for all then she didn't know what was.

"You ready?" Luca asked, and Lissandra took a deep breath in and nodded.

"As ready as I'll ever be."

Chapter Six

Gabe tapped his earpiece.

"Perimeter still clear, boys?"

The reassuring "ayes" filtered through, and he rolled his tense shoulders, ignoring the disapproving look of the balding vicar. He paid the man enough for the use of this church. Nestled away in the Hampshire countryside between Winchester and Southampton, it had proven the perfect place for what he'd had in mind: Small, ancient, and above all cash-strapped. A heavy influx of his money had ensured this wedding would take place and a few rules had been bent in the process. Namely the reading of the banns under an alias.

The last thing Gabe wanted or needed was to alert Andrini and/or Ollivanti to his plans to marry Lissandra. As far as everyone else was concerned the girl had disappeared off the radar, and that's the way he wanted to keep it.

"I don't mean to rush you, but will the bride be arriving soon?"

Gabe adjusted his cufflinks and looked down his nose at the smaller man. Reverend Albert shifted from foot to foot under Gabe's silent scrutiny. Small eyes set too close together under his bushy eyebrows darted about nervously, and dots of perspiration broke out on his upper lip. He'd nicked himself shaving that morning, the red mark prominent just under his lips, and Gabe barely suppressed a smirk.

"She can take as long as she likes. It's her day."

The man exhaled sharply and nodded so enthusiastically his combover moved and fell into his eyes.

"Of course, it's just that—"

"Just what?" Gabe interrupted him with a snarl

that made the portly man take several steps back. "I've paid you handsomely for the exclusive use of this church, so if we're still standing here in six hours, then so be it."

The vicar gulped, nodded, and dropped his head.

"As you say, but if I might be permitted to say, sir, if she hasn't turned up by then, I dare say she'll have changed her mind."

Gabe growled his annoyance at the mere suggestion, and Albert's bottom lip quivered in fear. Gabe could smell it on the man. Fear and greed. He might be a so-called man of the cloth, but he'd dropped all pretenses of needing to do things by the book, when Gabe had started talking money. It sure made the world go 'round and folks lost all of their so-called principles for the right prize. Gabe hadn't even needed to put the proverbial screws on the guy. It seemed his reputation preceded him.

"She won't change her mind." While his voice rang out with clear authority, echoed around the old stone walls, he wasn't all that sure she wouldn't. Sure, she'd signed the papers, and sure, his men would ensure she got to the church, but no one could force her to say, "I do". Somehow, holding a gun to her head to get her agreement would give the wrong impression, and old Albert, here, might just faint on the spot.

Gabe turned his back on the man and tapped his ear again.

"Any sign of them yet?" he asked.

"Not yet, boss, but Stone rang through they've left the motorway. Won't be long now, I reckon."

Gabe relaxed his tense shoulders and expelled a long breath. That was something. Feeling this discombobulated was not a sensation he relished. Perhaps he should have stayed close to her. At least then he would have a clearer reading of her state of mind.

However, it would also have been sheer torture for him, and it would have been nigh on impossible to keep his hands off her luscious ass. He'd had to make do with reports from his men, and the odd phone call to hear her voice.

Gabe swore under his breath, earning himself a sigh from Albert, and scrubbed his hand over his face. Where the fuck were they?

"Incoming, boss." The warning in his ear preceded the sound of several cars pulling up outside and he breathed easier.

"Hope you're ready, vicar. They're here."

The other man smiled, nodded, and puffed out his chest in a vain effort to make himself appear either taller or more important. Gabe didn't care too much about either motif because Stone appeared at the open door, smirked at him, and made his way up the aisle to stand next to him.

Gabe nodded at him.

"Got the rings?'

Stone pretended to mull this over for a few frantic beats of Gabe's heart, and then clearly interpreting Gabe's furious expression, laughed and patted his jacket pocket.

"Relax, boss, of course I have them. You're in for a treat, by the way. Your future missus is stunning."

Gabe grunted at him, and Stone laughed out loud, before he muttered something under his breath that Gabe didn't get, because the movement by the door caught his attention.

A flash of white lace, some whispering, and then Mavis appeared. The old dear was grinning from ear to ear, as she, too, walked up the aisle to stand on the bride's side. It was farcical really, when you thought about it.

His best man was his second in command, and the bride's person was his housekeeper. There had been no time to alert anyone else, and even if there had been, Lissandra hadn't wanted anyone there.

"I highly doubt you'd let my father give me away, and my best friend is backpacking 'round the world and I can't reach her, so just forget it. As you keep telling me, there's no need to pretend this is a love match, right?"

It had been just as well he hadn't been in the room because she'd have earned herself a trip over his knee for sure. The minx didn't know it yet, but one of the first things he would do as her husband would be to turn her ass red for all the sass she'd been giving his men and Mavis.

He forced a smile on his face for Mavis's benefit, as she drew up next to him, and then any conscious thought fled his brain at the vision that slowly walked up the aisle. Lissandra clutched her bouquet to her chest in a white knuckled grip that spoke of her nervousness, but the steps she took were slow and deliberate. Head held high, her glorious mass of dark hair was pinned up at the sides and left to fall down her back. A gossamer veil sat on top, and the delicate lace of the gown he'd chosen for her hugged her curves in all the right places.

He scowled at the warpaint on her face. She didn't need any of that crap to look beautiful. He'd dock that make up person's fee for sure. The only place not covered in much were her lips. Traces of lipliner remained, but it was damn obvious that she'd worried the rest of the stuff off the plump flesh. As her gaze connected with his, she missed a step, but caught herself before he had to intervene, while her pink tongue darted out to wet her lips. Gabe swallowed a groan.

Soon, he'd have the right to claim those lips, to

mark every inch of her skin in his possession, and he hardened to the point of pain. Thank God for waistcoats and jackets, with this hard-on. Good old Albert might just die of a heart attack before he had a chance to pronounce them man and wife, and that wouldn't do. It wouldn't do at all.

The light scent of her perfume—peony, magnolia, lotus, and others he couldn't quite place—tickled his nostrils, as she stepped closer.

"You look stunning, little one." He bent his head to whisper those words into her ear, and Lissa froze. "Breathe, and smile. You don't want the good vicar here to think you're not doing this of your own free will, now, do you?"

Lissandra nudged her chin up, threw him a glance from under her eyelashes, and dutifully curved her lips into the semblance of a smile, and handed her bouquet to Mavis.

"Ready?" Albert asked, his eyes darting from Gabe to Lissa and back again. When Gabe raised an eyebrow he hastily dropped his gaze to the order of service in his hands and cleared his throat.

"Right, then, in the presence of God, Father, Son, and Holy Spirit, we have come together to witness the marriage of…"

The familiar words of the ceremony washed over Gabe, and he bit his tongue to not interrupt Albert, as he launched into his spiel. One that meant little to Gabe, but Lissandra clung to every word the vicar said, murmuring her affirmations to the prayer, and for her sake Gabe followed suit.

When it finally came to the part for her to say, "I will", she hesitated. Gabe's gut churned, and that damn vicar's eyebrows drew together in a frown, as he leaned forward to talk to her.

"Is everything okay, my dear? If you don't want this now is the time to say so."

Lissandra shook her head, and Gabe swore under his breath, while Stone reached for his gun. Albert went a lovely shade of white and green, and grasped his dog collar with one hand as though it was strangling him. Gabe knew how the man felt. His own cravat seemed like a noose tightening around his neck. It took mere seconds, which felt like hours, until Lissandra whispered her reply.

"I'm so sorry, I didn't mean … that is. I will. I will marry Gabe." She blinked rapidly as though to hold in tears, and Gabe's guts twisted for entirely different reasons. Giving into the real need to touch her, he grasped her chin and turned her head so that he could read her expression. Sure enough, moisture shimmered in her expressive eyes, but she also looked determined as she offered him a wobbly smile. Her breathing sped up under his silent scrutiny, and he murmured his approval at her actions.

"Good girl, I promise I'll take good care of you."

Albert cleared his throat, Stone gave a short laugh, and Mavis giggled as though she was a schoolgirl. Gabe registered their reactions but took no real notice. He was too enthralled by the slight blush which warmed Lissandra's cheeks and the way her eyes softened, took on a dreamy, hopeful quality, as she held his gaze.

"Right then," Albert continued. "Let's pray."

Neither Gabe nor Lissandra bowed their heads during the short prayer designed for them both. Their attention fixed on each other, they both said "Amen," where required.

Mavis's clear voice reading a passage from the Bible broke the spell, and Gabe reluctantly released his hold on Lissandra's chin.

"Thank you, Mrs. Jackson for this. Now, I would normally have a few things to say…" Albert blanched at Gabe's warning growl and took up his Bible. "Right yes, let's carry on then." He looked toward Stone. "Have you got the ring?"

"Rings, you mean?" His right-hand man, and the closest person Gabe had to a friend, pulled the box out of his jacket and handed the matching platinum bands to the Vicar.

"Please take each other's' hands and repeat after me. 'I, Gabriel Henshaw, take you Lissandra Raphaella Andrini…'"

****

Oh my God, oh my God, oh my God.

Those three words continued to bounce around in Lissandra's brain on a loop, even as her subconscious registered the solemn vows which bound her to Gabe until "death us do part".

His deep, gravelly voice pledged himself to her, and she blinked back tears when he slid the wedding ring onto her finger. Mavis then handed him the engagement ring which she'd pulled off her finger only moments before they'd entered the church, and Gabe slid that next to the plain band.

"There, all mine now." The murmured words for her ears only made breathing difficult. Somehow, she made it through her vows, and managed not to cry when she gave him his ring. It was utterly ridiculous to be this emotional about a simple ring, but she hadn't expected him to wear one. Judging by the astonished expression on the vicar's face, that had come as surprise to him, too. Lissandra knew she was reading far too much into this, but she couldn't help herself. From the minute his heated gaze had swept over her when she'd started to walk down the aisle to her doom—as she'd been referring to her upcoming nuptials in her head—this had felt too much like the real thing. Sure, whenever she'd pictured her wedding in her mind she'd always imagined being on the arm of her Papa, the church filled to the rafters with her family and friends, but then again, in her dreams Mama had also still been alive and crying softly into her hankie, overcome with emotion at her only daughter getting married. A far cry from the stark reality of this tiny, if beautiful, church in the middle of seeming nowhere, with just Gabe, Stone, Mavis, and the vicar in attendance. If you forgot about Gabe's security detail, which surrounded the church.

Lord knows what her now husband must have thought could happen, but he clearly wasn't taking any chances on this marriage not happening.

"...I therefore proclaim that they are husband and wife."

A shudder went through Lissandra as that proclamation broke through her befuddled state, and she grasped hold of Gabe's hand, grateful for his strength, which kept her upright as the vicar prayed over them both.

"Those whom God has joined together let no one put asunder. You may now kiss the bride."

"Finally." That one grumbled word gave her a moment's notice, before Gabe pulled her flush against his body. One arm went around her waist, the other hand into her hair as he tipped her head up and his mouth descended upon hers.

She'd been prepared for a rough meeting of lips, but not this. No, this was...

Lissandra gave up trying to analyze anything, as Gabe's warm, full lips brushed over hers in the lightest of touches. His stubble tickled while he increased the pressure of his mouth against her and ran his tongue along the seam of her lips in a quietly insistent invitation for her to yield to him.

She wanted to resist, keep her mouth shut and go stiff and unresponsive, but her traitorous hormones had other ideas. Surrounded, owned by his big body, his sheer presence and strength pulled her into his will. Every sharp inhale of air through her nose brought more of his intoxicating scent into her lungs. The hands fisted in his jacket loosened, and as though they had a will of their own, crept up and around his neck. Gabe grunted his approval against her lips and increased the gentle nibbles and licks of her mouth.

"Let me in, wife." Those murmured words spoken into her ear, after he left her mouth and kissed his way up her jaw to nibble on her earlobe, made her gasp. Gabe wasted no time in pressing his advantage. His mouth slanted back over hers, and his tongue invaded, claimed, cherished in bold strokes as he explored her mouth with breathtaking intensity.

Gabe kissed her as though he owned her, and in those few scintillating moments he did. Nothing else mattered but the slide of his tongue against hers, his groan when she kissed him back, and the way his hands slid to her ass, and lifted her up against him to deepen the kiss.

Eventually, loud throat-clearing broke through the haze of lust and desire. Gabe released her lips, grazing his teeth along her bottom lip, and the fire in his eyes threatened to burn her alive.

"What?" His furious snarl aimed at the vicar should have made her jump, certainly made the man of the cloth pale and put his hands up. Stone hooted in laughter, and Mavis found the study of her shoes most interesting. Her shoulders shook in silent merriment, as though she, too, found this whole thing ridiculous. One proper look at Gabe, and Lissandra, too, had to smile. He looked like a little boy deprived of his favorite lollipop.

That would be you.

Her inner hussy reminded her, and Lissandra's sense of humor won out. She giggled. Once she started she couldn't stop, and soon the three of them were laughing.

"Really, I must say... This is..." The vicar's protestations were too much, and Gabe, too, eventually smirked.

"Heaven forbid one has fun in church, right?" He sobered, pulled Lissandra into his side and swatted her bottom just once. "You best not be laughing at me, *wife.*"

While the words were stern the twinkle in his eyes belied that tone, and Lissandra did her best to get her merriment under control.

"I wouldn't dream of it, *husband.*"

Another much harder swat connected with her backside, and Lissandra gasped. By rights she ought to be outraged at this blatant display of ownership, but, after that mind-blowing kiss, every feminine cell in her body simply sighed in submission.

"Quit staring, vicar, and let's sign the register. I've got a honeymoon to get to."

"Right, of course, if you'll follow me over here to the register..."

The portly vicar made a sharp turn and strode off as though a pack of demons were after him, his ceremonial robes billowing behind him. Lissandra swallowed another completely inappropriate giggle at that thought. The reverend wasn't far from the truth, considering the reputation of the man she'd just married. A man who propelled her along next to him with a bruising grip on her elbow. Mavis and Stone followed close behind. A huge wooden door to the side of the church opened and shut behind them all, and Lissandra shivered in the much cooler air of the almost windowless room. A tiny stained-glass window high up under the rafters seemed the only natural light source. This place brought to mind old fashioned dungeons with its gloominess, until it was illuminated by a strip of harsh fluorescent light hanging off the domed ceiling. Rows of old leather-bound books stood next to each other in the tall book case to the right of the antique desk—its wood dark and scarred—further testament to the ancient origins of this church. The vicar sat on the leather chair, which groaned as though in mortal agony, and opened the current volume of the registry.

"I prepared all of this earlier, so if you could check the details on the printout and then please transfer them over, and sign here, and here." He indicated the various spaces with his podgy index finger. "Groom first, please."

Gabe, mercifully, let go of her, and proceeded to sign his name with bold, confident strokes. Like the man himself, his signature was distinctive and took up the entire space given. Hers seemed rather small and insignificant in comparison, and the parallels to her life weren't lost on Lissandra.

"Very, good, now the witnesses please," the vicar said.

Gabe pulled her off the chair and in front of him, his arm wrapped around her waist, his chin resting on the top of her head, as they stood in silence watching Mavis and Stone bear witness to the legality of their union.

"Are we really going on a honeymoon?" Lissandra inwardly rolled her eyes at the breathy whisper she managed to produce. Talk about giving away herself away. Gabe's hold on her tightened, and he shifted slightly until his breath whispered over the sensitive skin under her ear.

"Of course, we are, little girl. Don't mistake my keeping my distance up 'til now for disinterest. You're mine now, and I have every intention of claiming what's mine the minute I get you on our own. Every little bit of you." He flexed his hips, and the solid ridge of his erection left her in no doubt as what he meant.

"Oh."

Gabe's dark laughter sent shivers down her spine, as he bit down lightly on the fleshy part of her earlobe. The flash of a camera blinded Lissandra in that moment, and then Mavis grinned at her.

"Now that is a grand picture. I'll take some more outside, where the light is better."

"Like hell you will, woman." Gabe grumbled next to her, as he took their copy of the marriage certificate off a relieved looking vicar, and they left that tiny room behind.

Lissandra blinked in the bright sunshine that greeted them outside the church, and despite Gabe's protestations he paused for a little while to allow Mavis to snap away merrily with her camera. One warm hug from the old dear, and crude catcalling, whistles, and lewd suggestions from Gabe's men later, Lissandra found herself back in the state of the art SUV that had spirited her away from her father and into Gabe's clutches. Only she wasn't on her own this time. Gabe slid in next to her, the doors locked, and they drove off to goodness only knew where.

She didn't dare look at her brooding husband and did her best to ignore her heart threatening to beat itself out of her chest.

The very air seemed sucked out of the interior with his presence, and Lissandra closed her eyes and wrapped her arms around herself while she scooted into the corner as far away from him as she could.

Oh my God, what have I done?

Chapter Seven

Gabe frowned at his new wife. Huddled in the corner, as far away as she could get from him, she looked like a frightened, stiff little mouse, rather than the vibrant, passionate woman who'd come alive in his arms during the kiss they'd shared in the church. He could still taste her, hear the soft whimpers of her submission as her curves molded into him.

Fuck it.

Those memories weren't helping one little bit, and his still hard dick jerked, aching to be free of its restraint, to sink into his wife, dammit. He reached down to adjust himself, and Lissandra flinched. Even though there was no room, she appeared to have folded herself even more into the corner, and his mood darkened.

"For heaven's sake, woman, stop acting as though I'm going to pounce on you any minute now, and rape you in the back of the car."

A terrified gasp came from his new wife this time, and Gabe scrubbed his hand over his face in frustration. He knew he could force the issue, and in truth, had she been anyone else, he would have made her suck him off to relieve the ache in his balls, but she wasn't one of his girls. She wasn't an experienced submissive either, who would get off on his ordering her about, nor one of the many women drawn to his wealth and status, and willing to do anything to get in in his pants, and, they hoped, his good graces. She also, most definitely, wasn't an Andrini plant, sold to him under pretense to spy out his operations. That much had become abundantly clear during his time away from her, and his detailed investigations into Andrini and his connection to Ollivanti. While it was abundantly clear those two were up to something, he still didn't know what it was, which was why he'd chosen to spirit Lissandra away.

The yacht would provide the perfect, secure hideaway for both of them, and a real chance to truly get to know each other.

Gabe sighed and held out his hand palm up, patiently waiting for her to take it.

"Come here, Lissa." He purposely dropped his voice an octave, let it take on that edge of command he adopted in a scene, and Lissandra jumped. Her gaze sought his, and she swallowed hard.

"What if I don't want to?" Her breathy question shot straight to his dick, and he adjusted himself for the umpteenth time with a groan.

"Wife, you promised to obey me, not only in your vows, but in our contract, and my patience is wearing thin. While I would never force myself on you, I will spank that insolent backside of yours." Another one of those cock-hardening gasps, coupled with the most endearing blush, which spread down her neck and made him ache to find out how far down that went.

Fuck him, if she wasn't turned on. Her nipples practically waved at him, hard little points poking through the delicate lace of her wedding dress, and the bouquet she was still clutching in a white knuckled grip trembled. Her little teeth worried her bottom lip, and her breaths grew shallow. Aroused, confused at her reaction to him, and afraid all at the same time. Such an interesting contradiction she was, and all his to do with as he pleased.

"You wouldn't, not here. I mean your driver, he…"

Gabe raised an eyebrow and smirked.

"The partition is up, and even if it wasn't, he's seen far worse. Wouldn't bother him at all, but I'd wager it would disturb you greatly to have him see your ass, and to witness how wet you're already getting at the mere mention of my hand on your backside."

Lissandra shook her head and squirmed on her seat. He caught the tightening of her thighs, and relief lightened his tense shoulders. He hadn't read the situation completely wrong then. His new wife might be an innocent, and she clearly struggled with her instinctive reactions to his words, but she also responded to his dominance, no doubt craved it on a subliminal level.

"How dare you, I don't. I mean, I'm not … that's just wrong."

"Why?"

Her eyes widened at his one syllable question, and this time when he held his hand out again she took it. A gentle pull brought her closer to him, and he buried his other hand in her hair to hold her still. His slight tug on the soft, fragrant tresses brought forth another moan from his wife, and bending his head, he hovered his lips over hers.

Their breaths mingled, hers choppy and far too fast, his more even, yet harsh, as his dick forcibly reminded him where he wanted to be. Drinking in her scent, made ten times more potent by her fear mixed in with her unwilling arousal, meant he had to taste her again, and fuck the surroundings.

"Why what?" he murmured, before he closed the distance and kissed her. She didn't even try to resist him, opened her mouth on a whimper and kissed him back the minute their tongues touched. Like it had before in the church, passion flared between them, raw, breathtaking, immediate, all-consuming. Her bouquet fell to the floor, and her hands went around his neck, her fingernails digging into his skin, as their kiss grew ever more passionate. She climbed onto his lap of her own accord, straddling him, and Gabe groaned as his roaming hands encountered the silky flesh of her inner thigh.

Fuck him, she was wearing stockings. The heat of her pussy called him, as his fingers traveled higher, encountering the damp gusset of the tiny strip of lace covering her. Her hips bucked against his questing fingers, her gasp music in his ears.

With the last remnants of sanity Gabe still possessed as lust short-circuited his brain, he pulled away slightly to study her, while he kept up his gentle exploration of her slit through the fabric. She grew even wetter under his fingertips, and eyes still firmly closed tried to kiss him again.

He pulled her hair, and she moaned.

"Please, I need… God, please don't stop."

Another, far harder tug to her long tresses made her open her eyes, and Gabe groaned. With pupils so dilated only a small ring of blue remained, she looked like a woman on the edge, begging to be fucked.

"Please what?" He ground the words out through gritted teeth, tugged her head back more, and ran his nose along the delicate arch of her neck, inhaling deeply. Fuck, she smelled so good. If he didn't put a stop to this, he would soon be past the point of no return, and she deserved more than a quick fuck in the back of his car, dammit.

Then again, it *would* mean she was finally his in every way, and if there was a welcoming committee of any kind at the marina, they'd at least have had this moment. What did they say? A woman never forgot her first, and by hell, he'd make sure she'd never forget this moment for fucking sure.

"Little one, what do you call me?"

He bit down slightly, and she groaned when he soothed that sting with his lips and kissed his way back to her mouth before he pulled back to study her once more.

Lissandra licked her lips, making him want to kiss her, and his cock jerked in his pants. He was in real danger of coming on the spot like a fucking teenager, and that hadn't happened to him in a long time. Then again, he couldn't recall a time when he'd wanted a woman as much as he wanted his wife.

Brows drawn together in confusion, Lissa seemed to mull this over, and he knew the minute it dawned on her what he was getting at. Her eyes softened, her breathing sped up, and she whispered her reply.

"Please, Si… Daddy, please, I want you."

Fuck!

She dropped her head, as though embarrassed at what she'd just said, and Gabe damn well near swallowed his tongue. That dynamic had never featured much on his radar, but hearing her call him "Daddy" in that breathy, needy voice, while she grew even wetter against his questing digits, stroking along her still covered slit, hell yeah.

"Say that again, baby girl."

She closed her eyes and tried to shake her head, but he was having none of that.

"I said, say that again, or you will earn that trip over Daddy's knee." He grasped hold of her lacy underwear, twisting it while he spoke, until it pulled tight against her slit and clit, and she whimpered her need.

"Please, no, Daddy. I want, oh God, I'm so close. This is so wrong. I … oh…"

Gabe flexed his hand, and the delicate fabric gave way with an audible rip, giving him unhindered access to her sweet cunt. Her fingernails dug into his neck where she was holding onto him, her thighs quivering around him, as he slid his index finger into her tight, wet channel. Her internal muscles clenched around that digit, and her hips bucked, instinctively seeking the added friction she needed to tumble over that edge.

"That's my good girl, take what you need from me." He claimed her mouth with his, swallowing her groans, as he started to thrust that one finger in and out of her channel, while circling her clit with his thumb. That little bundle of nerves swelled, hardening under his ministrations. Gabe wrenched his lips off of hers and pulled her closer, while he continued his efforts to make her come. Her internal muscles rippled around the digit buried inside her cunt, telling him how close she was, as her arousal coated his hand, and her hips went wild, yet still she teetered on that edge.

"I can't, I … he'll see."

Gabe added another finger, stretching her, and she mewled her need, head buried in the crook of his neck, her harsh inhalations such a fucking turn-on.

"Let go, baby, he can't see a thing. Trust me, come for your Daddy, right now." He pushed in as deep as he could, flicked her clit, and bit down hard on her shoulder. As he suspected, that bite of pain was what she needed to go over, and he caught her scream of surrender in his mouth while he pumped his fingers in and out of her channel allowing her to ride out her release. When she stopped shaking he tried to extricate himself, but Lissa moaned and rubbed her hot little pussy all over his groin. Gabe groaned, and his cock jerked in need. He grasped hold of her hips to hold her still and growled his instructions.

"Stop moving, baby, or so help me I'll fuck you right here and now. You don't want that."

The cutest pout appeared on her face, she wrinkled up her little nose and looked up at him.

"Please, I do. I'm still so…" She blushed, and his

chest tightened in emotion at her confusion. "You're so hard and big, and that can't be comfortable, and I need … *please,* Daddy."

Fuck him, when she pleaded so nicely, he was fucking putty in her hands, and truth be told, if he didn't come soon, he'd lose the plot completely. Gabe forced a smile on his lips, and he must have succeeded somewhat, because Lissa smiled back at him. She ran her hands down his waistcoat and with his support scooted backward slightly, to enable her to undo his trousers. The tentative touch of her fingers as she traced the length of his erection was pure torture, and Gabe growled low in his throat.

"Let me, girl."

Her eyes widened when he shoved her hands away and yanked down his trousers and boxers just enough for his cock to spring free. One hand around her back, he held her up while he lifted his ass to shove the offending material down more. Gabe grasped the base of his shaft and kissed her, hard, and fast, while he urged her closer. Like the good girl she was she scooted closer her knees either side of his thighs, until the heat of her pussy branded his dick. Lissandra whimpered when the tip of his cock slid through her wet folds, and Gabe broke the kiss and held himself perfectly still at her entrance. Their gazes locked, and he gritted out his instructions through clenched teeth.

"I don't want to hurt you, so go at your own pace. Slide that tight little cunt down Daddy's cock and ride me. Show me how much you want this."

His fingers dug into her hips, and he cursed the fabric of her dress which obscured his view. He'd have liked nothing more than to strip her naked and to be able to see her ride his dick, but he sensed that would have been a step too far for her. She seemed to gain confidence by this intimate cocoon her dress provided for them both, and there was something incredibly erotic about fucking her surrounded by virginal white lace, which no doubt made him a right perverted, sick bastard. She deserved so much better than this, so much better than him, but she was fucking his now, and he wouldn't ever let her go.

Brows drawn together in concentration and with her little pink tongue sticking out, breathing roughly, her exposed skin covered in the fine sheen of perspiration and flushed in need, she looked very young, and so fucking hot, it took every ounce of self-control he had to not take over. To force her hips down, to make her take her his cock, to thrust upward and bury himself balls deep inside the wet, warm haven of her body, to pound into her tight virgin pussy and to empty himself deep inside of her. Gabe wouldn't last long, not as revved up as he was already. His steadily leaking pre-cum joined her own arousal, aiding the broad tip of his shaft to slide into her tight entrance.

Gabe swore, when she stopped, panted, and shook her head.

"It hurts… You're too big. I can't." She tried to lift off him, but Gabe held her firm with one hand, while he slid his hand up his shaft until he found her clit. He gently rubbed along that swollen bundle, and Lissa jumped and groaned, as he slid in further, stretching her, inch by slow inch. He felt the moment he broke through her hymen, catching her cry of pain in his mouth while he kept up the lazy circles on her clit, and she sank down all the way.

It was torture and bliss, being inside of her, her walls squeezing his dick in a stranglehold. He murmured endearments in between kisses, nonsense to reassure her, while he held himself still, giving her time to adjust to his length and width. Gabe wasn't small. He never considered himself to be particularly huge either, but this was her first time, and as ready as she'd been for him, this had to hurt.

"Relax, baby, you're so tight, let me in. It's okay. Let me love you now and make it all better."

Lissa whimpered, but the tight hold on his cock lessened and she lifted up a little.

"Oh." That one word spoke volumes, and Gabe grinned at her expression.

"That's it, just go up and down, like … fuck … that's so it. That's my very good girl. Ride … fuck."

Hands curled into the fabric on her hips, Gabe threw his head back and tried doing complicated arithmetic in his head to stop himself from shooting his load too soon. The feel of her sliding up and down his shaft, as she slowly found a haphazard rhythm was too much and not enough. His balls drew up, and he clenched his jaw so tight it was a miracle he didn't crack a fucking molar, but she was in the driver's seat for this, just once, just for this first time.

Slowly, ever so fucking slowly, she increased her pace, grew cross-eyed with the effort as her own need built in waves which rippled along his dick, and drove him fucking insane.

"Oh, this, I don't know, please … oh God yes, yes…"

Seeing, hearing, and feeling her response to his experimental thrust upward as she came down finally gave him free rein, and Gabe grinned as he repeated that action. Lissa mewled in need, and Gabe thrust harder, deeper. Feet planted firmly on the floor, he scooted his butt further down the seat, tipping her on top of him. The slightly different angle meant he went deeper, and Lissa gasped in surprise as every thrust now stimulated her G-spot. She gushed for him as she came, and Gabe slammed up into her, seeking his own release at the speed he needed. Not that it took long. Her harsh breaths in his ear, the walls of her vagina rippling around his dick, meant his orgasm burst forth with toe-curling intensity. He thrust in deep and stayed there, while she collapsed on top of him, shaking in the throes of another, smaller climax of her own, as he pumped spurt after spurt of his seed deep inside her body with a grunt. By the time his dick had finally stopped twitching, his cum leaked out of her, and he smiled in satisfaction. As for his sweet Lissa, she buried her head in his neck and shook her head when he addressed her.

"Look at me, baby girl."

"No, I can't. We… God, I can't believe we just did that here, now, and…" The intercom crackled, interrupting her, and she froze.

"We're here, boss. Been here for a while, but you seemed busy, so…" Stone's amused voice came through loud and clear, and Gabe groaned under his breath.

He fumbled for the switch to open communications.

"Fine, give us five. All okay out there?"

"All clear, boss, take your time."

Gabe flicked the switch and shifted them both. His softening cock slid out of her, and Lissa winced.

"Poor baby, here, let me help you clean up a bit."

He moved her to lie back on the seat, while he tucked himself back in his boxers. The sight of his dick covered in her blood-streaked cream was such a visible reminder of what he'd just taken from her that he frowned. That possessive caveman inside of him rejoiced, however. While he'd had no real doubt of her innocence it was damn good to see the confirmation nonetheless. Taking her knees, he pushed them upward and out, flipped her skirt up and groaned at his first proper sight of her cunt. Red and puffy, it made a mouth-watering sight. Seeing his cum slowly trickle out her still quivering hole made him half harden again. If it wouldn't blow her mind completely and they weren't sitting ducks in the parked car, he'd take his time to clean her up by eating her out. Instead, he grabbed some tissues, unscrewed a bottle of water, and having wetted them proceeded to gently wipe between her legs. Lissa tried to close her legs, but she was no match for him.

"Shush, let me take care of you. There you are, this will have to do until we're on board ship." That brought her head up, and she got on her elbows to look at him. Heat crept in her cheeks, when he dried her off with yet more tissues and then dropped a kiss on her mound, before he pulled her skirt down, preserving her modesty.

"Ship?" she asked and swung her legs back 'round until she was sitting upright, once again the picture-perfect bride, if you ignored the high color in her cheeks, her ruffled hair, and, of course the ruined lacy ivory panties, which he picked up off the floor. Her eyes grew wide when he lifted the underwear to his nose, inhaled deeply, and then deposited them in his pocket with a wink.

"Yes, ship. Rule #1 of being Daddy's little girl." He watched her closely as he murmured the words, and the way her breathing sped up and her eyes softened was a true delight to witness. This was definitely what she needed. "No panties when you're with me. I want easy access to my little girl at all times."

Renewed heat rose in her cheeks, but she nodded.

"Good girl. Rule #2, trust Daddy to know what he's doing and not ask silly questions." She frowned at him, but she gave another tiny nod, and he smiled.

"Good girl, let's go then."

Chapter Eight

Lissandra couldn't get her voice to work, but her nod must have been enough for him, because his smile lit up his craggy features, and her heart gave a far too suspicious bump in her chest. Lordy me, when he smiled at her like that, called her his *good girl*, it was like a ray of sunshine burst across her, which was ridiculous to the extreme. However, Lissandra couldn't shake it, this need to please *Daddy*.

Jeez, why was that such a turn-on? And why did she feel the need to simply let go of everything and to let him take care of her? She barely knew this man, had been, if not forced, then coerced into this marriage, and they were about to go off to God only knew where, not to mention what they'd just shared. In the back of the SUV, no less. Who did that?

She suppressed a somewhat hysterical giggle at that thought. Surely, losing your virginity in the back of the car was the stuff of teenage fumbles, not mind-blowing sex with your much older husband.

Lissandra held her hands over her hot cheeks and concentrated on breathing. Maybe it was just as well that they got out of this car, because without Gabe's reassuring presence next to her, this all felt horribly wrong. That in itself ought to worry her, this hold he had on her. All those worries fled her mind, however, when the door next to her opened and Gabe held out his hand to pull her out into the open.

They were indeed at a marina, surrounded by gleaming yachts, the afternoon sun glinting off their polished chrome deck rails. She knew she was staring, probably had her mouth open, but this idyllic picture was too much. A gust of wind swept off the bay waters, lifting the bottom of her dress and making her painfully aware that she was standing here sans her underwear. She automatically squeezed her thighs together and dropped her gaze. Nevertheless, she caught Stone's knowing smirk.

Oh God, it was him driving us?

Oblivious to her discomfort, Stone threw the cigarette he'd been smoking onto the ground and extinguished it with the boot of his heel.

"Right then, she's all ready for you, boss. I'd feel better if you'd let me come with, mind you. The threat hasn't been eliminated yet."

Lissandra's stomach churned at that ominous statement, not helped one iota by Gabe's short, cruel laugh.

"They won't follow us into open waters, and if they do … I'll deal with it."

"On your own?" Stone's disbelief didn't help the whole business of drawing air into her lungs, and she forced herself to look up to see the men's expressions.

Gabe smiled at her and drew her into his side.

"By all means follow us, if it makes you feel better, but this is my honeymoon, and I intend to enjoy my wife without you fuckers breathing down my neck." His hand strayed to her backside during his response to Stone and squeezed one cheek. Lissandra jumped, and Stone laughed.

"What threat?" she asked. She inwardly grimaced at the wobbly cadence of her voice.

"Nothing for you to worry your pretty little head over, my sweet." Gabe, predictably, ignored her question and pulled her along the quay and down toward the walkway, at the end of which an all too familiar yacht gently bobbed in the choppy waters.

She came to an abrupt stop when the name came into view.

The Raphaella

"I—I don't understand. She sank. At least that's what Papa told Mama." She blinked away tears at the sight of a yacht with which so many of her happy childhood memories were associated.

Stone cleared his throat, and Gabe squeezed her hand.

"That's what he wanted you to believe. He sold her on to clear his gambling debts at the time. I managed to track her down a few years ago. She needed some restorations, and the inside has been completely refurbished, but yes, that's your mother's boat. Seemed fitting we use Valentina's boat for her daughter's honeymoon."

Lissandra blinked away tears, and Gabe made a rough sound at the back of his throat. She tore her gaze away from the yacht and to his face. The lines around his eyes appeared more pronounced than usual, and his expression could only be described as guarded as he watched her with a quiet intensity, as though her reaction meant something to him.

"I—I can't believe you did that," she said. Gabe's eyes drew together in a frown. It spurred her on to clarify what she meant, desperate to show her gratitude for his actions, and she didn't dare examine the motive behind this need to please him, to see him smile at her in approval. "I mean, I've got such happy memories of our time on here. Mama used to take me with her. She'd paint, and she was so happy. *We* were happy here." Slowly, Gabe's stern features relaxed, his dark eyes softening in emotion, echoes of her own tumultuous feelings, and she whispered the next words. "Thank you, Daddy."

The flash of heated lust in Gabe's eyes caused an answering burn in her lower belly, and she bit her lip to stop herself from moaning out loud.

Stone's low whistle behind her should have mortified her, but, caught in Gabe's intense gaze, she couldn't give two hoots about their audience. Like before in the car, she simply wanted to be with her husband, and the rest of the world faded away.

"Well, then, let's get you on there, baby girl." Gabe flicked her nose and before she could even grasp his intentions, he'd swung her up into his arms, and walked off down the walkway until he could step onto the yacht. Lissandra shrieked and flung her arms around his neck.

"Cast us off when I start the engine, will you, Stone?" Gabe threw that command over his shoulder while he carried her through to the interior. Lissandra could only stare at the luxury cabin in wonder. Decorated in deep reds and brown, the place looked warm and masculine all in one. An area to the side had clearly been set aside for his office space because it was dominated by a desk, and state of the art computer and surveillance system. An oval shaped seating arrangement made up the living area. She caught a glimpse of a huge TV screen on one wall, and then he rushed them through kitchen area. From what she could see of it, it had also been hugely improved upon, with a tall fridge freezer and gleaming cabinets, which included a full hob and oven, which seemed odd to the extreme. Surely, Gabe wouldn't cook for himself, would he?

All thoughts fled her brain however, when Gabe pushed open the door to the master cabin and her eyes took in the enormous bed that took up most of the space in the room. The room opened to a little covered balcony, on which she'd spotted her easel and paints.

Gabe slowly slid her down his front and pushed her down to sit on the bed.

"Stay here and out of sight, while I navigate us out of here. Take a bath, if you like. Plenty of water on board, and I can refill the tanks once we're in France, anyway."

"France?" she echoed. "That's where we're going?"

Gabe grinned at down at her.

"Among other places, though I doubt we'll leave the yacht. I have plans for you, little girl." Lissandra gasped, and Gabe's smile deepened, growing positively sinful as he traced her lips with his index finger. "I see we understand each other." He flicked her nose and hooked his thumb over his shoulder. "Bathroom is through there, where the second cabin used to be. Like I said, I had the *Raphaella* refurbished for my needs, so feel free to explore down here. Stay out of sight though, until we're on open waters at least." His voice dropped to that deep growl he adopted when he meant business, and Lissandra swallowed hard.

"Yes, Daddy."

Again, with that flare of emotions in his dark eyes that made her want to sink to her knees and please him. Lord only knew what was wrong with her. Maybe having awesome sex addled your brain to such an extent that you couldn't think straight anymore. Maybe that's why folks made such fools of themselves in the name of love, not that this, whatever this was between them, was love. Heaven forbid she should fall in love with Gabriel Henshaw. No, she just had a severe case of the hots for her husband, and her awakening submissive side couldn't help but respond to the dominance which oozed out of his very pores. That was the only reason why calling him *Daddy* felt so right.

"Good girl."

The approval in his voice made her feel ten feet

tall, and then he was gone. The engines rumbled to life moments later, and the yacht pulled away from its moorings. Out of the portholes, Stone's scowling figure was surrounded by more of Gabe's men, and then they all disappeared from view as they clambered into a smaller craft. What had Gabe said? Follow us if you must?

Unseen ice-cold fingers traveled down her spine, and Lissandra hugged her arms around herself. He never had answered her questions as to what threat Stone had been referring to. Surely, they couldn't mean her father. Unwanted tears filled her eyes, and she blinked them away. She would not think about that man now, she wouldn't. After the way he'd thrown her to the proverbial wolves, had lied to her, sold her to all intents and purposes, had lied all his life it seemed—this yacht a forceful reminder of that—Andrini didn't deserve her tears. He deserved to rot in a prison cell somewhere, for having used dear Mama as a human shield.

That thought brought Lissandra up short, because the anger and grief she still felt about her mother's untimely death had shifted from her unknown killer to Andrini. Even knowing that Gabe had been the one to order the hit on Andrini, she didn't see him as her mother's killer anymore. When that shift had happened, she couldn't say. It had snuck up on her over the last three weeks, and being here on her mother's ship just cemented that feeling. Gabe hadn't needed to bring her here. He hadn't needed to set up a studio for her in his apartment, nor bring some of her paints on board ship. He hadn't needed to do any of the things he had done, little and not so little, and he certainly hadn't needed to marry her. No one would have batted an eyelid, had he simply forced himself on her and then put her to work in one of his *establishments*. That's certainly the treatment she would have expected from one of her father's greatest enemies. Treatment she would no doubt have received had she fallen into Ollivanti's hands. She shivered at that mere thought. The little she knew about Gabe's rival and his reputation was enough to give her nightmares. Maybe he was the threat they'd been referring to?

She hugged herself and ruthlessly squashed down all thoughts of her father and rival crime lords and concentrated on the fact that she was now married. Holding up her hand, she admired the rings Gabe had placed on her finger.

Oh my God, I really am married.

The fact that she was, that Gabe had taken steps to protect her like that, it was … well, she wasn't entirely sure what that was or what it meant, but she knew one thing. She could never hate him. The urge to be near him set her feet in motion. Mindful of his instructions, she stayed below deck but positioned herself so that she could see him at the helm.

It was clear from his confident handling that he knew what he was doing. He'd shrugged out of his jacket and waistcoat, lost his tie, and rolled up the sleeves of his shirt, revealing strong, powerful forearms. Lissandra sighed to herself and sank down on the settee to watch him. When they left the English coast behind and hit the open waters of the Channel, Gabe looked over his shoulder. Surprise registered in his eyes, and then he smiled and held out his hand.

"What are you doing there, baby girl? Did I not tell you to go and have a soak?"

"I know, it was just…" Lissandra scrambled to her feet and stepped up on the deck with him. "It's lonely down there, I—"

"Stop right there." Lissandra froze at the furious

growl that interrupted her. "Put on that life jacket, before you take one more step." He pointed to a bundle of them by the wall, and Lissandra rolled her eyes.

"Really?"

"Yes, really, and don't take that tone of voice of with me." His voice dropped further, taking on that delicious edge of command which sent shivers of delight down her spine.

She couldn't help but push him a little further, however, even as she dutifully lowered the life-saving device over her head. "You're not wearing one, so why do I have to?"

She knew she was pouting, probably acting like a spoiled little brat, and sure enough, Gabe's eyebrow rose in answer.

"Do you think it's acceptable to argue with your Daddy, *little girl*?"

Oh, the way he emphasized those last two words… Her stomach fluttered in apprehension and need. Her pussy clenched, and she wanted nothing more than for him to take her over his knee and make good on the threatened punishment. Which no doubt made her all sorts of fucked up in the head, but so the hell what? What had he said in the car? It's not wrong if we both want it.

"No, Daddy, and I'm not arguing, not really. But the fact remains that you're not wearing one, so…"

Her words trailed off when his stern features softened, and he shook his head as though amused by her.

"Come here, girl," he said, and Lissandra scrambled to obey him. He held out one arm, and she snuggled into his embrace with a content sigh. Gabe hugged her close for a few precious moments and then proceeded to check her life vest. She could hear the smile in his voice when he spoke again.

"What's this all about, baby girl? If I didn't know better, I'd say you're itching for a spanking." Lissandra's breath caught in her lungs at that far too accurate assumption. "Turn around and put your hands on the wheel." She obeyed without hesitation and gasped when he pulled her flush against his body, and the solid ridge of his cock made contact with her ass. His large hands came over hers and guided them along.

"Ever steered a yacht before?" he asked.

"No."

"Hmm, not even as a child? Andrini or whichever captain you had never took you up on deck, when you were little to show you how it all works?"

Lissandra squeezed her eyes shut and shook her head, not trusting her voice to work right now. She would give away her current state of confused arousal for sure. This close to him all she wanted to do was jump him again, and wasn't that the darnedest thing.

"Well, then, we'll have to rectify that immediately."

Gabe launched into an explanation of how to steer the boat, which left her head spinning with information overload, not least because his close proximity was far too distracting. She must have managed to make the right noises, however, because Gabe murmured his approval, and eventually stepped away, effectively leaving her in charge of the yacht.

"There you go, you've got it now."

"I can't—don't leave me." Lissandra winced at the shrill squeak she managed to produce, and frantically looked over her shoulder, while she held the wheel in a white knuckled grip. As exhilarating as it was to be in charge of the yacht, it was also downright terrifying without his guidance.

"Relax, just keep a straight course, while I change

out of this monkey suit, and rustle us up some food."

"What?" Lissandra let go of the wheel, and the yacht lurched to the right. Instantly Gabe was behind her, taking her hands and placing them back where they ought to be.

"Shit, I can't do—ouch."

The unexpected swat to her backside really stung and catapulted her whole body forward with the force behind it.

"I'll not have foul language coming out of that sweet mouth of yours, and I wouldn't let you do this, if I didn't think you could." He grasped hold of her chin, and she swallowed hard at the steely determination edged into the lines of his face. A far too visible reminder of their age difference, not that she cared about that one iota. What she did care about was not earning his displeasure and she hastily murmured her apology.

"Sorry, I just panicked."

The harsh lines of his face softened, and his dark eyes blazed in unmistakable lust.

"We'll see how sorry you really are, when you're over my knee, taking your punishment, girl." He smiled at her sharp intake of breath, and leaning down, planted a hard kiss on her lips. As brief as the contact was, she felt the sheer force behind it down to her toes, and she was grateful beyond belief that she'd kicked off her heels earlier. Otherwise she'd have been in danger of swooning on the spot, and he wanted her to hold the yacht steady and on course.

He tapped her nose and pointed to the compass in front of her.

"You know what to do. Don't let me down." With that he turned sharply and left her to it. Panic gripped her in a stranglehold, threatening to overwhelm her, but she forced the feelings down. She could *do* this. He wouldn't let her otherwise. The door to the cabin banged shut, yet she still felt his presence. Her skin tingled under his silent scrutiny, and when she risked a quick look over her shoulder, it was to see him indeed watching her from the inside of the cabin. A small smile played around his lips, as he gestured back to the expanse of the English Channel stretching out in front of her and twirled his finger in an unspoken command for her to turn her attention to what she was doing.

Lissandra loosened the death grip she still had on the wheel, took another breath in, and forced herself to concentrate on the task. Slowly, but surely the sheer magic of being at sea seeped into her bones. She'd all but forgotten how exhilarating it was to be here on deck, with the sea breeze whipping her hair around, the taste of salt on her lips, and the ability to go almost anywhere.

Mama had taken regular trips out to sea with a small Lissandra tucked away in the stern. Her love of painting had been born out here, watching Mama take them far out to sea before she dropped anchor and started to paint. Tears clouded her vision, but these were happy ones. She could almost feel Mama's spirit wrap around her, cradle her in her arms, as her whispers carried in the cool breeze.

"It will all be okay, Lissa, you'll see."

Chapter Nine

The crackle of the radio pulled Gabe's attention away from the vision that was his new wife at the helm of the yacht. He'd hoped that taking her on board ship would relax her, and seeing her now, a smile on her face as she raised her head into the sea breeze, he knew his idea had worked.

There was something surreal in seeing her on the deck, small feet bare, wearing nothing but her wedding dress and the life vest. He smiled, recalling her outraged surprise at his insistence that she wear it above deck. There was no chance in hell he would risk her safety, however. While the Channel was calm, visibility good, and not a cloud on the horizon, the weather could and frequently did change on a whim. Plus, should the unthinkable happen, she would float, enabling him to get to her.

"Boss, you're there?"

Stone's insistent voice, distorted by the radio, forced him to abandon his watchful post, and he crossed the short distance to his desk.

"Of course, I'm here. Where else would I be? Take it no one followed us?"

"No, you're all clear." Stone's sigh made Gabe grin.

"You sound almost disappointed at that."

A short laugh, and Gabe could almost see the younger man's sheepish grin. He would have run his hand over his shaved head, and shrugged.

"Well, I'd love to take them out, that's for sure."

Gabe sighed and focused his attention back on his new wife.

"Wouldn't we all, but I fear there's more at play here. Keep in touch and your eyes open. I'll be going off radar for a while."

Stone's grunt of annoyance came through loud and clear, but he didn't contradict him.

"Aye, boss, can't say I blame you, just be careful out there. We need you back in one piece."

Gabe didn't bother to respond and switched off communications. Keeping one eye on Lissa, he raided the freezer, and shoved the Mavis-made lasagna into the oven to heat up, before he joined her back on deck. The sea was starting to froth as the wind picked up, and he needed to be back in command of the yacht.

Lissa breathed an audible sigh of relief when he stepped up behind her and put his large hands over hers.

"Here, let me take over. It's getting rough out here, and Christ, girl, you're frozen. Get your ass back below deck and warm up."

Lissa shook her head and pressed back against him.

"No, please. I'm all right. Besides, you're so warm, and I want to stay up here with you, please?"

Gabe swallowed his instant denial, because, in truth, she felt far too fucking good in his arms, as she leaned her head back on his chest, and smiled up at him.

It loosened that knot of worry in his gut that the interchange with Stone had left behind. Like his second in command, he wished Ollivanti would play his hand already, so that he could deal with the threat. He forced a smile on his lips for Lissandra's benefit, and they spent the next half an hour in companionable silence, until the French coastline came into view.

"Is that France? Are we here?" The excitement in her voice and her bouncing up and up and down on the deck were contagious, and Gabe relaxed further. If they stayed away from the main tourist attractions, they ought to be safe from detection.

"Almost, little one. There's a little secluded cove I know not far up the coast from Cherbourg. We can drop anchor there. I don't know about you, but I'm getting hungry, and Mavis's lasagna ought to be ready by now."

Another happy bounce from his new wife.

"Lasagna? That's my favorite!"

One hand on the wheel, he wrapped his free arm around Lissandra's waist and pulled her flush into his body, while he dropped a kiss on her hair.

"I know, baby girl. The freezer is full of your favs. Mavis has outdone herself. We sure won't have to worry about food."

Lissandra giggled, a full blown happy belly laugh, which lit up her features and made her eyes dance in merriment.

"What's so amusing about that?" Gabe grumbled his question, but her laughter was too infectious to not at least smile, and he swore to himself there and then that he would do his utmost to hear more of that delightful sound. She was his now, come what may, and he wanted to protect and spoil her, like she should have been growing up.

"Oh nothing. I just had visions of either of us trying to cook and burning the yacht down in the process, which…" She sobered and frowned. "Wouldn't be all that funny. I sure can't cook."

Gabe shook his head and, releasing her, tapped her ass a few times in quick succession, before his attention was taken up negotiating the rising cliff face, behind which lay the cove he was looking for.

Lissandra squealed, rubbed her butt, and mock pouted her annoyance, even as she leaned into his side.

"What was that for?"

"That, little girl, was for making assumptions about me again. For all you know I could be a gourmet chef in the making." A quick glance at her showed her openmouthed expression, and warmth spread through his chest as she appeared to mull this over.

"Are you?" she finally asked, just as he was rounding the cliffs and the tiny cove came into view, and he dropped the anchor. The heavy object reeled out of its casing and splashed into the water. Lissandra hung her head over the rails, watching its descent, and laughed. "Wow, you'd never know that was here. It would be beautiful if the weather was nicer."

Gabe nodded his approval and shrugged.

"That's the Normandy coast for you. I intend to make our way to warmer climates over the next few days, but this will do for now." He held out his hand, and something unfurled in his chest when she took his proffered digits without any hesitation. Gabe yanked her to him, and his dick surged to life with renewed vigor when all of her delicious curves collided with his hard frame. Dipping his head, he claimed her mouth in a harsh, quick kiss.

Or at least that had been his intention, but when she opened to him, he had to take that kiss deeper. When she kissed him back, he was lost to pleasure. Kissing his wife proved as addictive as it was arousing, stirring the caveman inside of him, which wanted her tied to his bed, naked and begging for mercy.

He forced himself to pull away, and to release his hold on her.

"You heard me, baby girl. Scoot below deck. I'm hungry."

Lissa pouted but one raised eyebrow from him and she complied with a murmured, "Yes, Daddy."

Fuck him six ways 'til next Sunday, he would never grow tired of hearing her call him that, especially in that breathy, "come fuck me" voice. He watched her descend in front of him and groaned under his breath as he adjusted his dick.

Dinner proved to be a most uncomfortable affair for him, because watching Lissa enjoy the lasagna was sheer torture. The little noises she made, as she bit into her first mouthful … an auditory orgasm all by themselves.

To distract himself from his growing carnal desire for his wife, he wolfed his own food down and then started to ask her about her work.

"So, have you thought about where you might want to exhibit?"

The lasagna-laden fork stopped halfway to her bow lipped mouth, and her eyes lit up in excitement.

"Not really. I mean I've set up a website for the work I'm happy with so far, and I've had a few orders, so that's a start, right?"

Gabe smiled at her over his wineglass and nodded.

He'd put quite a few orders in himself, not that she needed to know that. Several of her paintings were in his private office, and he intended to get more for the casino.

"I know. You're very talented, baby girl."

Heat blossomed across her cheeks at his praise, and her expressive eyes lit up even more.

"Thank you, Daddy."

"Jesus, girl. Don't call me that unless you want me to act on it." Gabe groaned and readjusted himself for the umpteenth time since they sat down to dinner. The little minx noticed, and before he could grasp her intent, she pushed her chair away and approached him. The effortless way she slid to her knees in front of him and her coy smile told their own story.

"What if I am, *Daddy?*"

Gabe, too, pushed his chair back and angled himself to face her. Her gaze dropped to his groin, and her eyes widened. She licked her lips, and Gabe closed his eyes and took a deep breath in.

"You're playing with fire, baby girl."

"Maybe I like getting burned." She grinned up at him and slowly slid her hands up his legs. As innocent as that contact was it meant his dick jerked, and Gabe grasped the sides of the chair to stop himself from burying his hands in Lissa's hair and demand that she suck him off.

She was new to this, he had to remember that, and, besides, he wanted to see what she would do next. The slow, torturous progress up his legs grew more hesitant the closer she came to his groin and stopped completely when her fingertips traced the outline of his erection. His cock jumped, Gabe groaned, and Lissa looked up at him, clearly startled by his reaction.

"Don't fucking stop now, girl." The words came out much harsher than he intended them to, but, *fuck him*, her hesitant exploration was doing him in.

Lissa bit her lip, her brows drawing together in a frown, but she mercifully continued the far too arousing movements of her questing digits.

Gabe hissed through his teeth, and she stopped a second time.

"I don't want to hurt you."

She looked so earnest in her response that Gabe swallowed the laugh bubbling up at the back of his throat and shook his head.

"Then don't stop. Do what you want to do and get on with it, or you won't like the consequences."

Her breath hitched at that statement, and clearly emboldened by his words, she scooted closer still and proceeded to slowly free his aching cock. Her gasp when she pulled his underwear down and his dick sprang free was fucking music to his ears. The chair creaked under the stranglehold Gabe had on it, and he had to clear his throat several times to get the words out.

"Now, you've got Daddy's cock what are you going to with it, baby girl?"

****

Lissa held her breath as Gabe's cock came into view. Her pussy clenched, and she grew ever wetter. While she'd known he had to be impressive, had the sore nether regions to prove it, seeing his shaft up close was still a revelation. Lissa had never thought that part of a man's anatomy particularly pretty, but Gabe's cock was…

Acting on instinct and driven by the very real need to taste him, to give him back some of the pleasure he'd given her, she traced her fingertips along the veins of his erection. Another hiss escaped the man in front of her, and his dark spicy musk increased. Moisture appeared at the tip of his mushroom flared head, calling her to lick it away. When she did, Gabe groaned, his cock jerking and seeming to grow even bigger.

"Jesus, girl, stop teasing and suck it."

The guttural tone of his voice and the way his thighs clenched spurred her on to repeat that action. His essence teased her taste buds, salty, yet not as unpleasant as she'd always assumed it must be. Besides his harsh breaths spurred her on, and hollowing out her cheeks, she sucked more of him into her mouth. His scent increased, and more of his pre-cum coated her tongue, encouraging her to keep going.

"Fuck, girl, you're a natural, that's it. So damn … fuck…"

She grinned around her mouthful of cock, while that organ grew bigger still, pulsing in her mouth as she took him deep and swallowed.

His grunt gave a moment's warning before his hands fisted in her hair and pulled her off his cock with a muttered curse.

"Enough, I'll blow down your throat at this rate."

Lissa gasped when their gazes connected, because the intensity of his stare sent her insides alight in need.

"Please."

A harsh grin lit up Gabe's face.

"Oh, you'll have Daddy's cock, my sweet, but on my terms, not yours." He let go of her hair and much to her dismay tucked himself back inside his trousers with shaky moves so unlike him, that she couldn't help her smile.

"Is something amusing you, girl?"

Oh, that voice, deep, dark, and commanding, it slid over her skin, urged her on to please to him, to bend to his will.

"No, it's just you don't look very comfortable like that." She flicked a glance up to his groin before she dutifully dropped her gaze to the floor.

"Hmmm, that would be all your fault, baby girl."

There was a teasing undertone to those grumbled words, which made her smile widen, and Gabe sighed.

"You clearly need a firm hand." He leaned forward, grasped her chin, and made her look at him. Her stomach flipflopped wildly at the determination she saw in his eyes.

"Please, Daddy, I'm all yours."

The smile her words caused lit up his features, made him look years younger, and the shimmer of emotion in his eyes took her breath away. He looked as though he cared, truly cared, and warmth spread through every fiber of her being. This was dangerous territory, for sure. This man was a ruthless killer, she knew that, and yet, here, now, and in this moment none of that mattered. The more time she spent with him, the more she was drawn to him. For better or worse, he was now her husband, her Dom, her Daddy, and with that came peace. The certain knowledge that he would indeed look after her, that she was his and that this connection between them mattered.

"Yes, you are…" His hold on her chin turned into a caress, as he swiped his thumb across her lips. "All mine."

His dark gaze grew more intense, until she felt utterly consumed by his presence.

"Breathe, baby girl."

Belatedly Lissa realized that she needed oxygen in her lungs and took a huge gulp of air, which made the man in front of her chuckle.

"Good girl, let's take this to the bedroom. I want you naked and tied up for my pleasure. As beautiful as this dress is, it needs to go."

He stood up and held out his hand for her take. Lissa slid hers into his much larger one without any hesitation. Gabe pulled her up and along to the bedroom with slow measured steps which only served to pitch her further into the maelstrom of fevered anticipation.

The door banged shut behind them, and with the setting sun bathing the inside of their cabin in an orange glow, this moment felt even more special. As though this marriage was real, and not just…

Gabe stepped behind her, ran his hands up her arms, raising them up above her head, before he curled her hands around the bed post.

"You're thinking mighty hard there, little one. Time to take you out of your head a little. Keep your hands there, while I peel you out of this dress."

He murmured the words in her ear, his breath

leaving goosebumps behind on her skin, while he rubbed his beard roughened jaw along her neck. The action tickled, and Lissa's shoulders came up as shivers raced down her spine.

She felt his smile in the butterfly kisses he trailed down her exposed back, while his hands followed the curves of her body, leaving heated awareness of him in their wake.

"Such beautiful curves." He flicked his fingers over her nipples, and Lissa didn't even try to hide her moan. "I'm going to fuck these tits." Taking a nipple each between his fingers he pulled, hard, and Lissa inhaled sharply, as that tug shot straight to her clit. "And you're going to let me do that, aren't you?"

His voice dropped further, as he crowded against her back, his hard cock a heavy presence against her hip.

"Answer your Daddy, girl."

"Yes, anything, please."

Her knees trembled as he slid his hands lower, cupped her pussy through the folds of her dress with one hand while he pulled down the zipper at her side slowly, until her whole back was exposed.

"Lower your arms."

When she did, he released his hold on her and tugged the fabric down her arms until it fell in a shimmering pool of lace by her feet. His sharp intake of breath was music to her ears, and when he stepped around her she could feel his hot gaze skim across her body.

"So fucking beautiful."

The whispered words settled around her like a warm hug. She ought to have been embarrassed standing there in nothing but her hold up stockings and bra. He ran his knuckles over her breasts, and then pulled the string holding the bra together at the front. The cups gave way, releasing her heavy breasts, and his renewed intake of breath sent more moisture into her pussy. The air grew heavy with the musk of their combined arousal as he studied her. The longer she stood there, feeling his gaze roam across her body like a physical caress, the wetter she became. Her breasts grew so heavy they hurt, her nipples tight nubs begging to be touched, while her pussy swelled, ached to be touched, to be filled by him.

He ran a finger over each nipple, and down the soft skin of her belly, until he reached her mound.

"Open your legs. Let me see how wet you are for me."

The air felt cool over her exposed swollen flesh as she dutifully spread her legs wider. His feather light touch across her labia brought a tremble to her knees, and she stumbled, only to be caught by him.

Held in his strong arms, Lissa closed her eyes, and breathed in her Sir, her husband, her *Daddy*.

"Please, Daddy, I need…"

His kiss stopped any further words she could have made, and she simply gave herself up to the onslaught on her senses, as he simultaneously deepened the kiss and lifted her. Lissa clung to his shoulders, breathless and needy, as he shifted them onto the bed, his bodyweight pinning her in place as he moved her hands from his shoulders and held them above her head.

"I know what you need, baby girl." Gabe lifted his head to study her, and her breath caught in her lungs at the expression on his face. "Trust me?"

Chapter Ten

The seconds ticked by as he waited for his wife's answer, marked by the beats of his heart. Christ, he was turning into a sentimental old fool where Lissa was concerned. But he needed her consent, to know that she was truly on board with this. Why this need drove him so hard, he didn't dare examine too closely.

He shifted his hips, to relieve some of his self-inflicted blue balls syndrome, and a moan escaped his girl's plump lips. Her expressive eyes widened, her pupils dilating further as her breathing got choppier.

"Yes, I do, please just—"

She melted into him, when he kissed her, her submission a sweet gift indeed, and Gabe couldn't wait one more second.

He broke the kiss and got to his knees to reach the rope tucked away at the headboard.

Another one of those telling gasps made him grin, when he held it up for her to see.

"Good girl. I'm going to tie you up now. Remember your safewords if this gets too much for you."

"Green, Daddy." The speed with which she replied made his chest ache in emotion, and he smiled down on her, as he proceeded to wrap the rope around her wrists. Every tug, every knot, brought more whimpers of need from Lissa, and pitched him effortlessly into the dominant headspace he craved.

He took his time, checking the knots and drinking in her sweet moans and sighs, as he fastened a chest harness to frame her amazing tits, and then brought the rope around her hips to secure her lush thighs.

By the time he was finished, the sheet under her butt was soaked through with her arousal and Lissa, herself, had drifted away, if the unfocused look in her eyes was any indication.

So, fucking responsive and perfect for him. As though she'd been made just for him. Sitting back on his heels Gabe let his gaze roam over his wife's ample curves, while he kept up a steady stream of reassuring words to keep her floating in her happy space. Was there anything more delightful than to see your woman's flesh held in by ropes, marked by your hands, with her helpless to take whatever he decided to do to her?

Christ, she really is mine.

His dick jerked with that possessive thought, and Gabe groaned. With her legs splayed open all her juicy cunt was on display. Her clit stood proudly erect at the top of her hood, testament to how turned on she was. Her lips looked swollen and so very pink and needy, while her little hole quivered, expelling more of her cream. Gabe did what he'd wanted to from the beginning. Grasping hold of her ass cheeks, he bent his head and tasted heaven. Lissa's thighs quivered around his head, and another gush of her sweet musk was his reward, as were the incomprehensible sounds spilling from her lips, as he ate her out. Every lick of his tongue resulted in more of her arousal for him to taste, until Gabe couldn't stand it anymore. Drinking in her taste, her very essence, he took her cum all the way back to the other hole he intended to claim. If not today, then soon. This woman would be his in all ways.

Lissa groaned long and hard when he pushed his tongue past that tight ring of muscle, while he set his thumb to her clit and rubbed hard. His sweet girl did not disappoint in her response. She tumbled into an orgasm so intense she soaked his face, as her whole body shook in her climax. Gabe looked up her bound curves and grinned.

Head thrown back, eyes tightly closed, she panted

her release, seemingly lost in a world of pleasure.

"That's my girl, you ride those waves. There's plenty more of those to come."

Reaching across her he pulled out the butterfly vibrator he kept in the drawer. It was a matter of moments to secure the device to her pussy, and Lissa screamed when he turned it on. Her eyes flew open, and her whole body went rigid as he adjusted the speed to maximum pleasure and her sensitive tissues responded.

"Oh my God, no, not again. I can't … God, yes. *Yes.*"

Gabe crawled back up her body, until his dick rested just at her entrance and smiled down on her.

"Yes, you can, as many times as I say you can. I'm going to fuck you now. Eyes on me."

When she complied, he flexed his hips and sank into bliss, as her pussy walls trembled around him, milking his cock in rhythmic ripples as she rode out her orgasms. With their gazes locked he pulled almost all the way out and then rocked back into her body. In this moment they were one, linked together not only by their bodies, but their minds, their connection a palpable force between them, as he increased his space.

Sweat gathered between his shoulder blades, dripping into his eyes, as he lost himself inside his wife, gathering the speed he needed to chase his rapidly building orgasm. The bed shook with the force of their coupling, as he truly let go, secure in the knowledge that she was with him every step, shaking around him, her incoherent whimpers the biggest turn-on yet. His balls drew tight, and he had to close his eyes, as the force of his own climax forced a guttural shout from his lips.

"Fuck, yes, you're mine. So fucking good, baby."

The room spun, and he pushed in deep, and stayed there, filling his girl up to the brim with his seed, while he buried his face in her neck. He had the foresight to switch off the butterfly still clipped to her before he collapsed on top of her. They fought for breath together, her heartbeat a thundering presence under his ear, as he used her tits for a cushion, and willed his legs to move. When he could draw even breaths into his lungs, he lifted off his girl to find her still trembling in aftershocks. Flushed and breathless, she looked utterly done in. Tender protectiveness welled up inside him, and he brushed his lips across hers while murmuring to her.

"There, now, baby girl. Let's get you out of all this, shall we?"

A needy whimper was his only response, and her wince as he removed the butterfly tore at his soul.

"I know, sweetheart. I was hard on you, forgive me." He proceeded to unwrap her ropes one by one, and by the time he was done, and massaged her arms to get the circulation going, she seemed more with it. The caveman in him loved seeing the marks left behind on her skin. He traced the harness marks on her rack with his fingertips, and Lissa's breathing sped up again.

"Daddy?" Her whisper brought his attention off her breasts, and when he looked at her, tears were shimmering in her expressive eyes.

"Welcome back, sweetheart." He cupped her face in his hands and rested his forehead on hers.

"Did I do okay?" The hesitant question tore at his heartstrings, and, pulling back a little, he smiled down on her.

"More than okay, my love." Her full lips trembled in a smile, and he kissed away the tear running down her cheek. An action which made her cry harder and cursing under his breath, Gabe pulled her onto his lap and into a clearly much needed hug.

"I'm sorry, I … I don't know what's wrong with

me." Lissa clung to him as she uttered those heart-wrenching words, and Gabe held her tighter.

"Shush, my love, it's okay. I know. It will pass. Just let me hold you for a while. Cry if you need to, it's okay. I've got you."

How long Gabe sat holding his precious bundle of curves on his lap, while whispering nonsense into her hair, he couldn't say, but, eventually, she calmed down and the stranglehold she had on his biceps lessened. He was half expecting to see crescent shaped gouges in his skin when he slowly extricated himself out of her grasp.

Reaching across to the nightstand he grabbed the glass of water and lifted it up to Lissa's lips.

"Here, slow sips now, mind you. I don't want you to be sick."

Lissa eagerly complied, and when she'd drained most of the glass she sagged back against him, while her baby blues focused on him. Too wide and innocent, those azure orbs drew him in and almost made him utter the words burning a hole in in his throat.

She was too fragile to hear them now, and besides, he was a goddamn sentimental old fool for even thinking them. This … this dam of emotions which threatened to burst forth, he hadn't counted on. Then again, perhaps he shouldn't be surprised. Lissa was far too good for the likes of him, and he should probably rot in hell for having her tied to him like this, both physically and emotionally, but so be it.

She *was* his now, and he wouldn't ever find the strength to let her go again.

He forced his lips into a semblance of a smile for her, even though his jaw ached with the force required to unclench it enough to enable him to do so. He must have managed it, however, because his precious girl smiled up at him. The way she looked at him…

Fuck.

As though he'd hung the sun and the moon for her. Gabe was all too painfully aware that he would no doubt try to do just that if she asked it of him. The need to look after her, to protect her at all costs was like a knife digging into his side.

"Better, little one?" He inwardly grimaced at the hoarse quality of his voice.

Lissa nodded and laid her head on his shoulder.

"Yes, just … why did I do that, Daddy?"

Gabe took a deep breath in and willed his cock to behave, because that fucker was hardening by the second, now that he knew she was okay. When she called him *Daddy* in that breathy, "come fuck me" voice… Well, fuck him from here to next week. He wanted her again.

"It's not unusual for a submissive to experience heightened emotions after a scene, Lissa. Like I said I was hard on you, and this was your first proper scene, so I'm not surprised." He took another deep breath and cupped her chin to make her look at him. "I'm sorry, if I was too hard, but you're so beautifully responsive, I…"

Words failed him at her smile in response. It lit up her whole being, made him feel ten feet tall, and the knot in his gut unraveled slowly.

"You weren't, Daddy. It was…" She chewed her bottom lip with her little white teeth, and the cutest frown appeared between her eyes as she mulled over what she was going to say.

"Jesus, girl, don't do that." Lissa jumped at his growled command, and he forced another smile on his lips while he proceeded in a gentler tone of voice. "And for the love of God, don't call me *Daddy* unless we're in a scene because it makes me want to do all sorts of other perverted things to you, and you're up not for another round yet." His cock jerked under her ass, and she gasped when she noticed. "Ignore that. He's like a fucking teenage boy around you, it seems."

Her expressive eyes widened in pure mischief, and the little minx wiggled her hips and giggled. *Giggled*!

Gabe growled his annoyance and swatted her ass just once. Not really hard enough to leave the faintest of marks, but he got his point across for sure.

"Enough, girl, behave."

Lissa sobered and murmured an apology. Her face fell when he picked her up and put her back down on the bed.

"Stay here." He dropped a kiss on her nose in an effort to reassure her. "I'm going to run you a bath, and there is chocolate dessert in the fridge with your name on it. Just the ticket for sore li'l subbies if you ask me." He winked at her to show he wasn't annoyed, and her little frame visibly relaxed.

"Chocolate does sound heavenly, Da... I mean Gabe." The most delightful blush spread across her cheeks when he got off the bed and her gaze dropped to his cock. Fully erect again, that fucker bobbed up to his navel, and Gabe's hands shook as he grabbed a pair of joggers out of the wardrobe and pulled them up and over his erection.

"How you can still blush is beyond me, girl, but I love to see it. Now stay and relax. I'll be back in a jiffy."

It took longer than he anticipated to run the bath, not least because he felt compelled to light several candles and forgo the harsh artificial light in that room to illuminate the space. By the time he'd brewed her some tea, set up the chocolate mousse on the side, and made it back to her side she was asleep.

Gabe stood and watched the rise and fall of her

chest for a little while before he picked her up. A moan came from his girl, and her arms lifted around his neck as she snuggled back into his neck.

"Come on, sweetheart, I know you want to sleep, but we need to clean you up."

"Not fair, was cozy."

Gabe swallowed a laugh and then stepped into the bath with her in his arms. There had been no time to take off his joggers and besides, he didn't trust himself with her all wet and naked in his arms. Far better to have a barrier between his cock and her sweet cunt.

Lissa giggled again when she realized. Giggles which turned into moans and sighs as he set to wash her down gently and then proceeded to feed her the mousse.

The water had run cool by the time he stepped out from behind her, pulled off the soggy joggers and wrapped a towel around his hips. The little minx watched him from under hooded eyes, a lazy, cat-that-got-the-cream, look on her face, and he shook his head at her sass.

"Behave, I'm going to change the sheets and then come and get you. *Don't* fall asleep."

A yawn was her response and a sleepy, "I'll try, Daddy."

Fuck him, he was never going to lose that damn boner at this rate.

****

Lissa smiled to herself as Gabe stalked away, muttering to himself. With her belly full and her body glowing in the aftermath of his care, she shut her eyes and let her mind wander. Who knew such utter bliss was possible? Not her, for sure. The care Gabe had showed in looking after her, the way he held her, looked at her with such emotion in his gaze… A girl could get used to that, crave it even. It was almost better than sex … almost.

Nothing compared to the orgasmic torture he'd subjected her to. Her pussy tingled in remembered pleasure and her sore bits clamped down on thin air, as memories of being utterly owned by him swamped her. Her breasts grew heavy, and her nipples peaked, aching for his touch. The urge to touch herself was almost irresistible, but he hadn't given her permission to do so. Somehow, she doubted he would look too kindly on that, and the need to please him, to see the approval in his dark features, and to be the cause of that private smile he reserved just for her, drove her hard.

The cynical side of her told her to get a grip. For all she knew he smiled at every woman he bedded like that. The mere thought of other women made her gut clench, and she sat up straighter, hands balled into fists. She recognized the acid churning in her belly for what it was. Jealousy, pure and simple. Red hot and all consuming, it took her breath away, and made her scowl at him when he reentered the bathroom.

"Whoa, there, girl, since when do you look at Daddy like that?"

The censure in his deep voice made her feel even more wretched, pulled the proverbial rug out from under her feet, and she sought refuge in anger. Anything to stop the images of him with a succession of women bombarding her brain.

"How many women have you had?"

Gabe blinked as though surprised at that question, and her stomach churned anew when he widened his stance and crossed his arms over his chest. Only he could look utterly menacing like that when clad in nothing but a towel. A drop of water fell out of his still damp hair, and she followed the path of that drop as it made its way down over his hairy chest, danced along his six pack for a while and eventually disappeared into the towel.

"Jesus, girl, how can you ask me that while you're looking at me like that?"

The towel tented in front of her eyes, and Lissa's breaths grew choppier, as her body grew pliant and wet for him.

"Get out of the bath, baby."

He held his hand out for her to grasp. and when she took it, yanked her out of there and in front of him. He wrapped a large, warm, fluffy towel around her, before he pulled her into his frame and kissed her.

Not just any kiss either, but tender, yet demanding ownership of her mouth, which left her breathlessly clinging onto him for support. His hand fisted in her damp hair, and the sweet sting of pain only served to excite her further. Lord help her, she'd turned into raving nymphomaniac around him it seemed. By the time he released her mouth with an animalistic growl that reverberated through every fiber of her being, she was so ready to jump him again.

Not that Gabe let her, of course. He studied her instead, his face all harsh angles and dangerous intent, and she murmured her apology.

"I'm sorry. I don't know why I said that." Lissa dropped her gaze to his collarbone unable to stand the intensity of his gaze any longer.

Gabe sighed, and hand still wrapped in her hair guided her out of the bathroom and back to the bedroom.

"I should pummel your ass for this, girl, but I have a better punishment in mind for you." He released her and stepped away. "Drop the towel, girl, and get on the bed on all fours, butt up in the air, shoulders down."

It didn't even occur to Lissa to not comply with that demand because this was Gabe in stern Daddy mode, and heaven help her if she didn't want to please him. Craved this side of him and the freedom to be found in submission.

"Good girl." That grumbled praise made her smile into the fresh covers, and she held her breath as she heard him rummage around. The pop of a lid coming off made her stomach flip over in anticipation. The bed dipped, and then he was behind her, his body heat seeping into her, as he grasped her butt cheeks and squeezed hard. Her pussy clenched, and Gabe laughed.

"Such a naughty little wife I've got. You're so turned on my cock would slide right back in here wouldn't it?" He slipped one hand lower, through her wet folds, until he could slide two fingers knuckle deep into her channel.

Oversensitive muscles protested that move, even as the slight sting of pain made her embarrassingly wet. Gabe thrust those digits in and out of her pussy a few times. The wet noises should have been mortally embarrassing, but this was Gabe, her husband, her Daddy, and under his appreciative murmurs at her response there was no room for shame. Just red-hot arousal which made her pant in need and meant her hips took on a life of their own, seeking more of him. She pushed against his digits, and Gabe laughed.

"Yes, so very naughty. You'd let me fuck this sweet cunt again, wouldn't you, girl?"

"Yes, Daddy, please, please…"

Spirals of desire radiated out from his fingers in her cunt, and Lissa was so close, so damn close again, it wasn't even real.

"Yes, you want Daddy's cock again, don't you, girl? How about in here?"

He slipped what felt like one well lubed finger into her butthole, and Lissa gasped at the strange sensation. Something cold dribbled down between her ass cheeks and then there was more pressure as Gabe added another finger.

"Oh, God, I can't. I never … fuck."

Gabe pushed another finger inside that forbidden place, stretching her, and Lissa could barely breathe. That felt so wrong, yet so right at the same time.

"I was going to wait to claim this hole, but I think I'll fuck you right here and now. What do you say, my sweet? Will you let Daddy sink his big fat cock into that tiny hole?"

Gabe's voice dropped an octave taking on that deep, dark delicious growl which meant she had to obey him.

"Have you been a good girl and used those butt plugs I told you to?"

Lissa screwed her eyes shut and swallowed hard. She'd balked at the demand at the time, but curiosity had won out in the end. So, yeah, she'd dabbled.

A hard swat to her ass took her breath away, and she moaned the loss of his fingers in her butt.

"Answer your Daddy, girl. I need to know if you're ready for this. I don't want to hurt you."

The concern behind those grumbled words, his voice harsh with need, proved her undoing, and she somehow managed to get the words out of her parched throat.

"Yes, I did, but I only used the first two."

The kiss between her shoulder blades took her by surprise, and then his fingers were probing, stretching her to the brink of pain.

"I see, well we can work with that. I'll be careful, but I need to be in you."

He pushed in deeper, twisted his fingers, awakening untold nerve endings, and Lissa groaned.

"Please, green, Daddy, please, I need… Oh God, so full."

Speech became impossible as the pressure in her butt increased.

"Relax, baby, blow out, and push against me. That's it. That's so fucking it. Fuck."

Through the haze of pleasurable pain, Lissa smiled at the words delivered in staccato pants of air. To know she affected him like this was a heady aphrodisiac indeed. It made her determined to take any kind of pain for him, to do this for him, even if it killed her, even if she wouldn't be able to sit for a week without wincing.

In the end there was little pain, as he bottomed out inside of her, his harsh breaths in her neck testament to how much this turned him on, and then he started to move. Slowly at first, and then with ever increasing speed. Muscles stretched, nerves tingled, and Lissa flew headlong into an orgasm so intense she saw stars. Different from the ones she had before, yet no less intense, she shuddered and screamed, dimly aware of Gabe following her over that cliff into ecstasy. They collapsed together on the bed with Gabe rolling them onto their side, his cock still deeply lodged in her butt. Eventually it softened and slipped out of her. Lissa couldn't help her wince of pain, which brought Gabe's concerned face into her view.

"You're okay, baby?" he asked.

"Fine, I just … I never knew it was possible to come like that." Heat stained her cheeks, and Gabe's expression grew tender.

"Oh, sweetheart, anal orgasms are entirely possible if you know what you're doing. You, my sweet, are beautifully responsive." He kissed her, and Lissa sighed into his mouth.

"If you say so."

That response earned her a mock glare, before he got out of bed and padded away. She didn't have time to wonder what he was up to, before he was back, warm washcloth in hand and proceeded to clean her butt and thighs gently.

"There, that'll do," he said as he flung the washcloth on the floor and tucked her into his side, as he stretched out with her under the covers.

"Now, go to sleep, girl. I don't know about you, but I'm fucking knackered now."

Lissa grinned and snuggled into his chest.

"So, was I better than these other women you've had?"

Gabe's deep sigh made her hold her breath, especially as his muscles tensed. He didn't grow angry though, as she thought he might, just blew out a breath and scrubbed a hand over his face.

"Girl, I'm no saint. You know that. Yes, there has been more pussy in my life than I can count, but they didn't mean anything. None of them were my *wife*."

The emphasis he put on that one word gave her a warm glow inside, and she smiled into his chest as she twirled her fingers around his chest hair and tugged.

"Watch it, girl."

Lissa pushed herself up slightly to be able to see his expression, and everything inside her just melted at the tenderness in his gaze. Oh, sweet Jesus, *this* Gabe she could so easily fall in love with. Maybe she already had?

"So, is that your cock-eyed way of saying I'm different?" she asked.

"Of course, you're fucking different, woman. Those others were just holes to fill."

She flinched at the rude words, and Gabe kissed her nose.

"Forgive me, you know what I mean. Why all these questions, babe?"

Lissa swallowed past the sudden lump in her

throat and forced herself to ask the next question.

"I just wanted to know. What about my mum?" She couldn't bring herself to look at him, and she hurried on lest she run out of courage. "I mean, I heard Papa say he took her away from you so…"

"Your father is a cock-sucking asshole who never deserved your mother, Lissa, and no. She was different, or she would have been. I never fucked your mother, babe. We were friends, and I loved her like a sister, that's all. Jesus, girl, do you honestly think I could be here with you like this, if we'd ever been an item?" He wrapped his hand back in her hair, forcing her gaze up, and she could read the sincerity in his eyes. "I might be a monster, but even I'm not such a cold-hearted bastard."

Lissa gasped and reached out to run her fingers through his beard.

"I don't think you're a monster, Gabe."

He blinked once, and then smiled.

"Ah, you don't know me that well yet, my sweet."

He released his hold on her, and Lissa snuggled back down into his side. She wanted to deny that notion, but she was all too painfully aware that he was right. They'd spent little time together so far, and what there had been of it had been emotionally charged to say the least. Maybe that's all this was and the ache in her chest had nothing to do with her having fallen in love with her husband after all. Silence fell between them, and eventually his even breaths told her he must be asleep. It took her a hell of a lot longer, for sure.

Chapter Eleven

Lissa woke up with a smile on her face, stretched and winced. Lordy, everything down there was tender this morning. Still, definitely the good kind of aching. She moved over to Gabe's side of the bed, only to find it empty. She rolled her eyes at the immediate wave of disappointment that assaulted her.

Jeez, she had it bad, and of course, he wouldn't be there. The hum of the engines and the gentle rocking movements of the boat meant someone had to be steering it. As they were the only two people on the yacht, logic dictated Gabe must have gotten up at the crack of dawn to move them on. Where that man got his energy from was beyond her.

She turned a little more to avoid the sun shining right in through the little balcony attached the bedroom and frowned. Then again, what time was it exactly? She sat up properly and spotted Gabe's note propped up next to a travel mug on the nightstand. A big bold arrow pointed upwards with two words.

Drink this!

Her heart skipped a few beats when she picked up the mug to reveal another note. Having popped open the lid, she inhaled deeply as the wonderful aroma of coffee filled her nostrils. She then took a sip and read that note.

Morning, sweetheart. Didn't want to wake you. Once you've had this coffee, and I can be sure that you won't kill me, come and find me.

G x

PS: If you come above deck wear a life vest.

She grinned to herself as she drank up and traced that one kiss left behind on the paper. Such a small thing to do, yet it meant the world to her.

Having taken care of the morning necessities in

the bathroom—the run-down candles made her smile widen—she pulled on some leggings and a t-shirt, twisted her long hair up into a messy bun, and went in search of her husband. As she thought he was at the wheel, and the sight of him stalled her breath anew.

With the wind blowing through his hair, and clad in a long-sleeved shirt and jeans, he looked much younger than his age. Were it not for the gray streaks in his hair and beard, he could have passed for someone in his late thirties. Not that his age mattered to her. Other folks might think he was old enough to be her father, and technically he was, but so what?

She loved him.

Oh my God, I do love him.

Far from sending her into a panic attack, that knowledge settled around her like a comforting blanket. Those large hands of his, handling the wooden wheel with expert ease might be used to kill people, but they'd given her nothing but pleasure. *So* much pleasure, that she grew wet just remembering it, and she squeezed her thighs together to relieve the sweet ache in her pussy. A look at the clock on the wall gave her an answer to her earlier question. It was almost lunchtime, and her stomach rumbled loudly. The view out of the portholes showed nothing but a wide expanse of sea, and another giggle bubbled up inside her.

This was just so exciting. Just the two of them sailing away. Not for one moment did she feel unsafe. Gabe clearly knew what he was doing, and this enforced proximity meant they could truly get to know each other. Starting with some food.

A rummage through the fridge unearthed bacon, mushrooms, and eggs, the perfect ingredients for the one thing Lissa could make to perfection. She set to work humming to herself, so engrossed in her task that she didn't notice the yacht wasn't moving anymore until Gabe's large hands landed on her shoulders.

She jumped, almost flinging the omelets onto the floor rather than their waiting plates, and Gabe's low laughter washed over her.

"Easy there, baby girl. That actually looks delicious, and I'm starving."

He nuzzled into her neck, and Lissa shut her eyes and simply enjoyed this moment of tenderness between them. It was over all too soon, as he stepped away and, grabbing the plates, put them down on the table for her.

When she joined him, he grinned at her and tucked into his omelet with a groan of delight, which gave her the most ridiculous happy glow inside.

To mask her reaction to him, she picked up her cutlery and started eating.

A comfortable silence fell between them until Gabe pushed his plate away, patted his stomach, and fixed her with a stern look, that made her stomach flip in anticipation. She knew *that* look, and she squirmed on her chair.

"I thought you said you couldn't cook, baby girl?"

"I, well, this is just an omelet, hardly cooking, Daddy." Her whispered reply made his eyes heat in lust and some other, much deeper emotion that meant she grew wet for him all over again. He inhaled sharply and crossed his arms over his chest. The action made his biceps bunch under the fabric of his shirt, and Lissa barely suppressed a sigh of contentment. This was her husband, and right now she couldn't have been happier if she tried. One eyebrow cocked up at her reaction, and when he spoke his voice took on that delicious edge. The one which meant she would do anything for him.

"Have I not told you not to call me that unless

we're in a scene, girl?"

Lissa tore her gaze away from his muscles and nodded.

"You did, Daddy."

A deep animalistic growl came from the man sitting opposite her, and she swallowed past the lump in her throat, as every feminine cell in her body sighed in submission.

"Topping from the bottom, girl?" he asked, and she shrugged.

"I don't even know what that means."

A sigh was his answer this time.

"Come here, girl."

He uncrossed his arms and patted his lap, and Lissa wasted no time taking him up on that invitation. She scooted onto his lap and snuggled in when his arms came around her in a tight embrace.

"Better?" The deep rumble of his voice vibrated through her, and Lissa snuggled in closer, closed her eyes, and whispered her answer.

"Much, thank you."

His cock hardened under her butt cheeks, and Lissa's breathing grew heavy as she wriggled against it. A sharp slap to her thigh stopped her.

"Behave yourself, minx. You're not up for a repeat performance and, besides, I want us to have crossed the Bay of Biscay by this afternoon. I've got a table booked at a charming little restaurant in La Rochelle."

That got her attention, and, pushing her hands against his big chest, she sat up more. The fact that he let her, smiled down at her, wasn't lost on her, as he kissed her nose.

"Like that idea, I see?"

Lissa swallowed her snarky comeback. Her

Daddy wouldn't appreciate that, and she sure didn't want to spoil the moment.

"I thought we'd just stay on the boat?"

Gabe ran a hand through his hair and studied her for the longest time before he spoke.

"That had been my original intention, but I find that I want to show off my wife. And I think you'd enjoy exploring, wouldn't you, sweetheart?"

The unexpected endearment made her grin like a loon, and Gabe's stern features relaxed into a smile.

"Thought so, plus I'm pretty sure you won't be trying to make a run for it the minute we're on dry land, right? Not that you'd get very far, if you tried, girl." His voice dropped on the last few words, took on that edge which would have terrified her before with that silent threat, but now she simply smiled and nodded.

"Why would I run?" she asked. "Maybe I quite like the perks that come with being married to you."

Gabe threw his head back and laughed before he wrapped his hand into her bun and tugged her head back. The sharp zing of pain settled straight in her clit, and she gasped.

"Are there now, girl?" He sobered and studied her with that grim intensity which never failed to get her wet. "And what would those be? Do enlighten me."

"You do own a mirror, right?" she countered, and Gabe's eyes narrowed.

"Meaning?" She jumped a little at that clipped reply, but she carried on with her train of thought. It seemed imperative to make him see. Not that she had the courage to confess her feelings—she wasn't entirely sure he would welcome such declarations—but she had to show him that she'd changed, and that she appreciated all the effort he'd put in on her behalf.

"Well, look at you. Any woman would be happy

to call you her husband, and then there is all this." She waved a hand around the yacht, and his gaze grew tender. "I mean, you didn't have to do any of this. Papa all but sold me to you." His hold on her hair grew painful and she winced.

"Andrini doesn't deserve that title, and I don't want you mentioning him again, are we clear?"

Lissa blinked back tears, and the hold on her hair lessened, turned into a soothing caress as he slid his fingers to her nape and kissed her. A mere brush of his lips across hers, as he murmured his apology.

"Forgive me, but I don't want to think about that fucker or his cohorts while I'm on my honeymoon and neither should you."

He pulled back slightly to study her, and Lissa offered him a wobbly smile.

"Neither do I. I'm just saying that you're so very different to how I thought you would be, and..." That eyebrow of his rose again, and Lissa faltered in her attempt to explain herself.

"I'm just gonna shut up now. Can we go back to you just holding me, please?"

Gabe's tender smile in answer to her hesitant question warmed her from the inside out, and she snuggled back into his embrace.

"What did you mean earlier by topping from the bottom?" she eventually asked when she couldn't stand the silence between them anymore.

"It means you're trying to get me do something you want. You'll find I'm not that easily manipulated, and if you try that again you'll earn yourself a trip across my knee and *not* the fun sort."

He nudged her chin up with one hand until she had no choice but to look at him. The swirling emotions in his dark gaze took her breath away, as she waited for him to continue speaking.

"However, you're new at this, so I'll let it pass for now. In future, if you need something from me, ask. I'm pretty good at reading body language, but while we're working out our dynamic, I'm bound to get things wrong, and I need you to tell me if I do." The concern behind those grumbled words made fresh tears fill her eyes, and Gabe swore softly.

"Jesus, girl, don't do that. I don't like it when you cry."

He released her chin and scrubbed a hand over his face as though he truly didn't know what to do with her reaction right now, and Lissa swiped the useless tears away.

"Not even if they're tears of happiness?"

A noncommittal grunt was his response, but he tugged her back into his chest and simply held her.

"This is nice," she said as she hugged him back and his chest shook in silent laughter. "I didn't like it when I woke up on my own."

Another sigh came from the broad chest she was snuggled up against, and he hugged her closer.

"I figured you wouldn't, but I had to get moving and didn't want to wake you. I did leave you a note, sweetheart."

There he went again with that simple endearment that made her heart leap for joy. She was such a sap, for him at least.

"I know, thank you." She sat up more to find him studying her again. When she smiled at him, his answering grin softened his harsh features, and it was her turn to sigh.

"As much as I'm enjoying this, we do need to get going if we want to make that reservation, so, you're good now?"

Lissa nodded and hopped off his lap.

"Yes, thank you for the hugs, Daddy."

"Anytime, baby girl."

With that, he turned and went back above deck, and Lissa made herself busy clearing up the lunch dishes. After a shower and having changed into a light summer dress in deference to the much warmer weather they were experiencing she joined him on deck with her life vest on, just in time to see him negotiate the old harbor of La Rochelle.

One they were on dry land, the beauty of the place took her breath away, as he pointed out landmarks and they soaked in the atmosphere together. From the cobbled streets of the old town to the bustling shops, the intimate restaurants they discovered and the magnificent structure that was the Saint Nicholas Tower, doing the tourist thing with Gabe was fun and exciting.

If she found it odd that he avoided the casino, she kept her opinions to herself. Clearly Gabe wanted to disassociate himself from his usual surroundings back home in London as much he could, and that was just fine by her.

Their journey along the coast continued, as the days wore on, and with each new place they discovered, she felt closer to him. And then there were the delights to discover in the privacy of their yacht. Who knew submission could bring such innate piece? Far from it being demeaning, it was empowering, and as they settled into their dynamic, Lissa had never been happier, or more creative.

Reams and reams of paper were filled with her paintings, because the artist in her needed to capture all the sites. Seeing Gabe's approval of her skills also gave her a much-needed boost. All too soon their time was up, and they were heading back to Southampton.

The change in his demeanor the closer they came to England burst the bubble of happiness Lissa had been floating in. Something was clearly bothering him, but any attempts of getting him to talk about it, were rebuffed. Lissa sought refuge in her painting, as they moored one last time before returning home.

****

"Boss, we have a problem."

Gabe scowled at Stone's worried face as he fired up his computer for the first time since they left England behind. Back in the secluded cove they'd started their journey, all that separated them was short trip across the Channel this morning.

"Meaning?" He barked that question, and across the yacht Lissa jumped. He could just about see her engrossed in her painting. She scowled at the blue slash across the middle of her painting of the yacht, and Gabe sighed. He'd caused that, and it would take her hours to correct that mistake. Then again, if she was busy with that it might be a good thing all 'round.

When he'd woken up that morning, he watched her sleep for the longest time, conflicting emotions making his chest feel tight. The faint rope marks left behind on her skin made his inner caveman strut. He loved leaving his mark on her body, and he loved her reaction to his visible reminders of his possession of her even more.

As he traced the fading half-moon of a bite mark on her left breast, he tensed. Lord knew what awaited them back in England. Would his precious girl still feel the same way about their dynamic when it came under society's scrutiny?

He wanted nothing more than to stay on the yacht with her. To hell with business and his responsibilities back home. Seeing Lissa come out of her shell and blossom into the radiant, happy young woman she deserved to be had been a joy to witness. She thrived under his dominance, and it was his pleasure to meet her needs by being her *Daddy*. Her gift of submission served to ground him, to satisfy his need to care for and protect her like a husband should. Truth be told, he couldn't fool himself any longer. He had fallen head over heels in love with her. He'd found the perfect counter foil for his darker needs and desires, and the thought of losing her burned a hole in his gut.

If she ever found out how much she meant to him, she would have the perfect ammunition to bring him to his knees. Not that he truly believed she would do that. Unless his senses were completely off, his baby girl needed him as much he needed her, and the way she looked at him when she didn't think he was noticing soothed his damaged soul.

Silly girl. As though he ever did *not* notice her. Her very scent was imprinted in his psyche, which should probably worry him a great deal. To love someone this much made you vulnerable. The one thing he could not afford himself to be, yet he couldn't bring himself to care about that either. Hence, he hadn't been in touch with Stone until now.

"What sort of problem?" He tore his gaze away from Lissa, not before sending her a reassuring smile when she glanced across, clearly concerned by his earlier snarl at his laptop. She wouldn't be able to see who he was talking to, but his wife wasn't stupid.

"There's a warrant out for your arrest, boss."

Gabe gave a short laugh and scrubbed a hand over his face.

"Is that all? What for this time?"

Stone didn't share in his amusement, and the light scent which signaled Lissa drawing nearer ensured his amusement fled.

"Hi, Lissa, great to see you." Stone fixed his attention behind Gabe, and sure enough, a hesitant Lissandra appeared on the screen behind him.

"Sorry, I don't mean to interrupt, but I figured if there's a problem, I should know it, too." Her voice, while wobbly, carried that grim determination Gabe had come to know well.

"Nothing the boss and I can't handle, right, Gabe?" Stone's attempt of reassurance fell flat, as Gabe knew it would. Lissa frowned at his second in command, crossed her arms under her chest, and he swallowed a groan. Even when covered in her painting apron, she looked far too damn sexy, and despite the imminent threat he hardened in his pants. A trace of blue paint marred her cheekbone as though she'd swiped her fingers along it, and he wanted nothing more to clean that up for her, before he tied her up and took her out of her head for bit.

He did neither, all too aware that she had a right to know what was awaiting them at home. Plus, he could sense her worry positively pouring off her little frame, and he needed to make that better for her. With that thought uppermost in his mind he pushed the chair back from the desk and patted his lap in an unspoken invitation.

The speed with which Lissa complied and snuggled into his hold lessened that building knot of fury in his guts.

Stone seemed to have other ideas, if the way his eyes narrowed were any indication.

"Erm, boss? Should we be having this conversation in front of … erm…"

"My wife? Yes, we should, as I'm pretty sure this will concern her, too, right?"

Stone's sigh spoke volumes, and Lissa tensed in his arms. He dropped a kiss on the top of her head, which caused Stone's eyes to widen.

"Right, well, it does, but I figured you didn't want to—"

"Spit it out already, Stone."

Gabe's snarl made Lissa jump, and he hugged her a little tighter, while nuzzling into her neck. Her automatic head tilt to give him better access made him smile despite the situation, and he indulged himself by nibbling on her earlobe.

Her breathing sped up, and her little moan in response made him even harder. If only he could say *fuck all this shit* and simply lose himself in the delights of her body, but that wasn't an option anymore and wouldn't be until they'd sorted this out.

"Boss, I'm sorry, this … pay attention, will you?"

Lissa tensed anew, and Gabe swore softly as he fixed his attention on his second in command.

"You've got my attention, so spit it out already. What are they trying to pin on me this time?"

Stone shook his head, threw a worried glance at Lissa, and grumbled his answer.

"Kidnap, rape, attempted murder, to name but a few, boss."

Lissa's horrified gasp rang in his ears, and Gabe took a few deep breaths into calm his rioting emotions.

"Right."

Lissa struggled in his arms, and he reluctantly released his hold on her. The fact that she didn't immediately jump off his lap, utterly horrified, soothed his churning gut a little.

"We've got Parkinson on it, of course, but there isn't much he can do at present. They've got an impressive number of witnesses together to make their case."

Gabe gave another short laugh. It was that or pace the room, and with his baby girl still sitting on his lap, seemingly frozen in shock, he couldn't do the latter.

"What witnesses?" He ground the question out through gritted teeth, while he drew circles over his baby girl's tense back.

"Andrini, for one."

"Papa?" Lissa's response was barely a whisper, but both men heard it anyway. Stone's expression softened as he fixed his gaze on Lissa.

"Yeah, I'm sorry, he's one of the chief witnesses, Lissa. He claims the boss abducted you and attempted to kill Andrini while the fucker, sorry, Lissa, was trying to protect his only daughter. Blasted ass sure can lay it on thick."

"Fuck this shit." Lissa leaned into Gabe when he grunted that answer, and the savage beast inside him calmed down instantly.

"But that's not true. All they have to do is ask me. I'll put them straight, right, Daddy?"

Stone blinked once and shook his head at Gabe.

"Not as easy as that, Lissa. There's other witnesses, too. Most of them Parkinson can hang, but there's the vicar who married you." That made Lissa sit up and pull away from Gabe, and he swallowed another curse.

"Fucking wanker wants more money, is that it?" Gabe asked.

"Reckon he got more, a hell of a lot more, or Ollivanti put the screws on him. You were right before, boss." Stone paused as though he wasn't sure how much to say in front of Lissa, and at Gabe's silent nod continued with a sigh. "Ollivanti and Andrini are thick as thieves. There's a number of Ollivanti girls who've come forward to claim you've raped them, boss."

Another one of those utterly horrifying gasps from Lissa, which made him want to take her far away from all this crap. She didn't deserve to be associated with the dark side of his business. The allegations weren't true, but would she believe them?

"It's all a pack of lies, Lissa. The boss wouldn't touch Ollivanti pussy with a barge bole, let alone rape anyone."

Lissa didn't respond other than to hang her head. Her hair hid her expression from both men, and Gabe's stomach churned at her silence. He would be left with a fucking ulcer at this rate.

"Lissa, you know that, right?" Stone's voice grew more insistent, and he scrubbed a hand over his shaved head, clearly at a loss as to what to make of her lack of response. Gabe shook his head at him, and Stone frowned.

"Anyway, Parkinson will make mincemeat of them, but there's someone else whose statement might make a difference."

If that was possible Lissa tensed even more, and Gabe's chest tightened to such a degree it hurt to breathe. He was going to lose her, he just knew he would, because she wasn't handling this well. Not that he'd expected her to jump to his immediate defense, but this stillness, the waves of shocked terror which he sensed coming from her, they made breathing difficult.

"Do enlighten me, Stone." Gabe grimaced at the hoarse quality of his voice.

"I'm sorry, boss, it's Ange."

Gabe shut his eyes and murmured his reply.

"Fuck."

Chapter Twelve

"Who the fuck is Ange?"

Lissa couldn't help her angry shout any more than she could have stopped herself from jumping off Gabe's lap as the sharp, immediate, all-consuming poker of jealousy pierced her heart like a poisonous arrow.

"She's nobody, Lissa." Over the ringing in her ears she heard Stone's attempt to smooth things over, but she didn't believe a word of it. Gabe's response to that woman's name had been too immediate for her to be nobody.

"I wasn't born yesterday, Stone. You wouldn't have mentioned her if she wasn't important. If she was a nobody then, surely, Gabe's solicitor could disarm her easily as those other girls who've come forward." Hands on hips, she turned her back on Stone's worried face and sought reassurance from her husband. Not that she found any.

Instead of the reassuring smile she'd hoped to see on her *Daddy's* face, she looked into the closed off expression of Gabe the killer. His usually so warm eyes had turned to cold, expressionless mirrors that wouldn't let her in. His sensuous mouth was an ugly sneer, and hands which had given her such pleasure curled around the edge of his desk in a white knuckled grip so hard that the wood creaked under his fingers.

She ought to have been terrified. The old her would have been, but this Lissa simply grew angrier herself when Gabe wouldn't answer her, ignored her question completely and fixed his attention on Stone instead.

"Thanks for the heads-up, Stone. I'll cast off now, and we'll be with you soon. Let the fuckers try to take over. It won't work."

"Usual drill, boss?" Stone asked, and Gabe nodded.

"Kill them all if you have to. But Andrini, Ollivanti, and that bitch are *mine*."

Lissa gasped and stepped away from him as Gabe ended the call and slammed the laptop shut with so much force, he must have surely cracked the screen.

"Gabe, what do you—"

"Nothing." He interrupted her, and Lissa took a few steps back when he rose to his full height and glared down on her. Gone was the tender, passionate man she'd come to love over the last three weeks and in his stead stood a stranger. *This* Gabe she had no doubt could kill her at a moment's notice, and yet, strangely she still wasn't afraid of him. He wouldn't harm her. How she could be so sure of that she didn't know, and maybe it was just wishful thinking on her part. The deeply in love with this man part, who wanted/needed to believe he was better than *this*, clung on to that belief with a need that smacked of desperation. Because, if she didn't hold onto that, then what was she left with other then the fact that she'd married a monster?

"Please, Daddy, talk—"

His furious growl stopped her, and she swallowed hard when he advanced on her. Eyes blazing in so much cold fury it made her shiver, but she nudged her chin up, determined to hold his gaze, to not give in to the rising panic threatening to engulf her.

How was it even possible to still need him this much? She wanted nothing more than for her *Daddy* to take her in his arms and to tell her that everything would be all right.

"I told you not to call me that, girl. Especially not now." He stopped mere inches away from her. Hands either side of her face he crowded her against the wall.

Rather than let herself be intimidated by his sheer presence, Lissa rose on her tip toes and ran her hands up his chest and over his bunched biceps. The muscles tightened under her fingertips, and Gabe swore under his breath.

"Who is Ange?" she asked.

Gabe shook his head and stepped away from her. The physical distance from him hurt, not least because he ignored her, got on deck and fired up the engine of the yacht. It rumbled to life under her feet, and Lissa blinked away tears. The sensible thing would have been to take his dismissal, and to not probe the sleeping monster, but Lissa had never been sensible.

Sidestepping the life vests, she followed him onto the deck and held on for dear life as he turned the yacht at a steep angle to leave the cove. Gabe glared at her, but that was it. A fact which hurt far more than his previous actions and told him his state of mind clearer than anything else. He always made such a big deal about her need for a life vest, normally, when she was above deck when the yacht was on the move, that his lack of response stung.

Ignoring the unease churning her guts, Lissa stepped up behind him, when the boat straightened, wrapped her arms around his torso, and clung.

"Talk to me, please. I'm not leaving until you do." His chest heaved under his harsh breaths, but he didn't respond. He didn't shake her off either, and Lissa took comfort in that, as she simply held the man she loved. Never in all of her life would she believe that he raped anyone, and whoever that Ange was, whatever her motive was, she would scratch the bitch's eyes out if she ever met her.

How much time passed, with her holding onto him, the silence heavy and oppressive between them, she would never know, but eventually Gabe spoke.

"You should go back down. You'll freeze up here."

Sure enough, the unpredictable English Channel lived up to its name. Clouds had gathered above, and the first spits of rain hit her skin like icy needles, and still she clung to his broad back. Fear for their future cemented her feet to the deck.

"I'm not going anywhere until you tell me who she is."

"Jesus, girl, fine." Gabe swung around with an exasperated huff, disengaging her arms from him at the same time. His dark eyes lit up in concern for her one precious moment, before the mask came back down. "She's a bit of pussy I used to fuck from time to time."

Lissa blinked at the harsh words. Gabe reached out to her with the hand not on the wheel and cupped her face briefly. A flash of regret crossed his features, so brief she'd have missed it had she blinked, and he withdrew his hand. She instantly missed the contact and wrapped her arms around herself in a vain attempt to stop the shivers wrecking her body.

"She's also one of my working girls, so mud sticks, as they say." He let that statement sit between them and turned his back on her.

"Did you—" His deep growl stopped her from probing further while his reply turned her blood to ice.

"If you seriously have to ask me if I raped that bitch then … fuck." He ran a hand through his hair and completely closed himself off. She could almost see the bricks going up around him, and it broke her heart all over again.

"I wasn't going to ask that. It's just that—"

"Spare me, girl. Go and tidy yourself up. You're a fucking mess. No need to give the assholes more ammunition to hang me with."

The words stung, like he no doubt meant them to, and gathering the last few shreds of her leftover dignity to herself she fled below deck. Fine, if he wanted to be like that, then let him.

See if I care.

The problem, of course, was that she *did* care far too much, and as Southampton eventually came into view and with it their welcoming committee of armed police, her composure fled completely. No sooner had they docked, they were raided, as though they'd known exactly when they were expected. It was like a scene from a freaking Bond movie and seeing the man she loved spread eagle on the floor, being cuffed while several armed coppers trained their rifles on him was surreal in the extreme. Someone was shouting, and she didn't realize at first that those sounds were coming from her, until they yanked Gabe to his feet and he came back into view.

He headbutted one of the coppers, kicked the other, and then he was in front of her for one precious moment, resting his forehead on hers, before unseen hands yanked him away from her.

"It's gonna be okay, baby girl."

The grumbled promise grounded her like nothing else could, as she watched him being led away. He nodded to someone in the gathering crowd, and Lissa's gaze briefly connected with Stone's. She easily recognized a few others of Gabe's men in the crowd, which helped to make her feel marginally better, as she, too, was led away, surrounded by police officers. It was good to know they were around even if in the background and she had to trust that Gabe had some sort of plan to get them all out of this mess.

Surely?

"Mind your head, Miss Andrini."

The sympathetic smile on the WPC's face who slid in the back of the cop car with her grated on Lissa's last nerve. Not least because she kept looking at the all too visible fingerprint marks on her forearms. Faint remnants of Gabe's rope work on her wrists also remained, and she wished she'd had the foresight to grab a cardigan before all hell broke loose. Then again, why should she cover up? She had nothing to be ashamed of. These marks were consensual, for fuck's sake, and they still had the power to turn her heart over in longing for her husband.

"That's not my name. It's Mrs. Henshaw, and I demand to know what this is all about. Why have you arrested my husband?"

The woman's smile faltered, growing thoughtful while the two coppers in the front of the car gave a short laugh.

"You want the whole list? About time we could pin something on him."

Lissa glared at the backs of their heads.

"He hasn't done anything wrong."

Another short laugh and her gaze briefly connected with the ice blue gaze of the uniformed cop driving, while his plain clothed counterpart swiveled around in the chair to look at her. Amber eyes assessed her, and his bushy brows drew together in a frown.

"Miss Andrini—"

"For fuck's sake, the name is Mrs. Henshaw, and you can all stop looking at me as though I'm some fucking victim. I'm not, and whatever lies my father fed you, it's just that. *Lies*. You can't believe a word that man says." She ran out of steam as the reality of her situation sank in and slumped in her seat. "I want Daddy."

She hadn't been aware she uttered those words out loud, until the woman cop reached across and patted her arm.

"It's okay, this has all been a bit of a shock. We'll just need to take your statement at the station, take some DNA evidence of your injuries, and then you can be reunited with your father."

An ice-cold hand grasped hold of Lissa' heart, and she shook the other woman's hand of.

"No, you don't understand. I don't want *him*."

The woman blinked once, and Lissa screwed her nose up in disgust.

"As far as I'm concerned Andrini lost the right to call himself my father years ago. I never should have … I want my Da…" She slammed her mouth shut to stop herself from saying it again and blinked away tears.

They would never understand. She wasn't entirely sure she understood it all herself yet, so it would probably be better to keep her mouth shut, lest she inadvertently say something to incriminate Gabe further.

At least that's how it worked on crime shows, right?

"Yes?"

Lissa ignored the woman's gentle probing and shook her head.

"No comment."

It was something she reiterated ad nauseum once they were at the station. She had absolutely no intention to tell these people anything.

The brief meeting, she had with Gabe's solicitor, Parkinson, was equally as infuriating.

His simple instructions were not to say anything at all. That didn't work for her either. How was she supposed to refute this silly notion that Gabe had kidnapped her if she didn't say anything?

"That's insane. I've got to tell them the truth. That Andrini sold me to him and…"

Her ire left her at the gray-haired man's sigh, and she fell silent.

"Surely you can see how that would look? The less you say the better. It truly is, trust me. Also, and it pains me to remind you of this, but you did sign an NDA."

"How dare you!"

Lissa erupted into a furious snarl.

"As if I ever would sell him out like that regardless of a stupid piece of paper. Besides, hasn't stopped that Ange from singing like a fucking canary, has it?"

Parkinson blinked repeatedly and taking his spectacles off his long nose he made a big show of cleaning the perfectly spotless lenses with his handkerchief, until Lissa wanted to scream at him to look at her.

"Damn it, answer me."

Parkinson replaced his spectacles with exaggerated care and sighed.

"He made her sign one of those, right?" Lissa asked, not at all sure she actually wanted to know the answer to that question.

"She's an employee, so yes, she did. It's part and parcel of the employment contract."

"I see." Lissa frowned, not sure she really saw anything at all, but now was her chance to get some answers.

"Where exactly did she work?"

Parkinson regarded her steadily over the rim of his glasses, and just when she thought he wouldn't answer her he sighed.

"At the casino. She's been there for years in the

strip club section. By all accounts she's very good at it, 'cause she's still there. Most girls don't last long once they slide down the wrong end of thirty." He grimaced as though disgusted by his own words, and not for the first time Lissa had to wonder why this straitlaced, conservative man was Gabe's solicitor. Then again, he was one of the best, if not *the* best, so that had to be why.

"Nothing to do with my *husband* having a relationship with her, then?"

Why she felt the need to stress her own status in Gabe's life like that she would never know, but it got through to Parkinson all right. A faint blush stole across his cheekbones, and the tips of his ears turned pink in his all too obvious discomfort.

Lissa would have found it quite amusing to see in other circumstances. Now she just wanted answers and rolled her eyes at the man.

"With all due respect, Mrs. Henshaw, I've never known your husband to hold down a relationship with any woman, not until you came along that is." That simple statement sat in the room, and Lissa mentally hugged the words to herself like a reassuring blanket. "Gabe has always been too focused on the business side of things, and from what I can understand Ange was nothing more than one of several *ladies* used for mutual … erm, pleasure … shall we say." His ears positively glowed now, and Lissa shook her head in wry amusement.

"He just used them for sex, that's what you're trying to say, right?"

Unbidden, Gabe's face swam into the forefront of her mind when they'd been discussing his previous partners on the yacht, and a wave of longing so intense it took her breath away hit her. She wanted him back, dammit. Wanted those carefree times on their honeymoon when the rest of this fucked up world didn't intrude on their relationship.

"Well, yes, erm … quite. That is."

Lissa took pity on the man and waved a hand at him to stop him.

"It's okay, I get the picture. What I don't understand is why she would suddenly turn on him and bite the hand that feeds her. It doesn't make sense."

Parkinson cleared his throat and consulted the thick file in his hand.

"Well, as to that, I suspect it's a simple matter of needing the money. She knows her days at the casino are numbered, and by all accounts she didn't take the news of Gabe's marriage very well. I have several statements from fellow employees here that she flew into something of a rage. Plus, further investigations show her to be knee deep in debt. Rather ironic really, because I'm sure she could have come to Gabe for a loan, if she was in financial trouble. She'd have had to earn it back of course, but—"

"On her back?" Lissa interrupted the man, and he frowned at her.

"I wouldn't be privy to the particulars of such a transaction, but I can assure you, Mrs. Henshaw, that it is not your husband's make up to force women into prostitution. They always have a choice as to what employment they take up with him in any of his various *establishments*."

Lissa suppressed a completely inappropriate giggle at that word. One way to call the brothels he ran, she supposed. While she'd known Gabe was no angel, the true nature of his vast criminal undertaking hadn't been apparent to her until the detective in charge of her case had thrown picture after picture a her in an effort to get her to talk to him. To incriminate her husband to admit that he'd kidnapped and abused her. Well, he could damn well sing for it. At least the latter part wasn't true.

"I know that. I might be naïve but I'm not stupid, and I'm fully aware of the caliber of the man I married, Parkinson. What I want to know is what you're going to do to get Gabe out of this mess, and what I can do to help."

Which had resulted in her keeping mum and enduring the myriad of tests, physical exams and psychological assessment they were throwing at her.

The latter of which resulted in her waiting in this room for a shrink to come and assess her.

"You'll like Ms. Booker," Parkinson had said. "Please be honest with her. It will help Gabe's case."

Lissa highly doubted that, as the door finally opened to reveal a petite, stunningly beautiful brunette with an hourglass figure to die for. Subtle, expensive perfume permeated Lissa's senses, as Rhonda Booker smiled at her and took a seat opposite Lissa.

"Lissa, you don't mind if I call you that, do you?" She held out her hand for Lissa to shake in a strong grip that made her palm tingle.

"No, I guess not. As long as you don't call me Miss Andrini we're good."

Rhonda laughed and winked at her.

"Ah yes, I heard about your dislike to your father. We'll get to that in a minute."

Lissa crossed her arms under her chest and glared at the other woman.

"Oh, we will, will you. It's not my name anymore. I'm Da... I mean Gabe's." She inwardly winced at that almost slip of the tongue and the considering look Rhonda shot her way from under one perfectly arched, raised eyebrow made her squirm on her seat.

Just like Daddy looks when he's cross with me.

That thought brought heat to her cheeks and meant she had to drop her gaze, all too aware of the silent dominance this woman exuded without even trying.

"Much better, girl, and please lose the antagonistic stance. No doubt what you need is a trip over your Dom's knee to ground you right now, but I'm here in a professional capacity and thus can't fulfill that need. Besides, knowing Gabe Henshaw he wouldn't appreciate my interference."

That brought Lissa's head up, and the amused concern she read in the woman's warm brown eyes soothed some of her internal anguish.

"You know Gabe?" she asked.

Rhonda flicked a strand of her long hair over her shoulder and smiled.

"By reputation mostly, though I've seen him in action at the club my boy and I frequent on occasion, when he's on dungeon duty. He's a good Dom. That's all I need to know for the purposes of this assessment. What he gets up to professionally is not for me to judge."

"Right." Lissa wasn't quite sure what to make of that statement. "He goes to a club?" she asked.

Rhonda smiled, reached across the table and patted her hand.

"If it helps, we haven't seen him there in months, and certainly not since you appeared you on the scene, so that should tell you something, Lissa. Now, enlighten me as to the nature of your D/s relationship with him, so that we can put an end to this silly downtrodden, abused victim stuff the police are trying to pin on you, shall we?"

Lissa swallowed hard and nodded.

"How can you be so sure I'm not that?" she asked in return. Rhonda's eyes narrowed, and a shiver went down Lissa's spine.

"Are you?"

"No, of course not. It's just, you don't know me at all and..." She stopped speaking as Rhonda's other eyebrow shot up.

Oh dear. She knew that look only too well, and her submissive side cringed.

"I'm sure your Dom told you not to make assumptions and to verbalize your feelings, so speak. I will draw my own conclusions from what you share with me, once I got to know you a little better. How's that?"

Lissa nodded and did the only thing she could do. She talked. It felt unbelievably good to get everything off her chest. To know that the other woman *got* it. That she listened to her without judgment and finally that all these feelings and desires were indeed normal. That there were other women like her in a Daddy/little girl dynamic, which took on as many different forms as there were unique couples in this world. That her need to be cosseted and cuddled and yes, spanked to feel right in herself, didn't mean that there was something wrong with her, and as long as everything they did was consensual and brought her pleasure, that's all that mattered.

"It was lovely to meet you, Lissa. Thank you for being so open with me." Rhonda held out her hand again as they parted company, and Lissa barely resisted the urge to hug the woman. "Good luck with everything, my dear. Parkinson is one of the best, and he's got my Jack on his legal team, too. I'm sure as I can be that they will get your Dom out of this nonsense kidnap charge. As for the other, we both know that's baloney. Henshaw is many things, but a rapist is not one of them."

With that she left with a few clicks of her Louboutins, and Lissa was on her own. Eventually, she was indeed released into the bright glare of a midday sun, with Parkinson by her side. No sooner had they negotiated the last step down from the police station when a pop sounded. Parkinson clutched his shoulder, where a sickening, red stain spread. A car screeched to a halt in front of them, and then the world went dark as something coarse and foul smelling was shoved over her head. Whatever it was, robbed her of her ability to see and think clearly as her mind grew fuzzy. She was dimly aware of the sound of shouting—was that Stone's furious voice she heard?—more rapid gunfire, and then the air knocked out of her lungs as she was thrown into the confined space of what felt like the boot of a car. Sure enough, there was the thud of the door being slammed shut and the squeal of tires, as her prison lurched from side to side. Lissa hit her head as she rolled into something cold and hard and then, mercifully, she couldn't feel anything anymore.

Chapter Thirteen

"What the fuck do you mean she's gone?" Gabe glared at Parkinson's senior partner, and the younger man swallowed hard. He didn't back down, however, but held Gabe's gaze. Were it not for the silent understanding in his amber eyes drawn together in concern, Gabe would have planted his fist in Jack Delaney's face. The old him might have well done so, regardless of the fact that he was still incarcerated and assaulting a member of his legal team would not exactly be helpful in getting him out of this hellhole.

Besides, it never helped to shoot the messenger, and with Parkinson laid up with a gunshot wound to his shoulder it would fall to this young pup to get him out of this fucking mess.

"I know it's a shambles, but they got to them seconds before your men arrived. I can only assume someone here talked to..." Delaney glanced up to the camera mounted in the corner of the room and frowned. The light was off, so it shouldn't be recording—Gabe was allowed these moments of privacy with his legal team—but he appreciated the man's caution. Ollivanti had his fingers in many pies, and he'd long suspected that the asshole had a mole in the police department.

"Let's just say, it's too much of a coincidence that she was nabbed like this."

"Fucking coppers ought to do their job properly instead of holding me in here on trumped up charges." Gabe, too, glared at the camera as he spoke, and Jack Delaney gave a humorless laugh.

"We're working on that, Mr. Henshaw. Bail has been set at a quarter of million pounds, and as soon as the funds have cleared, we can get you out of here. That was the original purpose for this meeting with you."

Gabe's churning gut settled somewhat at this unexpected news, and he took a proper look at Delaney. In his late thirties, he wasn't really a youngster, and he did have the reputation for being a shark. Clearly well-deserved as Parkinson alone would have never achieved that so easily.

"Just like that?" Gabe asked.

Delaney ran a hand over his stubbly jaw, and amusement lit his eyes this time.

"Well, let's just say with good old James out of the picture I could pull in some not exactly ethical resources. I figured you wouldn't mind if I brought in some extra help in the form of McLeod Security. They're not cheap, but they are the best. They have also accumulated quite a file on your competition, shall we say, so their intel is invaluable."

Gabe pushed his chair back on his legs and whistled through his teeth. He'd heard of them, of course. Crossed paths with some of their operatives on more than one occasion and had been suitably impressed by their professionalism.

"Didn't think they would want to come to my aid." He gave a self-deprecating smirk, and Delaney shrugged.

"Zane McLeod is an old buddy of mine, and, besides, they're not doing it for you, but for your wife. My fiancée Rhonda is the psychologist assigned to assess the accuracy of your wife's statement, shall we say. She took a liking to her, and Lissandra is the true victim in all this." He put his hand up in a conciliatory gesture when Gabe slammed his chair back on all fours and growled his annoyance. "Take it easy, Henshaw, I don't mean she's *your* victim, but she's clearly being used as a pawn, and that doesn't sit right with any of us. Plus, like I said, McLeod has a file a mile long on the people involved, so we can use their intel."

Gabe grunted his acknowledgement of this all too accurate assessment and swallowed down bile. He couldn't think of the implications behind her disappearance. If he did, if he allowed himself to imagine who might have their filthy hands on her right now … *fuck.*

I'm going to kill the whole fucking lot of them.

Jack, clearly sensing Gabe's mood, sighed. "I can imagine what you're plotting, but as your legal counsel I'm going to have to strongly advise against any violent course of action. It's one thing getting you out of here for trumped up kidnap and rape charges, but murder is another thing entirely."

Gabe smirked.

"Who says anything about murder, Delaney? Accidents happen, after all."

The younger man shook his head.

"I'll pretend I didn't hear that, and, to get back on topic, your man Stone is working with Zane directly and fully aware of the situation. They'll find her." He hesitated and glanced up at the camera again. Still no sign of any activity there, but, man, this guy was good. "You just hang tight for now, and don't do anything foolish in here."

Gabe had to laugh at that.

"Define foolish."

Delaney rolled his eyes and picked up his briefcase.

"I'll leave that up to your interpretation, Henshaw."

Gabe, too, stood and held out his hand for Delaney to shake.

"Thank you."

Surprise briefly registered in Delaney's eyes,

before he took Gabe's hand in a firm shake.

"Wait until you see my bill before you thank me."

Gabe laughed, genuinely amused this time, and Jack winced when he punched him in the shoulder.

"Right, I best get going. Want me to pass on anything to Parkinson?" he asked.

Gabe shook his head and released the man's hand.

"Just tell the old coot to get better, and I'm glad it's only a flesh wound."

Jack's eyes again lit up in surprise, and in truth Gabe surprised himself with the concern for his solicitor. Yeah, he'd known the guy for years, but they hadn't ever seen eye to eye. He used him because he was the best, and he needed the respectability Parkinson and Co. represented. What the hell was going in with that hollow feeling in his gut at the thought of the man getting hurt while in his employ? He was getting soft in his old age, dammit.

"I'll be sure to pass that on." One last searching glance from Jack Delaney later, he rapped on the door to be let out, and Gabe himself was led back to his cell. It left him plenty of time to plot his revenge on the fuckers involved, and by the time he was finally released on bail, he was baying for blood.

"Boss." Stone slid a thick file across to him, when Gabe got into the SUV and his second in command drove off. "That's all the intel we got from McLeod. Some interesting stuff in there regarding Ange. Looks like she's been double timing us for some time. No idea how we missed it, to be honest. Think we need an overhaul on our security procedures."

Gabe nodded and swallowed a growl. That bitch was the least of his concerns right now. She'd made her bed, and she could fucking lie in it.

"Figures, but nothing an *accidental* overdose won't take care of. Where is Lissandra?"

Stone's hold on the steering wheel grew white knuckled, and Gabe's damn chest hurt with the effort required to keep on breathing. If Ollivanti harmed one hair on her body...

"He hasn't put her up in the auctions, we know that much." Stone threw him a glance as Gabe released a long breath.

"Thank fuck for that." He punched the dashboard in frustration when he drew a blank in the file regarding her whereabouts.

Stone sighed.

"I've got all our contacts on it, as has McLeod. She can't just disappear, and—" He smirked, and Gabe glared at him.

"What's so fucking amusing, Stone?"

"We got Andrini. Figured you'd want to conduct that interview yourself, boss. He's at the docks."

"Fuck, yeah. Put your foot down."

Stone grinned.

"Figured, you'd say that. He claims no knowledge of anything, of course. There's a copy of his TV interview in there, where he pleads for the return of Lissa. Fucking pathetic, I tell you, but it complicates matters somewhat. We can't just kill him, or you'll be back in prison faster than we can say wanker."

Gabe only half listened as he opened up the laptop and Andrini's ruddy face filled the screen. The asshole was actually crying.

"Should have taken up a career in acting," Gabe grumbled, and Stone laughed. "Still, a man that distraught wouldn't think twice about jumping off a building, right?"

That comment made his second in command grin.

"Like your way of thinking, boss. Are you sure Lissa would be on board with that, though? He's an asshole, but he *is* her father."

Gabe scrubbed a hand over his face and sighed. Stone had a point, but he couldn't let that fucker live. For as long as he did he represented a threat to Lissa, and Gabe would do anything to protect her.

"Doesn't matter. He's fish food, just as soon as he tells me what I need to know."

Stone whistled through his teeth, and Gabe ignored the ache in his gut. He wasn't at all sure Lissa would forgive him for what he had to do, but he was going to do it anyway.

Andrini reeked of fear, piss, and sweat when Gabe entered the abandoned warehouse where they'd strung him up. One eye already swollen from the punches his men got in before him, he hung from the meat hook in the ceiling like the pig he was. Too bad Gabe couldn't gut him like one.

It would be fun indeed to see his entrails all over the floor, to be eaten by the rats which scurried in the corners.

"We meet again, Andrini."

The man's head came up, and a stain appeared in his crotch when recognition dawned in his one good eye. Stone spat on the floor in disgust and handed Gabe his favorite hunting knife.

"I don't know anything. I don't. I've already told your goons that. I—argh."

The stench of urine got stronger, as Gabe pressed the knife to the fucker's throat and then slowly slid it down his meaty body, until it rested on the guy's balls.

"You don't speak unless it's something I want to hear, or I'll cut those puny things off and make you eat them. Where the fuck is my wife?"

In a rare and foolish show of defiance, Andrini spat in his face. Gabe simply grinned, wiped the spit off his face, and slammed the handle of his knife in the guy's balls.

Andrini yanked on his restraints and howled in pain, and Gabe stepped back.

"Wrong answer, asshole. Where is she?"

"Don't … know … fuck … aaaargh."

A well-placed kick to the knee cap shattered that part of Andrini's anatomy, and the sickening crunch echoed around the empty space.

Gabe waited until Andrini's agonized screeches stopped before he spoke again.

"Like I said, wrong answer. I can keep this up all day, and I'll break every bone in your fucking body if I have to."

He got right into Andrini's face, drinking in the man's desperate fear. It soothed the raging beast inside, the one that needed to inflict some serious damage, to make the assholes pay for daring to take what was his.

"Don't … Ollivanti … no, don't—argh."

The fucker's collarbone snapped under Gabe's hands this time, and Andrini bit through his tongue. Blood spattered down his front, and Gabe shook his head in disgust.

"I fucking know he's got her. Where is he keeping her, Andrini?"

By the time Lissa's father finally passed out, there wasn't much left of him to break, and Gabe swore under his breath. He cut the rope holding Andrini up, and the guy fell to the floor in a gloopy mess.

"Throw him off the top of his house."

He slumped against the wall and frowned at his bloody hands. Far from making him feel better, Andrini's punishment left a hollow feeling in his gut, not least because they were none the wiser.

"Guess, he really didn't know, eh? Who next?" Stone asked. "Ange?"

Gabe shook his head and shoved his hands out of sight. Lissa would be disgusted at the state of him. Right now, he looked like that damning picture she'd painted of him at the start of their relationship.

"That bitch won't know. Why is she still alive anyway? Get her dealt with already."

Stone's whistle brought several other members of his team out of the shadows and together they bundled up Andrini's broken body and carted him off.

"Don't wanna do it yourself, boss? I thought you might?" Stone asked.

Bile rose in the back of Gabe's throat, and he shook his head.

"If I go near that cunt, I'll fucking strangle her for her duplicity."

Stone nodded. "I get that, but she might know something. Bitch has been in deep with Ollivanti for the last six months, and…" Stone's brows drew together as his phone rang and he answered it.

"Zach, what's up?"

Gabe pushed away from the grubby wall.

Stone's expression grew murderous as he listened.

"Right, gotcha, yeah, that makes sense. We'll meet you there." Stone ended the call and grinned at Gabe.

"What?"

"That was Zach, one of the McLeod Operatives I've been working with. He's got a lead on Lissa's whereabouts, and I bet he's spot on. Ange used to meet up with one of Ollivanti's men in a seedy strip club in Soho, on occasion. Well, several different clubs, but the one Zach's been staking out has a cellar. They use it as a play party dungeon type thing. Been to a few when I was bored out my skull before they closed the place down. It's soundproof and... Fuck, he's right, she's gotta be there."

Gabe swore under his breath.

"Bring the car round."

"On it, boss."

****

Lissa drifted in and out of consciousness, only dimly aware of her surroundings. This last place they'd brought her to, chaining her up against the wall like some fucking animal, seemed to be some form of sex dungeon. Her stomach rolled anew, threatening to bring up the little water they'd allowed her to have as her imagination went into overdrive. What would have been an exciting place under Gabe's dominance now seemed menacing, dirty, perverted, not least because the man assessing her from under hooded lids gave her the creeps. Similar in age to Gabe, and impeccably dressed, he had cruel, merciless eyes, and she knew without being told that this was Ollivanti himself.

A woman cried softly somewhere in the room, and the sounds of flesh slapping on flesh as someone else had sex registered over the ringing in her ears the last slap to her face had caused. Her cheek burned, and she tasted blood from her split lip. When had he hit her?

Time had lost all meaning, not helped by the drugs they'd pumped into her system.

A slap to her other side jerked her head 'round, and she winced at the resulting jolt of pain.

"Answer Mr. Ollivanti when he asks you a question, bitch."

Spittle flew in her face, and she tried her best to focus on the cruel face of the musclebound asshole who seemed determined to wake her up by beating her. Blood pooled in her mouth, and she spat it into this asshole's face.

"Fucking cunt."

The punch to her belly winded her, making her see stars, and she hunched over as much as she could in her restraints. The cuffs dug into her wrists, shooting yet more pain up her dead arms and into her strained shoulders. She almost wished for the oblivion of the drug induced sleep—almost. They'd clearly decided they wanted her awake for this, and disgust cramped her insides, as the unseen woman's sobs got louder, and the scent of sweat and sex assaulted her nostrils.

Yes, oblivion would be preferable to all of her senses coming back on line. Whether it was a by-product of the drugs they'd given her, or simply the adrenaline coursing through her system, everything seemed brighter, more vivid in that moment.

"Take it easy, Gordon. You damage her too much, we won't be able to sell her. I want her features recognizable when we film me fucking her brains out. That should get Henshaw going, eh?"

Ollivanti's smooth, cold voice slithered into her senses, and Lissa gagged. So that's why they wanted her awake then? Well, fuck them. He could take her body, but he would never own her. She blinked back tears and swallowed hard when his cologne invaded her nostrils. It was the same scent Gabe used, but on this man, it made her gag. It also brought Daddy's beloved face into the forefront of her mind, and she forced herself to look Ollivanti in the eye.

"He'll kill you."

Ollivanti's black eyes crinkled up at the corners seconds before he laughed in her face, brought his hand around her throat, and squeezed off her air supply.

"Bitch got spirit, I give her that. Henshaw might let you get away with that mouth, but I won't. Let's see how verbal you are when I've filled every one of your holes, shall we?"

He stepped away, releasing her throat, and Lissa gulped in enough air to whisper her response.

"Fuck you!"

Another punch, to her side this time, sent a renewed wave of pain through her body, and she bit her tongue in an effort not to cry out at the agony left behind.

"Show the boss some respect, cunt."

Alcohol-laced breath blew in her face, seconds before the goon ripped her top, exposing her lacy bra.

She closed her eyes, determined to block out what was happening to her. A sharp pain to her nipples forced her eyes open to see Ollivanti's cruel hands holding them in a tight grip.

"Impressive tits, I give you that." He pulled harder, forcing Lissa on her tiptoes to try to alleviate the pain, and he laughed. "That's better. I have ways to make sure you know exactly who's fucking that lush pussy of yours." He kept hold of one of her breasts while he pulled her leggings down and cupped her mound. "Nice and dry, just how I like it. I'm going to make you scream, girl…" He laughed and winked at her. "And bleed." He licked up the side of her face, and Lissa used the last of her waning strength to headbutt him. More pain exploded in her head, yet she had the satisfaction of seeing his nose bleed.

Ollivanti's dark eyes blazed in fury, and he raised his arm to hit her. Lissa braced herself for a punch that never came, as a door burst open and Daddy's deep voice boomed around the dank room.

"Get your fucking hands off of her."

Oh, thank God.

****

Gabe saw red, seeing his precious girl strung up against the wall, with Ollivanti's filthy hands all over her. He yanked the asshole off her and sent him crashing against the opposite wall where one of his goons was raping a girl far too young to be caught up in all of this. Track marks marred her skin in the same way as they marked Lissa's pale flesh. He wrapped his arms around her to hold her up and bellowed his instructions to cut her loose.

She was too pale, too still in his arms, as though she'd fainted, but then again, that might be for the best as his men filed in, knives drawn and slit the throats of Ollivanti's men one by one. Stone had Gabe's rival pinned against the wall, knife to his throat, but he wouldn't kill him. Not yet. That would fall to Gabe, once he'd tortured the evil slime and made him pay for what he'd done to Lissa.

First, though, he had to get her out of here and away from all this ugliness. That part of his life should have never fucking touched her. He breathed a sigh of relief when they found the keys to her cuffs and his girl was free. He scooped her up in his arms and turned his back on the chaos behind him.

Fuck, that had been way too close. If he'd lost her... Gabe pulled her closer, inhaling deeply of her sweet scent, as Lissa, coming back around, wrapped herself around him, as though she, too, never wanted to let him go. Shivers still wracked her body, remnants of the terror she'd witnessed, the horror he'd pulled her away from, as he made his way up the stairs, through the abandoned club and out the door. He nodded his thanks at the team from McLeod Security who'd guarded the outside, barely registering Zane McLeod's grim smile in acknowledgment. He owed that guy big time for his intel on Ollivanti.

Stone ran ahead, yanked open the car door, and Gabe had never been so grateful for the quick actions of his own team, as the doors locked, and the SUV speeded them off to safety.

"No, I don't. Please no."

Lissa hung on tighter, her tears wetting his shoulder when he tried to slide her off his lap, so that he could buckle her in.

"Please don't let me go. Don't ever let me go."

Gabe's cold heart splintered into a thousand pieces at the desperation in her voice. Swallowing hard against the emotion clogging his throat, he somehow managed to force out words.

"Shh, it's okay, baby girl. I've got you. You're safe now. Those bastards will never touch you again." He pulled her tighter, his hands exploring her curves to reassure himself that she was indeed unharmed, that he hadn't been too late, despite evidence to the contrary.

Her sobs eventually stopped.

"I knew you'd kill them."

Gabe kissed the top of her head and grasped her chin to enable him to read her expression. What he saw made him want to turn the car around and rip Ollivanti apart with his bare hands. Her pale skin was already bruising, one eye so badly swollen she could hardly see out of it, and blood still seeped out of the cut on her split lip.

"I haven't yet, baby girl, but I will, as soon as we've got you checked over. Where does it hurt, sweetheart?"

Tears clouded her beautiful eyes, and she sniffed.

"Everywhere, but it doesn't matter. I want to see."

Gabe frowned, and Stone, too, looked puzzled at

her whispered words.

"Want to see what, baby?" Gabe asked.

Lissa struggled to sit up more and winced as he loosened his grip on her to enable her to do so.

"When you kill him. I want to see him die. The things he said." She closed her eyes and shook her head, and when she opened them again, Gabe's stomach churned at the determination on her face. "I never knew evil had a face until him."

Gabe kissed her nose, about the only place he didn't fear hurting her more, and shook his head.

"You don't want to see that, little one, trust me."

"Yes, I fucking do. I … shit." She burst into tears once more, and Gabe simply held her tight, while murmuring nonsense into her hair. The fact that she let him, clung to him until she fell into an exhausted sleep, meant more to him than he could ever hope to articulate, and in this moment in time he didn't need to. It was enough to know that she was safe in his arms.

He carried her to her his place, only putting her down to enable Mavis to fuss over her. His housekeeper shooed him away when he hovered over them both.

"Go, scoot. I've got this. The last thing your girl needs is for you to see her like this. I'll take good care of her. Go, do what you have to and come back when it's done. Give the fuckers who did that to her a kick from me, too, please."

That vehement comment brought a grim smile to his face. It was a surreal day indeed when the two women in his life urged him on to be his violent self. Not that he felt like damaging anything right now. He was too fucking worried about Lissa, as he paced the length of his living area, watched over by an equally worried looking Stone.

"Boss, sit down. You're making me fucking

dizzy."

Gabe ignored him as the doctor finally came to see him.

"Well, how is she?"

"Battered and bruised and she'll feel like hell for a few days, but no permanent damage as far as I can tell. I've taken some blood samples to determine what drugs they used on her, but hopefully, there won't be any ill effects from that either."

Gabe blew out a sigh of relief, and the old doc smiled.

"Relax, she's young and healthy, and as far as I can tell you got to her before they could do any real damage."

"She wasn't?" Gabe ran a hand over his face and swallowed past the lump of dread in his throat. "I mean, he had his hands all over her, and—fuck, was I too late?"

Doc Samuels sighed and shook his head.

"She wasn't raped as far as I can tell if that's what you're asking me. Like I said, all things considered, she was lucky. Cuts and bruises, and no doubt she would benefit from seeing a counselor, but she should make a full recovery in time. What she needs right now, though, is rest and lots of TLC. I trust you can do that, Mr. Henshaw."

Gabe heard the implication loud and clear, and he nodded his acknowledgment.

"Of course, I can. Thank you, doc."

Samuels smiled.

"Good, I'll let myself out."

Stone swore loudly and profusely once the front door banged shut behind the good doctor and then grinned at Gabe.

"Thank fuck for that, boss, eh. Now, what are we going to do with Ollivanti? Got him strung up in the same place we'd stored Andrini."

At the mention of that asshole, Gabe's mood darkened again, and he snarled his reply.

"Let's go and gut a pig."

Chapter Fourteen

Lissa woke up to the murmur of voices, and she stretched. Her heart beat faster when she recognized Daddy's deep baritone. He didn't sound happy, but then he never did these days. She blinked away unexpected tears and, padding across to her en-suite bathroom, glared at her reflection in the mirror. Two weeks on from her ordeal some bruising still remained on her face, but her physical injuries had all but healed. Thank goodness none of the drugs they'd pumped her full with had left any lingering after effects either. Thanks to daily counseling sessions with Rhonda Booker, she'd also more or less stopped waking up screaming in the night.

Of course, that meant she saw even less of Gabe. While he'd refused to sleep in the bed with her, according to his logic...

"You need your rest, baby girl. I'll be just next door."

...He always appeared to rock her back to sleep when she had one of those nighttime screaming fits. In those moments she could almost believe that nothing had changed between them. His strong arms provided a safety net, a cocoon from the outside world where nothing could touch her, until she woke up on her own again.

Try as she might there was distance between them. While the rational side of her knew that he was busy— now more so than ever—her heart still cramped painfully. She wanted the closeness back. The easy rapport they'd established on their honeymoon before the ugliness of Gabe's life had invaded their cocoon. Before her eyes had been truly and irrevocably opened to the true nature of Gabe's business and what it took to stay on top of it. To the dangers lurking around every corner. To the fact that he'd killed her father.

Her grip on the washbasin turned white knuckled as her father's face swam into her consciousness. The tears he'd shed in the interview the news program had led with when they announced his apparent suicide.

Mavis had clucked her tongue and switched the telly off while she'd pulled her into a hug.

"There now, you don't need to see that, my dear. No point in upsetting yourself all over again."

Lissa had pushed the older woman away.

"I'm not upset. It's okay, Mavis, and I know full well that wasn't suicide. Gabe killed him, didn't he?"

Mavis blinked repeatedly, seemingly searching for the right words, and Lissa had shaken her head.

"It's okay, you don't have to answer that. I know he did. For starters Papa was too much of a coward to throw himself off a building. If that's even what happened."

"You seem very sure of that, Lissa."

Gabe's deep voice had made her jump. At his nod, Mavis had hastily left them on their own, and she'd drunk in the sight of him. Clad in jeans and a t-shirt, he'd looked so much like he'd done on the yacht, it had taken every ounce of her will to not throw herself into his arms. Maybe she should have done just that. Maybe that would have helped with the growing distance between them.

She hadn't, though, held in place by the intensity of his gaze as he studied her.

"I'm sorry. You weren't meant to find out like that."

Lissa had shrugged and feigned a nonchalance she'd been far from feeling.

"Why didn't you tell me?" she'd asked.

Gabe had run a hand over his face and looked uncomfortable.

"There didn't seem to be a right time, and you're still recovering, and—"

"Bullshit." His eyes had widened at her interrupting him like that, and she'd expected him to pounce. Needed him to, in fact. She ached for his touch, his dominance to keep her grounded, to know he didn't see her any differently now that she was soiled goods.

Oh sure, they hadn't actually raped her, but she still felt their grubby hands all over her when she closed her eyes and she needed to know that her Daddy saw past that.

Only he let it pass, didn't pull her up for her rude reply, and that hurt the most of all.

"The doc said I'm fine. I'm not that fragile that I can't cope with the truth, Gabe."

"I know that, so ask me."

Lissa had shaken her head, and Gabe had sighed.

"No, it wasn't a suicide, just like Ange's death wasn't an overdose, but they both had it coming. They put you in danger, and that meant they had to die. My only regret is that I didn't see the life draining out their eyes while I had my hands wrapped around their miserable throats."

She hadn't been able to help her gasp. It hadn't been shock, exactly. Not at what he'd done anyway, more shock at herself at how pleased she was at their death. When had she become this bloodthirsty?

Gabe clearly had read her reaction differently though because that godawful mask had come back down over his expression, and his lips had curled into a sneer.

"Told you, you'd married a monster, babe." Even the way he said that endearment hadn't sounded like the Gabe she knew, and, turning his back on her, he'd left.

Lissa shook her head and swiped away the utterly useless tears which ran down her cheeks. They'd never achieved anything after all.

The door to her room cracked open, and Mavis stepped inside with a breakfast tray like she did every morning. Lissa smiled at the housekeeper, and Mavis set the tray down on the nightstand.

"Ah, I'm glad you're awake. Gabe sent me in here to wake you up. I'm sorry, dear, but the police are here, and they won't leave until they've taken your statement."

Lissa pulled her robe tighter around herself and helped herself to a much-needed cup of coffee.

"It's okay. I'm surprised they waited this long."

Mavis twisted her hands inside her apron, a surefire signal of something bothering her, and Lissa put her cup down with a frown.

"What is it? Out with it, Mavis, what aren't you telling me?" she asked. "I'm sick and tired of folks pussy footing around me."

Mavis blinked once and sighed.

"Well, it's just. They've threatened to arrest Gabe again, unless you give your statement. He's been putting them off, see, and—"

"Oh, for the love of God."

Lissa shot to her feet and out of the room, determined to put an end to this charade. Her steps faltered when she entered the living room to find Gabe and Stone surrounded by several uniformed police officers while the detective who'd been responsible for her being subjected to all that questioning before smirked. What was his name again?

Dickinson? Yeah, that was it. Dick by name and dick by nature.

Gabe's eyes narrowed when he spotted her, and the dickwad police officer spun around when she cleared her throat.

"Officer Dickinson, I had hoped I'd seen the last of you. Would you care to explain to me why you're in my home and manhandling my husband to boot? Mavis call Delaney, will you? I'm sure this police brutality is worth a complaint to Dickinson's superiors."

She put her hands on her hips and stared the policeman down. He might be taller than she was, and she was all too painfully aware that she was standing here clad in nothing but a robe, but fuck it all to hell and back. This was her home, and she'd had enough of this shit.

****

"Now listen here, Miss Andrini, I—"

Gabe held his breath as his little wife positively exploded in fury. He knew she would, had known it from the minute she'd burst into the room as though the hounds of hell were after her. It had been there in every line of her body, which was vibrating in fury. Color marred her cheekbones, hid the remaining bruises there, while her impressive tits quivered and strained against the robe with her harsh intake of breaths.

He should rot in hell for noticing that right now, but his dick hardened anyway. It was just so unbelievably good to see her this riled up. Ready to go into battle for him, no less. For a while there, he'd feared her spirit had been broken. She'd clung to him like a fragile bird, seemingly afraid of her own shadow. It had damn well nearly killed him to keep his distance, and as for the nightmares… *Fuck,* they made him want to kill all the people who'd hurt her all over again, starting with himself. Gabe was all too painfully aware that none of this would have happened had he not insisted on marrying her. He'd made her into a target, and he would never forgive himself for that. He couldn't let her go, however, either. He loved her too fucking much for that, and seeing her reaction now, maybe it wasn't too late for them.

Hope blossomed anew in his chest, chasing away the shadows which haunted him.

Stone, too, had the hugest grin on his face. His second in command had been equally worried about her. All his men had, truth be told. Nothing seemed right without Lissa in their midst.

"For the last freaking time, my name is *Mrs. Henshaw*. How hard is that to get into your thick skull? I'm assuming you can, in fact, read, and as you waved my marriage certificate under my nose the last time we met, when you accused my husband of kidnapping me, I know you've at least seen it." She took a much-needed breath, and her eyes softened when they connected with Gabe's across the room. "One of the happiest days of my life."

That did it. Gabe couldn't stand the distance between them anymore, and shoving the coppers out of the way, crossed the room to pull her into his arms, and growled his response into his ear.

"Mine, too, baby girl."

She sank into his embrace and clung while seemingly all hell broke loose behind them. Stone, too, shook off the two coppers holding onto him, and it was the signal for the rest of his men to turn the tables, as it were. They formed a protective semicircle around Gabe and Lissa, and Dickinson turned a nice shade of purple in his outrage.

Let him splutter away. Gabe didn't take any notice of his threats. Besides, thanks to McLeod's investigations, they now had the means to prove without a doubt that Dickinson had been taking bribes from none other than Ollivanti himself. Delaney was on his way over with the evidence, and this whole thing would die a death right here or Dickinson himself would get very familiar with the inside of a police cell.

Of course, Lissa didn't know any of this, which made the fact that she'd come to his rescue even more special.

"Let me go, I need to—"

Gabe shut up her protests by the very expedient method of kissing her. Her gasp of surprise granted him access, and he wasted no time in deepening the kiss. Gabe put all of his pent-up emotions into it, determined to show her how much she meant to him. Lissa went pliant in his arms. Her hands locked behind his neck, and she clung to him, kissing him back with a fervor and need that matched his own. By the time he forced himself to release her lips, they were both breathing hard, and the sweet musk of aroused woman hit his nostrils. He ran a hand under the hem of her robe to grasp her bare ass cheek and his dick jerked. Fuck him, she was naked under there.

"Daddy, please, I need to—"

"Hush now, baby girl. I know what you need, and that isn't standing here listening to this asshole."

He pulled back enough to read her expression, and confusion warred with arousal in her expressive eyes.

Fortunately, Delaney arrived at this moment in time. In any other circumstances the knowing smirk as he ran his gaze all over Lissa would have earned the man a punch, but Gabe was far too pleased to see him.

"About time, Delaney, what took you so fucking long? Go tell Dickinson here, why there will be no arrests made today, will you? At least not mine."

"That will be my pleasure, Gabe." The younger man winked at him and turned his attention on a sputtering Dickinson.

Gabe had heard and seen enough. He needed to reconnect with his wife, and Delaney and his men could deal with this easily enough. The uniforms could a be problem, but everyone had a price, and Gabe bet his last penny that they were probably in on it already with Dickinson. The man had been careful to cover his tracks. In the end it was his own greed that had been his downfall. He didn't earn enough to afford the sports car he'd splashed out on in cash, after all, and the fool didn't play the lottery, so that excuse didn't wash.

"I don't understand. I—mph."

Gabe threw her over his shoulder, which earned him a cacophony of wolf whistles from his men, and strode off to his room. Belatedly, he remembered her previous injuries and swearing under his breath he carefully slid her off his shoulder and set her back down on her feet the minute they had some privacy.

He ran his hands over her ribs and shook his head at his stupidity.

"Shit, I forgot. Are you okay? I didn't hurt you, did I? I—"

The shove to his chest caught him off guard, and he stumbled back a step.

"For fuck's sake I'm fine. Will you explain to me what the hell is going on?"

There she was, his little spitfire. Gabe hid his relieved amusement and, crossing his arms over his chest, raised an eyebrow and widened his stance.

"Is that any way to talk to Daddy, baby girl?" he asked, dropping his voice on purpose.

Lissa's eyes widened, growing soft as her submissive side instantly responded to the steel in his voice, and warmth flooded his chest. Shit, he loved this woman, and he would tell her just as soon as they'd sorted this out.

"I'm sorry, I thought, you didn't see me like that anymore. I—"

She blanched at his furious growl in response and dropped her gaze to the floor.

"I'm sorry?"

"So you should be, girl, and if I wasn't still worried about your ribs you'd have just earned yourself a trip over Daddy's knee and not for the fun kind of spanking."

A needy whimper came from Lissa's full lips, and Gabe pulled her back into his arms.

"Is that what you were thinking? That I didn't want you anymore, sweetheart?"

Lissa nodded into his chest, and he wasn't at all surprised to feel the fabric dampening with tears. He steered her over to the bed, to enable him to sit down and draw her onto his lap. As she sank against him, hugging him back, the world righted itself again.

"I thought you saw me as damaged goods now." Had he not been so focused on her he might have missed that far too quiet whisper of a reply. Cupping her chin, he nudged her head up to read her expression. The raw emotion and desperate hope that shone back at him took his breath away and made him blurt out his own feelings.

"Nothing could be further from the truth. I love you, and I always will, no matter what happens."

Renewed tears sprang into her eyes, and Gabe grumbled his annoyance.

"Jesus, don't cry, baby."

Her little hands come up and tugged at his beard, while she shook her head.

"Big, old, bad Dom afraid of a few tears." She grinned up at him, and he knew his face sported a shit-eating grin of his own as he responded to her.

"Less of the old, girl. I'm in my prime, I'll let you

know." He kissed her nose, and Lissa giggled, further soothing his very soul. Who knew he had it in him to sound like a fucking poet? Just as well his men weren't here to witness him going all soft on his woman like this. He'd never live it down.

"Is it really all over?" she asked, and he nodded.

"Yes, my sweet. Dickinson was on Ollivanti's payroll. With that fucker gone, he'll be on mine, or he'll be living the rest of his life out in prison. Brass don't tend to do that well inside, so I'm confident he'll take the deal and this whole thing will be dropped."

"Oh, just like that?"

Gabe smiled at her surprise.

"Just like that, yes."

He let her mull this over for a little while before he spoke again.

"Now, what have you got to say to Daddy, baby girl?"

Lissa shivered, and he pulled her in a little closer, concerned that this was all too much for her after all, when she floored him completely.

"I love you, too."

Their gazes connected, and he couldn't doubt the sincerity shining back at him.

"And you're not a monster, not to me. You never were, and for what it's worth, I'm glad you killed all those people. Even Andrini." Her voice caught on that last word, and he hugged her closer.

"For what it's worth, I'm sorry I had to. I promise I'll do better from now on. No one is going to touch you again. You're mine, and I'm yours. To hell with the rest of the world."

Lissa shook her head and surprised him again.

"I don't expect that of you. I know you need to do *stuff.* With Ollivanti gone, I dare say you'll be taking over?"

She sat up more and searched his face, and Gabe ran a hand over his face.

"I can let someone else do that if you prefer." The mere thought threatened to turn his guts inside out, but he meant it. He'd do it for her.

"I wouldn't ever ask that of you. Besides, you look after your people. I'm guessing whoever was working for Ollivanti will need looking after, too, or … well I guess you'll do what you have to. Just don't get yourself arrested again, please, Daddy?"

Gabe's heart damn well nearly burst out of his chest hearing her call him that, and he nodded.

"I'll try my best, baby, but I'm done talking. I need to be inside of you."

Lissa bit her lip and straddled him with a speed that made him dizzy.

"Then have me, I'm yours."

The End

www.dorisoconnor.com

EVERNIGHT PUBLISHING ®

www.evernightpublishing.com

www.ingramcontent.com/pod-product-compliance
Lightning Source LLC
Chambersburg PA
CBHW031552240626
47153CB00002B/471